The Harder they Ride

CORALEE JUNE

BLURB

He turned me into a woman of extremes, living a life of intense passion and fierce emotions in the rugged landscape of West Texas.

When I cried, I drowned.

When I loved, I burned.

Declan Wilder, a man with a deadly past and a killer smile, made me feel alive like never before. Little did I know that he was a key player in the criminal underground rodeo circuit, where danger and desire went hand in hand. *Little did I know, he had been hired to kill me.*

When he aimed, he destroyed.

When he obsessed, he consumed.

Our love burned hot, an insatiable fire that threatened to ruin us both in a world of reckless outlaws and high-stakes games. Declan was my forbidden flame, a man with a dark past and a possessive streak that threatened to devour me whole. Still, I ached for him, even if it meant facing the deadly consequences of his criminal ties in the gritty and unpredictable wild of the West.

When we fell, we crashed.

When he claimed, he *ruined*.

I knew that I was destined to ride the thrilling waves of passion and adventure, even if it meant risking it all on a journey where love, danger, and villains collided.

CONTENT WARNING

Dear Reader,

I am excited to introduce you to my latest book, *The Harder They Ride*. Before you dive into this dark romance, however, I feel it's important to warn you it contains themes that may be triggering for some readers.

The Harder They Ride includes intense scenes of stalker behavior, rape, dubious consent, knife play, primal play, murder, violence, and gore. These themes are integral to the plot and, as such, may be difficult for some readers to handle. I encourage you to prioritize your mental health and well-being and stop reading if any of these themes become too overwhelming.

At its core, *The Harder They Ride* is a story about overcoming trauma and the power of love to heal even the deepest of wounds. It follows the journey of two flawed individuals as they navigate their complicated relationship and the obstacles that stand in their way.

If you or someone you know is experiencing trauma, please know that there are resources available to you. One such resource is the National Domestic Violence Hotline, which provides support and resources for women experiencing abuse. You can visit their website at www.thehotline.org or call their 24/7 hotline at 1-800-799-SAFE (7233).

Thank you for considering *The Harder They Ride* as your next read. While it may be a challenging read at times, I hope it will move and inspire you, and I encourage you to prioritize your mental health above all else.

XOXO,
CoraLee June

PROLOGUE

DECLAN

Tonight, the desert throbbed with an untamed symphony. Each step I took crushed the gravel under my boots, and the rustle of desert critters filled the air. The night was vibrant, teeming with life, the wind screaming through the canyon, carrying the pungent scent of sage and mesquite.

In some parallel universe, my father might have been here, watching, a proud smile tugging at his lips. My mother would've been a tearful contrast, heart clenched in fear for her boy venturing into the jaws of danger.

But death had robbed them of the chance to feel, to think, to exist.

The dead don't deal in emotions, and the living run

from them.

The land was pulsating, matching the wild rhythm of my heart, and I was stalking through its rugged beauty, like a predator on a hunt.

The underground rodeo, a grueling trial of strength and guts, lured in men hardened by life.

The deal?

To prove myself.

The reward?

Answers.

In the looming distance, a bonfire danced wildly, throwing monstrous shadows around. It roared its fierce existence, echoed back by the escalating shouts of the crowd. The air was thick, clogged with a potent cocktail of sweat and adrenaline.

As I neared the arena, shadowy whispers danced around me, tales spun from the heart of the desert. The bulls in their enclosures snorted, restless. The clanging boom of riders prepping added a metallic note to the sounds of the night.

"You think you're ready?" Hank's voice sliced through the noise, the question hanging heavily in the air.

My nod was curt—a silent declaration. Here, actions were louder than any sermon.

I vaulted over the fence, and the chilly cloak of the night wrapped around me. I took a moment, my gaze raking over the frenzied crowd—fellow riders preparing for the battle, spectators high on anticipation, silhouettes lurking in the shadows. Danger was woven into the very fabric of this place, and I knew with complete certainty that I was cut out for it.

No, more than that—I was born for it.

Walking up to the chute, the floodgates of my memory were thrown open. They lit up the darkest corners of my past.

The blood.

The sweat.

The echoes of lives crushed under my hands. They were a brutal testament to the path I had walked.

But the impatient snorts of the bull demanded my attention.

As I filled my lungs with the hot night air, I hoisted myself onto the bull's back. My grip on the rope was a vise.

And then, we were off.

The gate swung open, the bull lunging into the storm of cheers that erupted from the crowd.

The noises faded into a blur as I narrowed my focus on the ride.

The prize was within my reach.

This was my arena, my battleground. I was the hunter here. I was the goddamn king. No force on heaven or earth would stand in my way now.

CHAPTER 1
Dusty Boots and Rhinestone Dreams

CLOVER

"*T*hat'll be twenty bucks," a gritty man said, his gold-coated tooth shimmering in the descending sun.

As I rummaged through my bag, my heart pounded in my chest, resonating with the fear of being in this seedy part of town. This was the hub of the underground Nightfall Rodeo, the town's well-kept secret.

Law enforcement turned a blind eye to the unsanctioned event, too wary to interfere with the Dust Devils, the local gang orchestrating the spectacle. The danger wasn't exclusive to the bucking bulls.

My purpose here wasn't the thrill of the rodeo.

I was in search of my sister.

My stupid, naïve, lovable, reckless, fucking sister.

5

After handing over the money, I glimpsed the man's twisted smile. He motioned me toward the stands. His eyes shone with a secretive amusement in the sinking sunlight. "Better be quick, sweetheart. The betting ends in ten. And remember, no phones, no pictures. We like our secrets here."

"Understood," I murmured, my voice wavering with a mix of anxiety and excitement.

"Good girl." His eyes, as sly as a fox, raked over me. "Nightfall Rodeo ain't for the faint of heart. Just keep your head low and steer clear of the Devils. You're too pretty to be on their radar."

A shudder ran through me. This place evoked painful memories; I could almost envision my father's ghost smirking in the background.

I made my way toward the arena, and the crowd was electric, erupting into a frenzy every time a bull charged into the ring, wild and primal as the riders tried to tame them.

The spectators were a fascinating mix of rowdy small-town folk in sweat-stained overalls and knockoff cowboy hats. Their infectious energy hummed through me.

Before I could adjust to the chaotic environment, a sudden collision pulled me back.

A solid chest.

A towering figure.

A brooding stare fixated on me.

"Careful, gorgeous," a rough voice clipped through my senses as two powerful hands gripped my shoulders, preventing me from toppling over.

My heart leaped to my throat as I stumbled, looking up to meet the eyes of a man who was the embodiment of dark and lethal. His striking features were framed by a five o'clock shadow and a thin scar trailing down his right cheek. It was the cherry on top of his bad boy sundae.

We locked eyes, and everything else fell away, leaving just him and me.

He was beautiful. In a tragic, murderous sort of way.

"Sorry, didn't see you there," he murmured, the deep resonance of his voice made a delightful quiver shoot through me.

Stumbling over my words, I choked out, "No problem," heat flushing my cheeks under his heavy gaze. He reluctantly released me and a hiss escaped my lips.

A crooked smile tugged at his lips, eyes sparkling with amusement. "Well, I might as well introduce myself then. Declan."

His hand hovered midair in greeting, tempting me. His strong fingers reflected the hard work of a cowboy, the rough life of a rodeo rider. There was something about the steady control beneath his rugged exterior that was magnetic.

Swallowing my doubts, I extended my hand, my pulse thundering as our hands met, sparking an electric charge.

"I'm Clover," I whispered, trying to ignore the rush of excitement.

His intense gaze didn't waver. "Clover, what brings a pretty girl like you to a place like this? Did you come to see me ride?"

Surprised, I sputtered, "Do all the girls fall for that line?"

His deep chuckle stirred a flutter in my stomach. "I don't need to make 'em fall, darlin'. They tumble all on their own. Though for you, I might enjoy the chase."

I could feel my cheeks warm, a thrill spiking my veins. His brazen confidence, the dangerous allure—it was intoxicating. As much as I hated to admit it, he had me hooked.

A mischievous glimmer danced in his eyes as he continued, "Tell me, Clover, do you come here often? Are you a fan of the rodeo?"

I arched my brow and laughed. "Another cheesy line? No. I don't."

"So why are you here, then? Looking for a little excitement?" His words dripped with suggestive undertones. This man was a cocky flirt. Assuming. Bold. Presumptuous.

"I don't know," I confessed, my voice quivering. "I found a rodeo flier and a note in my sister's room. She's young and naïve, and this place . . ." I hesitated, glancing around the chaotic venue.

"And this place is a shit hole," he finished for me with a teasing smirk.

"That's definitely one way of putting it."

He chuckled again, low and deep, and I couldn't help but be affected by the sound. It was both thrilling and unnerving to be this close to him, to feel the heat emanating from his body and the intensity of his gaze.

I could tell that Declan was used to making women fall to their knees. But there was also something unguarded about him, a raw and unfiltered quality that was captivating.

"Is your sister a Devils groupie?" he asked.

I shook my head. "An aspiring rider."

His brows shot up in surprise. "I think I heard someone say there was a woman riding tonight. If you want to find her, check by the chutes. Though I suggest you stay away from there. The Devils don't like people snooping around."

"Thanks for the tip," I said, trying to keep my voice steady.

He continued. "And maybe after you play the hero

and drag your sister away, you'll let me buy you a drink."

I couldn't help the breathy laugh that escaped me. "I don't think that's a good idea."

"Fun things are rarely good ideas."

Before I could come up with a response, a horn blast roared through the air, marking the start of the next ride. His eyes stayed locked on mine, that smirk still playing on his lips.

"I'll be seeing you, Clover," he drawled, winking at me and striding off into the crowd toward the roaring arena.

As he disappeared into the mass of bodies, I had to shake myself. I wasn't here for heart-stopping cowboys. I was here for my sister.

I was seized by a sudden and overwhelming nostalgia. Memories hit me like a punch as I breathed in the rodeo air.

There was Dad and Avery and me, chasing the rodeo trail, my father, a fearless contender, and Avery, a starry-eyed spectator eager to carve out her place in the rodeo world.

Avery had her heart engraved with the desire to claim her fame. To take her spot in the arena and command respect from those who lived and breathed rodeo. But that glittering lure of adrenaline and notoriety had stolen our father from us four years ago, and that same ambition had led Avery here, today.

The roar of the audience reverberated in my chest as the first wave of riders retreated, tipping their hats and waving in a showy display of false modesty. I squinted against the bright floodlights, searching the sea of faces for my sister.

I knew Avery wanted a sister who could cheer her on and support her dreams. But each stomp of the hooves, every triumphant ride, only conjured sorrow in me.

For Avery, bull riding was an intoxicating adrenaline rush. For me, it was a chamber of grief.

I would drag her away from this dangerous obsession, even if it meant hauling her back home kicking and screaming.

"Ladies and gentlemen, prepare for a treat tonight. He's the wildfire of the rodeo world, gathering praise wherever he roams," came the announcer's voice, resonating through the arena. "Let's hear it for Declan Wilder!"

The response was instantaneous. Women shot up from their seats, their laughter carrying through the cheers, whistles, and applause.

As Declan stepped out and tipped his hat, the crowd swelled into a roar. His face was an unreadable mask, his gaze icy and methodical, gliding over the audience and arena.

Declan Wilder was a spectacle. The tight white shirt he wore did little to contain his broad shoulders and chiseled chest. His jeans, rustic and well-worn, clung to his muscular thighs. He was the epitome of rugged elegance, the rough, almost raw appeal of his attire colliding with his composed movements.

Declan's stance mirrored the creature's wild soul. Under his shirt, muscles flexed as he held the rope, his arms showcasing their strength. He was tension personified, a predator poised for a lethal strike.

An impish smirk curled his lips before he turned back toward the chute. In that moment, time seemed suspended, held hostage by his charisma.

As the gate burst open, the arena echoed with thunderous applause.

Declan, merging with the bull's movements, was a display of grace and power. Each twist, each turn of the bull made me gasp. Declan's body moved as one with the creature's wild dance.

His cowboy hat was flung aside, revealing a tousled mass of black hair that framed his face, drawing attention to his enticing lips, which were pressed in a firm, determined line.

A violent buck from the bull sent a shiver of apprehension through the crowd. His grip faltered, a heartbeat away from being thrown. But he held on, his body refusing to surrender.

I held my breath.

I fought the memories.

I ignored the whisper of trauma coaxing my soul.

Finally, the bell tolled, marking the end of the ride. Declan jumped off the beast, his eyes triumphant.

The crowd went wild, their cheers and applause providing the perfect backdrop for his victory.

Yet despite the thrill, my thoughts lingered on my father's last ride.

His lifeless form in the dirt.

The paramedics that rushed to his side.

The gasps that ripped through the crowd as he was thrown.

I remembered with painful clarity how my father's body lay sprawled in the dirt. The once vibrant and imposing figure, so full of life and authority, now lay six feet under, discarded by the harsh rodeo arena like a broken prop.

From across the arena, Declan's intense gaze met mine again, making my heart stutter. His eyes seemed to see into my very soul, reading my every thought and desire.

It should have been exhilarating.

Maybe it should have been fun. Or exciting.

But the smell of dust and manure, the relentless

buzzing of the crowd, the painful memories of my father's accident—it was too much. I felt like I was going to be sick.

I retreated toward the back of the arena, a sour taste of dread creeping up my throat, enhancing the nervous thrumming of my heart. The incessant buzz of the crowd became a grim soundtrack to the memories of my father's death.

"Where the hell are you, Avery?" I said out loud. Focusing on finding her was the only way my brain would survive being here.

Avery's familiar blonde tresses caught my eye across the way, her silhouette framed against the fence as she watched the riders in the ring. But before her name could escape my lips, a forceful grip clamped down on my shoulder, halting my steps.

A voice sneered into my ear, "Where do you think you're going, little lady?"

The pit of my stomach dropped as I turned to face the one who had spoken. I recognized him, though we had never formally met.

Hank, the notorious leader of the Dust Devils, towered over me.

Everyone knew to fear Hank. He was a modern outlaw. A dangerous mafia man running our small town.

His eyes, fierce and penetrating, and his breath, a

nauseating mix of stale tobacco and cheap liquor, made me stumble.

"I'm just trying to find my sister," I replied, clinging to the remnants of my determination.

"And who is your sister?"

I nodded nervously, not wanting to bring Avery more into this than she already was. "I'm not here to cause any trouble."

"I'm not sure I believe you."

Before I could answer, the sudden, jarring sound of a bull's roar sliced through the tension. A frantic scramble of riders made us both snap our heads toward the arena as a massive beast broke free from its enclosure, charging toward spectators with terrifying momentum.

"Fuck!" Hank yelled before storming toward one of his men.

The bull's wild eyes scanned the crowd, looking for a target, and in its wake, it left a mass of scattered people.

Hank, like everyone else, was momentarily distracted by the unfolding disarray. Sensing an opportunity to get the hell away from him, I darted into action. My heart hammered in my chest as I launched myself over the fence and toward the commotion, hoping to slip away unnoticed.

Straight toward the bull.

Straight toward trouble.

The ground beneath me shook with the bull's charge, its hot breath practically burning into my back. I stumbled, a sharp rock nearly throwing me off balance, as I felt its monstrous horns come dangerously close.

Just as I was about to get trampled, a hand yanked me out of the bull's path.

Declan.

His urgent shout pierced through the screams, "Come on, let's get out of here!"

His grip was a lifeline as we ran from the bull, the boom of the rampage receding behind us. He helped me through a crumpled portion of the fence, and we both sprinted toward the parking area.

Once we were far enough away, I took a moment to calm myself and look for Avery. Did she get trampled? Did she escape?

Declan's laugh made me pause. "You probably shouldn't run *toward* the bull."

I looked up at him with a scowl. "I was trying to get away!"

"Sure," he replied. "If by getting away you mean practically sprinting toward the bull."

In the distance, the bull was finally roped in and the crowd dispersed, leaving behind a palpable wave of adrenaline. Declan's proximity sent my heart into a reckless movement, a tantalizing cocktail of fear and desire swirling within me.

"Thank you," I murmured, my voice barely a whisper against the lingering dust and the frenzied cadence of hooves and boots.

A devious glint twinkled in his eyes as a smirk played on his lips. "Just couldn't let a wildflower like you get trampled, now could I? This world could do with more delicate things."

I blushed, then started scanning the dispersing crowd, looking for Avery's blonde hair in the mass of people leaving.

But my eyes landed on a familiar figure in the distance, and the curious look on his face froze my blood in its veins.

Hank stared at me like I was a problem.

Fear constricted my chest as I tried to make a run for it. But Declan's grip on my hand, once comforting, now felt like a vise, grounding me to the spot.

His voice, low and laced with concern, punctured my spiraling thoughts, "What's the rush?"

"I . . . I can't be here," I stammered, each breath a struggle.

His gaze intensified, his brilliant blue eyes narrowing. "Why not?"

Avery. I needed to find Avery. The mere thought of her in the company of the Dust Devils was unbearable.

"I should go," I mumbled hastily. "Thank you . . . for everything." The words tumbled out in a rush as I released myself from his hold and darted toward the parking lot.

This rodeo, this whole place, was a nightmare.

CHAPTER 2
Grit and Glitter

CLOVER

*W*orry twisted in my gut as hours ticked by. After the rodeo called it quits for fence repairs, I finally got Avery to reply to one of my texts, and she hurriedly promised to be home soon. I couldn't find her in the rowdy crowd and decided to meet her at home, but with the break of dawn, there was still no sign of Avery.

The damn girl was going to give me a heart attack one of these days. I was pretty sure she'd already given me a stress ulcer.

Avery liked to party. She liked to live life to the fullest. She *loved* to make me worry.

The creak of the front door snapped me out of my thoughts. My sister, smiling like an idiot, waltzed through the door without a care. Seeing Avery brought a wave of relief, quickly replaced by a surge of anger. "Where have you been?" I demanded, my voice filled with tension.

A mix of chill and excitement colored her cheeks, and her eyes sparkled as she spoke. "It was wild," she said, waving her arms and making her old plaid shirt lift up. "A bull broke loose and turned the arena upside down!"

I felt my anger spike again. "I know, Avery, I was there!" I shot back.

Her eyes widened. "You were there?!"

"Yes. I found the *damn* flier in your room and showed up. Was looking for you when the *damn* bull got loose. It was fucking terrifying—"

She grinned. "It was *so* much fun!"

"Are you insane? You could have been hurt!"

She rolled her eyes, typical Avery. "I'm not a kid, Clover. I can handle myself." I quickly looked her up and down, checking for injuries. Her worn boots looked like they had taken a beating and needed to be replaced. But Avery had a stubborn attitude. When she loved something, she refused to let it go.

"That's not the point!" I was practically yelling now. "Why'd you even go there? You know how I feel about rodeos. When I found that flier, my heart dropped."

Avery didn't back down; her eyes flared with defiance. "I wanted to ride. I've been pestering the Dust Devils for weeks. But why were you snooping around?! You could have messed up my chance."

Anger simmered inside me, ready to boil over. "Oh, wouldn't that be a shame," I spat out, sarcasm dripping from every word.

She glared at me, but it didn't douse my anger. "Seriously? I'm fully capable of making my own fucking decisions."

I felt my nostrils flare up. "Obviously not if you're hanging out at the Dust Devils' rodeo. This isn't a game, Avery. They're legitimate criminals."

She rolled her eyes. "Come on. The Devils aren't *that* bad. They gave Dad his start, and he got sponsors almost immediately!"

The mention of our father made me sick. "Dad always said the Devils were dangerous, Avery."

She shook her head in annoyance. "I'm not going to join their fucking gang, Clover. I'm just riding at their rodeo."

I pinched the bridge of my nose. "And where were you after it got shut down? Your text said you were heading home!"

Her comeback was quick, just as heated as mine. "I was bummed about missing my ride. I went out with friends. It's not that big of a deal. I still can't believe you showed up. Why did you?"

I couldn't believe she had the guts to ask. "Seriously, Avery? I was there for you," I snapped, "even though I hate everything the rodeo stands for." Anger reflected in both our eyes as I took a step closer and pointed at her. "But you wouldn't get it. All you care about is the rush, not the people who care about you."

I couldn't help but notice the stark differences between us as we fought. Avery's soft and delicate face looked nothing like mine. Her pale hair, always practical for work, in a bun. Mine was a cascade of light brown waves. She lived in her tough denim and plaid shirts, while I preferred pink, rhinestone tops, and vibrant scarves.

"That's not fair, Clover," she countered, her voice echoing around us. She was full of fire, but I was used to it.

"Am I supposed to watch you 'follow your dreams,' Avery?" I mocked. "Is that what you call risking your life?"

"I'm careful!" Avery stood her ground, her resolve shining in her eyes. "I need to test my limits. No one, not even you, can stop me. The Devils are the only ones who give women a chance. Everyone else just laughs at me."

The tension between us was thick, her words hanging in the air. She was right, in a way. I knew my fears shouldn't control her, but the thought of her dancing with the devils made my stomach churn.

"Dad died riding a bull," I muttered, my voice barely above a whisper.

Avery's tough shell softened, her rough and calloused hand reaching for mine. "I promise I'll be careful, Clover. But I want to do this. I need to do this."

The distinct contrast between us never felt more apparent. Avery, with her adventurous spirit and audacious dreams, worried me. She thrived on chaos, took risks, and laughed in the face of danger. On the other hand, I was the calm after her storm, always trying to pick up the pieces left in her wake.

This was our life—Avery, chasing thrill and adventure, and me, constantly trailing behind, the fear for her safety an ever-present shadow. This was our dance, a turbulent mix of worry, anger, love, and an unhealthy dose of frustration.

"I just worry about you, okay?" I finally choked out.

She let out a sigh and took a step toward me, wrapping me in her arms with a begrudging embrace.

Returning her hug, I took a moment to breathe in the familiar scent of hay and horses clinging to her. "I just love you so damn much," I breathed. "You've always been brave and stubborn, but you're also kind and strong."

When we finally broke apart, she spoke. "I love you too. Next time, you don't have to chase me down at the rodeo. I can handle myself."

I resisted the urge to argue with her again. She couldn't handle herself. She could barely remember to fill her gas tank up let alone deal with the risks of a criminal underground rodeo. She was naïve and reckless, but fighting about it got us nowhere.

I avoided answering her and instead looked around our modest home. It was small but ours, the only thing Dad left us when he died. We owned three acres, and our property backed up to some trails. The floors and walls were scuffed, our kitchen needed an overhaul, and the bathroom sink had a persistent leak.

But it was ours.

Avery had put up rodeo posters and pictures of her favorite riders. It wasn't my style, but it made her happy, and that was all that mattered to me.

Feeling worn out, I excused myself. "I'm gonna shower," I mumbled, heading for the bathroom.

"Hold up," Avery said, a hint of mischief in her voice before she started digging through her purse. "I got you something from the rodeo." She handed me a tiny stuffed bull, a red flag held in its mouth. "An apology gift."

My eyes rolled in response, but my lips betrayed a

smile. "Thanks, I'll add it to my pile of unwanted rodeo keepsakes."

I retreated into the sanctuary of the bathroom, turning on the shower as hot as it would go. I tried to calm my anger. Avery was impulsive and reactive. Fighting with her wouldn't fix things.

When I came out, Avery was already in bed, the toy bull clutched in her sleep-loose grip. My heart warmed at the sight.

Closing the door to her room, I made a quiet vow. No matter what, I'd protect my sister, even if it meant stepping into the rodeo arena myself.

～

*A*s dawn painted the world in a wash of eerie crimson, the crisp morning air stirred an ache in me. Life as a trail guide promised the allure of adventure and an escape from reality, leading wide-eyed tourists through the treacherous, intoxicating landscape.

In worn leather attire, I headed to the stables. My horses, an extension of my own anxious energy, snorted their greetings.

"Morning, Ginny," I cooed, offering the eldest mare a blood-red apple. She crunched into it appreciatively, and the familiar, comforting sound soothed some of my restlessness.

Strapping on my worn boots, I pressed my back against the cool metal of Ginny's stall. It was still early; dawn was just a blush on the horizon, making the stables a realm of half-shadow and murmurings of horses. I did some of my chores, then saddled Ginny.

With her reins firm in my grip, we left for an easy morning ride. A sense of serenity washed over me. Out here, I could pretend that the pile of bills and my sister's reckless antics weren't waiting for me back home.

Here, I could pretend I was doing okay.

I rounded a bend on the trail and spotted the ominous shape of an RV parked haphazardly. It was rare that people were out here, and my brow furrowed in confusion as I approached.

My heart pounded as a familiar figure stepped out.

Declan.

His eyes were sparkling with mischief and something darker.

"Well now, look what the wind blew in," he drawled, leaning against the RV, projecting a casual ease.

"Didn't expect to see you out here," I replied, nudging Ginny forward.

His sapphire gaze glinted in the rising sun. "Just looking for some peace, Wildflower."

I gave him a skeptical look at the evasive response and the tenderness of his nickname for me. "The Dust Devils too much for you?"

His laugh was low and silky, a sound that curled around me, pulling me in. "Oh, they have their moments."

The tension between us sparked and sizzled, a connection I should have resisted but couldn't. Our banter continued, a verbal sparring match as wicked as it was compelling.

I scoffed, my grip on the reins tightening. "Moments? Seems like terrorizing the locals is more their speed. Though I haven't decided if you're as awful as the rest of them."

Declan's expression grew more smug, his eyes burning with an intense glimmer. "To be honest, I'm just as bad, if not worse."

I narrowed my eyes, unyielding in my gaze. "Well, saving me last night puts you a notch above those devils, I suppose."

"Maybe I had ulterior motives," he replied, his voice husky and alluring.

I stepped off my horse, my heart pounding as I closed the distance between us. "And what motives would those be?"

He leaned in, his breath grazing against my ear. "You were a beautiful damsel in distress. Perhaps I was hoping for a more . . . intimate way of showing your gratitude."

My lips curled into a sly smile, the tension between us growing. "So, you think a kiss would be appropriate?"

He smirked, his eyes tracing my lips. "A kiss, or something even more daring. The choice is yours."

A flicker of uncertainty mixed with undeniable attraction filled me as I took a step closer to him, our bodies almost touching. "And what if I choose the more daring option?"

Declan's voice dropped to a low, seductive tone, his gaze never leaving mine. "Choose it and find out."

I cleared my throat and shook my head. "Well, aren't you a flirt?" I laughed, feeling nervous. It was strange how easily he got my heart racing, my legs trembling.

"No, Wildflower. I'm definitely not a flirt. I'm a man of promise."

I swallowed nervously, and he took a step closer.

Declan closed the distance between us, his presence enveloping me in a heady mix of need and temptation. His voice was a velvety whisper, laced with a hint of dominance.

"Choose the daring option, Wildflower," he murmured, his gaze locked onto mine.

I couldn't help but feel a delicious sense of anticipation, a curiosity mingled with the nerves that flared within me. His confidence was both captivating and intimidating.

I leaned back slightly, my voice betraying a hint of nervousness. "And what exactly does this daring option entail?"

Declan's eyes sparkled with wicked delight. "It's a dance on the razor's edge."

My breath caught in my throat as his words painted vivid images in my mind. The charm of the unknown tugged at me, and yet, a part of me hesitated. "Maybe take me to dinner first," I teased.

His response was instant. "Are you free tonight?"

Before I could respond, the RV's door creaked open, revealing a woman in a black lace bra, her blonde curls tumbling around her shoulders. Jealousy flared within me, a green-eyed monster that surprised me. I barely knew this man and we shared nothing but harmless flirting.

It still stung, though.

She had bruises in the shape of lips along her neck. Her casual intimacy with Declan made it clear he was taking *plenty* of women to dance on the razor's edge.

"I think I better go," I murmured, my pulse loud in my ears.

But Declan was quick to make introductions, his tone full of sly amusement, "Tara, meet *my* wildflower. Wildflower, this is Tara."

Tara's eyes flickered between us as she arched her brow, "Hello, Wildflower."

Flustered and seething with a strange mix of envy and anger, I managed a curt nod before mounting Ginny and steering her back down the trail. I shouldn't be flirting with a Dust Devils member, much less harboring feelings of jealousy. But as I rode off, a bitter truth settled within me: Declan was an enigma I couldn't simply ignore.

CHAPTER 3

Rodeo Royalty

DECLAN

I stormed into their hovel of a hideout, fury bubbling up from my gut. The Dust Devils, a rotten group of clumsy criminals, had recruited me for a job. And their leader, Hank, seemed hell-bent on making my fucking life miserable.

First, he wanted to test me by making me ride a bull. It was some shitty hazing ritual they all enjoyed. I'd done it countless times before, and the back of a bucking bull lost its rush years ago, yet I resented Hank's smug assumption that it would be a challenge for me.

Now, apparently, Hank had another task lined up.

The stench of inevitable conflict filled my nostrils, bringing a wolfish grin to my face. I was ready for a damned good fight.

Pissed off and ready to raise hell, I was practically begging for a fight. The Dust Devils in the compound gave me a wide berth, their nerves fraying as I strutted past.

My every move screamed dominance, my glare sharp enough to drill holes.

I made my way confidently toward Hank's private quarters, immediately coming face-to-face with a duo of burly bodyguards. Their icy glares and clenched fists were clearly designed to intimidate, but I felt anything but fear. Instead, a rush of adrenaline mixed with sheer bravado coursed through me. My grin was rapacious.

Breaking the silence, my voice held a growl of impatience. "Where's Hank?" The guards visibly tensed at my confrontational tone, fully aware of the whirlwind I could cause. My overall demeanor, coupled with a gaze as cold as winter itself, was a clear warning sign.

"He's inside. Been waiting for you," one of the guards managed to say, barely concealing the nervousness in his voice. I simply nodded, ready to face whatever Hank had in store for me.

As I pushed my way through the grand doors into Hank's private den, my heart pounded a fierce rhythm. There he was, the man himself, reclining on his worn seat of power. He looked like the devil bathed in a haze of smoke.

His smirk broadened into a grin as he spoke. "A toast to your initiation," he chuckled, his voice as rough as gravel. "You handled that bull like a seasoned cowboy." Hank theatrically blew a kiss toward me, his predatory gaze challenging me to look away. The room was alive with a palpable tension.

I could take him out, along with everyone else in this damned place.

But I had a part to play.

"Been riding since I was a boy," I replied, layering my words with an enticing blend of venom and charm.

"Good," responded Hank, his self-satisfied grin transitioning into something genuine. "Means you can handle yourself in a fight. Just the kind of enforcer I need right now." He settled back into his chair, deeply inhaling from his cigar, all the while maintaining eye contact.

"I'm not an enforcer. I'm a hired killer. My contract with you has an end date."

Hank smirked at my confident words. "We'll see."

I paused for a moment, scanning the room for vulnerabilities. The place was like a pressure cooker, the air heavy with cigar smoke and the musky scent of perspiration. I continued. "Why the need for the bull-riding initiation?"

Hank let out a bitter laugh. "It's all about the ride. Tells us everything. Who's trustworthy, who's cunning, who's got the nerve. It's our method of separating the men from the boys. You're on my payroll. That makes you a Devil," he retorted, his tone asserting ownership.

I clenched my jaw. The thought of being owned didn't sit well with me, but I had a role to fulfill. Hank's enemies weren't the only rats I intended to eradicate.

"I'm my own man, Hank," I responded, a devil-may-care smile playing on my lips. He was stepping onto my turf now, and he knew it. I was the man skilled enough, capable enough to kill. I was the one with the connections. The qualifications. The only leverage he had was information, and if he double-crossed me, I'd rip the information from his veins.

Though I preferred this easier method. "I've done your little initiation. Don't mistake why I'm here."

"Understood," Hank grudgingly admitted, though his gaze remained unyielding.

He signaled his henchmen, who promptly exited the room. The door shut heavily behind them, leaving us in solitude.

"So what's the job?" I demanded, my determination unwavering.

"I like your direct approach." Hank leaned forward. "I've got a situation that requires your particular set of skills. You come highly recommended. Efficient, discreet, professional."

"I deliver results," I confirmed.

"I want to witness it for myself. People talk all the time, but I need action, Declan."

I raised an eyebrow. "What do you propose?"

"Bring me a trophy," he proposed with a wicked grin. "A head. Kill someone in this sorry ass town. Show me you can handle the dirty work. Make it clean. Make it secret. Then the job's yours. Along with your information."

I moved closer, confronting his challenge. "I've already proven myself."

His eyes narrowed, a hint of amusement in his gaze. "You're impressive, no doubt," he admitted, taking a long drag from his cigarette. "But proving your worth doesn't necessarily mean you're the killer I need for this particular job."

I widened my stance, my smirk speaking volumes. "My reputation says otherwise."

His laughter was a harsh grating sound. "Then one more won't hurt, right? I'll handle any fallout. It's a form of insurance, keeps my men in line."

His condescending tone irritated me.

Hank's mouth twisted into a wolfish grin. "I like

you, Declan. You don't shy from taking what's yours, from doing what's gotta be done. I can see that hunger in your eyes. That's why you're gonna find some poor bastard in town, kill him, and gift me his head. We both know you'll go to any length for my intel." He tapped his forehead with a finger. "Show me you're all in."

I tilted my chin up, arms folded across my chest. "I don't kill for free," I snapped, my tone oozing confidence.

Hank rumbled a laugh. "It's not for free. At the end of our contract, I'll pay what is due."

I shrugged, my lips twisting into a smug smirk. "Maybe I should charge more."

His gaze hardened. "We both know that the information I have is worth more than money," he warned.

I cocked my head, a spark of defiance in my eyes. "And I plan to collect," I shot back.

Hank's eyebrow shot up. "I'll tell you the name of your mother's killer, son. I'm a man of my word. But you have to prove yourself first. I don't fuck around. It's hard to trust a man driven by vengeance. It makes them harder to control. Harder to predict. I'm just making sure you're capable."

An inkling of doubt hit me, but I clamped down on it. Showed no cracks. "I'm ready for whatever shit-show you got lined up," I stated, my voice rock solid.

Hank grinned, nodding his approval. "That's the spirit."

"Alright then," I rallied, fire in my voice, "what's the gig after I kill some sorry fucker, hmm?"

His stare turned steely, a jolt of malice electrifying the air. Wasn't gonna let him grind me down with his talk. Had the fury, yeah, but more than that. I was a seasoned killer, a shadowy death dealer. I'd do the job, cash out, and collect the info I craved.

"I have a high profile problem I need to eliminate," Hank started, and I felt heat creeping up my neck, my body tightening like a sprung trap. His condescension was just gasoline on my flame. I was built for survival, unshakable, not even by this grizzled wolf.

"I don't need the backstory. Don't care about your grudge. Just need to get the hit done and be on my way." I had no plans to be in this town for long. I'd kill a few people. Fuck a few women. Then, I'd be on my way with the information Hank had.

"It's three hits," Hank corrected. "No loose ends, Declan. You got your RV set up on the trail?"

Hank was a greedy fucker.

I gave a nod.

"Good. Judge Mathis is treating his old lady to a trail ride for her big six-oh. The broad's crazy about horses." He barked out a laugh, the sound booming. "Set up on the trail, wipe 'em all out. The couple and the guide. Don't want anyone left to talk. Get it done clean, and I'll cut your check and give you that name you've been searching for. Make it look like a murder suicide."

I tilted my head. "You didn't say shit about a guide when you brought me on." My mind flashed to Clover. Fuck, she was gorgeous. I knew she'd be in my bed the moment I saw her. Now, Hank wanted me to kill her.

"What's one more? I can't have any goddamn loose ends. Judge Mathis double-crossed me. It's time he felt the full weight of what happens when you fuck with the Devils."

I sized him up, my face a stone mask, jaw clenched with a cocktail of rage and reluctant acceptance. I knew the futility of arguing. Hank held the reins. My voice was a frosty promise, "It's a done deal." I popped my knuckles, a cruel smirk playing on my lips.

Hank sank back into his chair, flicking his half-smoked cigar toward the ashtray. "Good," he replied, amusement twinkling in his eyes. "Knew I picked the right son of a bitch for this gig. You got four days to give me a head. Pull that off, and we can move on to the real job you signed up for." He pushed himself up, hand extended. "Your payday will be ready when you get back." I took his hand, eyes dissecting his every twitch. He retracted his hand, motioning me to the door. "Now get your ass moving!"

I ghosted out of the room, boots whispering over the polished floorboards. There was work to do, a mark to pick. Four days on the clock. Time to punch in.

Surrounded by the cesspit that was the criminal underworld, a wave of revulsion washed over me. These were the kind of scumbags I never wanted on my speed dial. But then again, I wasn't the type to lean on anyone.

I was a solitary beast, a ruthless hunter, a damn force of nature.

I learned a helluva long time ago, you can't trust a soul in this fucked-up world. Only got yourself to fall back on.

I couldn't help but dissect the fucker I was stuck working for—Hank. I'd seen his brand of sleaze before: a man all gobbled up by greed, senses numbed by the heady cocktail of power he sloshed around. Complacency had him by the balls, his defenses down as he bathed in his deluded sense of invulnerability.

I fucking loathed Hank and everything he embodied. The only reason I found myself tangled in his web of depravity was the golden nugget he held—the name of the bastard who killed my mom. That single tidbit had pushed me to the edge, forcing me to rub shoulders with the despicable dregs of society that swarmed around me.

As I continued my mental dissection of Hank's weaknesses, my focus sharpened. Every word he spoke, every movement he made, all meticulously cataloged and analyzed in my mind. I was a predator stalking my prey, patiently waiting for the perfect moment to strike.

CHAPTER 4
Lone Star Love Story

CLOVER

I navigated the shadowy, serpentine road leading to my friend Laura's home. The headlights of my car cast unsettling shadows that flickered and cavorted among the bordering trees.

"I got the ice cream ready!" she said on the phone while I smiled. She knew I needed a break. Avery's antics had been driving me crazy lately, and it was nice to hang out with someone who didn't need me to take care of them. Laura and I had been best friends for fifteen years.

"I'm surprised you snuck any ice cream into the house without Carson seeing," I teased.

"That boy already stole a scoop," Laura replied with a laugh, her tone full of happiness and warmth. "I swear my son has a sweet tooth alert system set up somewhere. The moment I walk through the door with anything containing sugar, he drops everything to steal it."

We both laughed. "I'll be there soon."

"Looking forward to it. Drive safe."

Following the call, I chucked my cell onto the passenger seat and pressed on, the car's engine and the road's white noise my only company. Reminders of Avery plagued me, a persistent worry gnawing at my consciousness. Out again, probably brushing shoulders with the wrong crowd—the Devils, maybe. My sister's penchant for flirting with danger was a constant source of anxiety, her reckless boundary pushing a weighty burden on my already heavy shoulders.

My responsibilities replayed in my mind like a broken record.

Work.

Avery.

And that crippling loneliness, an unwelcome passenger in the silence of the car, its presence more pervasive and tangible than ever. This stark solitude wasn't just a state of being; it was a harsh reminder of my isolation in a world of shared troubles.

I had Laura and Avery. But my sister was constantly out seeking the next thrill, and Laura was a single mom to a rambunctious six-year-old. Sometimes I just wanted someone to spend time with. To share the burdens with.

Someone to take care of me.

As I maneuvered through the path, my mind was a swirl of worry and anxiety, a veil of fog that separated me from the physical world. Lost in my own thoughts, my senses were numbed.

And then, in a blink, the tranquil night shattered.

A flash of brown and white exploded from the shadowy underbrush, a deer darting with heart-stopping suddenness onto the asphalt.

Shit!

My heart stalled as the world seemed to slow, the oncoming outline of the deer imprinted against the harsh glare of the headlights. A moment of suspended silence. Then came the devastating impact.

The deer slammed into the windshield with a thunderous crash, a gruesome chorus of shattering glass and a sickening crunch of bone. The animal's desperate eyes locked with mine for a horrifying instant before it was torn away by the brutal force of the collision.

Time seemed to slow as the deer collided with my truck, the terrible crash of impact blaring through the night. The animal was gone as quickly as it had appeared, leaving only shards of glass and a truck skidding out of control in its wake.

Frantically, I pulled the wheel to the right, but the truck swerved off the road, scraping into a ditch. The impact with the steering wheel knocked the wind out of me, causing a sharp pain to flare in my chest. My vision blurred as I gasped for breath.

Silence fell as the engine sputtered and died, the remnants of the crash lying starkly around me. Stranded, injured, and alone, I began to feel panic creeping in, filling the truck's cab and my mind with dread.

Every movement was met with a tremor of pain. With great effort, I grabbed my phone and pushed open the door, the twisted metal grinding against my strength. A quick inventory revealed a throbbing ankle, a scraped knee, and a backache. My head pounded, vision still fuzzy, but I knew it would pass.

My dad's old truck was now a testament to the accident, a broken windshield and sizable dent marring its exterior. Anger bubbled up, and I kicked the truck. This old piece of metal was more than just transportation—it was a piece of my dad. Now, it was just another thing in my life that was broken.

Between taking care of my sister and keeping up with bills, I was stretched thin. Laura's invite had been a lifeline. Now, it felt like another load added to my already heavy burden.

The growl of a motorcycle pulled me from my

thoughts. A sleek black bike pulled up, the rider stepping off with an air of effortless grace. The man was tall, his shoulders broad, and his face rough-hewn. His windblown hair gave him a rugged appeal.

Declan Wilder.

Why was it always Declan Wilder who crossed my path? His charm was a magnet I couldn't resist. We eyed each other, an exchange of silent assessments. His stare was penetrating, hinting at a darkness that made me tremble.

"Need help?" His voice was gruff, and I felt a jolt at his words. There was a certain electricity in the air, drawing us closer.

I hesitated, torn between wariness and attraction. He was a mystery wrapped in a good-looking package, but I was drawn to him, transfixed by his aura. With a slight nod, I allowed him to step closer. He moved with an ease and purpose that was almost mesmerizing.

His hand came up, pushing a loose strand of hair from my face. His touch sent a warm current through me, causing me to blush and lean into his hand.

Yet, amidst the tenderness, there was a twinge of fear. He was still an unknown, a tantalizing enigma.

His fingers traced the forming bruises on my arm, the contact sending a delightful chill through my veins. His gaze was overwhelming, a mix of concern and interest. "Are you hurt?" His voice was low, a husky rumble that sent a thrill through me.

I found myself unable to speak, the heat of his touch sparking an urge within me. His face softened with regret and concern. "I won't hurt you, Wildflower," he assured, his voice carrying a gentle growl.

He stepped closer, insistent on checking my condition. His touch was firm yet delicate, stirring a longing I couldn't deny.

Our connection in that moment felt electric, everything else fading into insignificance. "You're okay now, Wildflower," he murmured, his voice a soft rumble resonating within me.

I knew I should push him away, but his pull was too strong. His fingers gently traced my forming bruises, causing him to furrow his brow in anger. "You're pretty banged up. Anything else hurting?" he asked, his voice rough with worry.

Caught by his glare, I hesitated before admitting, "My head's throbbing a bit."

He put his hands on my shoulders, grounding me. "You could have a concussion," he grumbled, concern lacing his words.

"I'm okay," I managed to say. "Just shaken up from the deer."

His eyes examined me, checking for injuries. As his

gaze slid down, my veins buzzed. He reached out, his hands finding my waist. "I need to make sure you're okay everywhere else," he said, his voice a husky whisper.

His touch sent warmth through me. I struggled to keep my composure as he slowly moved his hands along my body, amplifying the charged atmosphere between us.

He stopped at my knees, his gaze seeking mine. "I need to check your legs, too. Is that okay?" His question hung in the air, filled with unspoken meaning.

I nodded, silently agreeing to his request. As he checked me over, the force of the moment was almost overwhelming.

Finally, he pulled back. "You might be sore tomorrow, but it looks like you're okay. Let's go look at your truck," he suggested. I watched him, drawn to the effortless strength and grace in his movements.

"Damn, this is pretty bad," he remarked, straightening up and turning to face me. "Your axle is shot. Your engine is beyond repair. You'll need a tow."

Fuck. More expenses. More bills.

"Thanks. I'll call for help," I replied, frustration etched on my face.

Declan noticed my expression and tilted his head, studying me intently with his dark, penetrating eyes. "You look like you could use a drink," he suggested, a slight smirk tugging at his lips. "Or maybe a visit to the hospital. I'm still worried about a concussion."

I let out a bitter laugh. "A drink won't solve my problems right now. I need a ride," I said, glancing at his motorcycle, an idea forming in my mind.

He raised an eyebrow, genuine concern furrowing his brow. "To the hospital?"

I shook my head, dismissing the thought. Hospitals meant bills I couldn't afford. Plus, I wasn't in terrible shape. "To my friend's house."

"A friend's house," he repeated, skepticism lacing his voice. He glanced at his watch, a flicker of jealousy crossing his face. "At this hour? What kind of man makes his woman come to him?" His voice quivered with an undercurrent of anger.

Bewildered, I furrowed my brow. "It's not like that."

A cynical smile played on his mouth, possessiveness seeping into his voice. "Are you sure about that?"

"Why does it matter to you?" I asked, curiosity piqued.

He stepped closer, his dark eyes locked onto mine, holding me captive. "If you were mine, I'd come to you," he growled seductively. "Hell, I'd probably never leave your side. I certainly wouldn't have let you drive this beat-up truck without airbags."

Embarrassment mixed with excitement, and a flush

crept up my neck. "Well, I'm not yours. I love this damn truck, and my friend has a little boy," I revealed. "It's hard for her to go out on school nights." It was odd that he was jealous when *Tara* was half-dressed in his RV just a few days ago.

His expression shifted to a look of surprise before his eyes narrowed again. "I see. It doesn't change the fact that you shouldn't be driving in your condition. Let me give you a ride. I promise I'll get you there safely."

I hesitated, weighing my options. Deep down, I knew I couldn't refuse his offer. "I could call someone else—"

"Clover. Get on the damn bike," he commanded.

I scoffed, not willing to be swayed so easily. "I barely know you. What if you're some kind of psycho?"

Declan's eyes darkened, his fist clenching as he leaned in, his breath tickling my ear. "Even psychos take nights off," he whispered, his words laced with both heat and peril.

My heart raced, uncertain if he was serious or if I was playing with fire. The gleam in his eyes stirred a blend of fear and desire within me.

"Come on, Clover," he said, his voice taking on a more earnest tone. "I won't harm you tonight. I just want to help."

I hesitated, the weight of his intentions still hanging in the air. But the sight of my battered truck pushed me toward a decision. "Fine," I relented, mustering a feigned confidence. "But don't you dare try anything funny," I warned, crossing my arms defensively.

Declan raised an eyebrow, an arrogant grin playing at the corner of his mouth. "Who, me? I'm the epitome of innocence," he teased, although the mischievous glint in his expression betrayed his words.

"I'm not joking," I retorted, my voice firm. "I've had a rough night, and the last thing I need is more trouble."

He held up his hands in surrender, his voice tinged with sincerity. "Alright, I promise, no funny business. I just want to make sure you're taken care of. You're in no condition to be wandering around alone."

I regarded him skeptically, the wariness still lingering within me. "Why do you care so much, anyway? You barely know me."

Declan's expression softened, and he sighed. "I'm not a monster. Any decent guy wouldn't leave a woman out here alone." But I knew Declan wasn't the typical decent guy; there was an aura of danger emanating from him that was hard to ignore. He stepped closer, his dark eyes filled with a fierce rush of power. "I just want to make sure you're safe."

I considered his words for a moment, torn between the logical choice and the captivating pull of the unknown. In the end, practicality won over curiosity. "Fine," I relented. I really needed to get to Laura's house. Not to mention, I didn't want to be stranded here while Avery was out at a party. "Laura lives off Dire Lane by the grocery store and that rundown bar. You know where that is?"

"Sure, Wildflower," Declan replied, his voice laced with a hint of amusement.

As I climbed onto the back of his motorcycle, a mixture of apprehension and excitement coursed through me. The engine roared to life, vibrating against my body as I tightly gripped onto Declan. The night air whipped against my face, blending with the adrenaline rushing through my veins.

Casting one last look at my battered truck, we started moving into the cloak of darkness.

CHAPTER 5
Love Bucked Me

CLOVER

*A*s we twisted and turned along the road, I found myself clinging tighter to Declan. The heat from his body seeped into mine, igniting something new within me. I felt a wild sense of curiosity bubbling up, testing the line between caution and recklessness.

Our ride was quiet, filled only with the sound of our breaths and the steady rumble of the bike. Everything else seemed to fade away, leaving just the two of us wrapped in the thrill of the ride and the strange attraction pulling us together.

I couldn't resist running my fingers along his back, feeling the hard muscles underneath his shirt. Our silent connection deepened with each new discovery my hands made. His body's subtle responses were a clear warning sign—we were crossing into terrifying territory.

When the headlights of the bike revealed a local bar instead of Laura's house, I was taken aback. "Why are we here?" I asked, trying to keep my annoyance at bay. We were just a couple of blocks away from Laura's place, my original destination.

A playful grin spread across Declan's face. "Relax, Wildflower," he said in a low, soothing voice. "Thought we could use a drink."

Without missing a beat, I retrieved my phone from my pocket, fingers dancing over the screen to text Laura about the car trouble and consequent delay. Not a cloud of doubt about Declan's intentions hovered in my mind.

I suppressed an eye roll. The idea of a hard drink seemed appealing after the whirlwind evening. Hell, I wasn't ready to say goodbye to him. Something about Declan Wilder captivated me. As we sauntered into the dimly lit bar, the murmurs dipped and heads pivoted, Declan drawing interest and speculation like a magnet.

Upon reaching the bar, Declan gestured for two neat whiskeys, the bartender nodding without questioning, as if already aware of his choice. Declan's silent command over the space was intense. The liquor's bite and subsequent warmth brought a welcomed flush, spreading from my throat to my chest.

Catching Declan's unwavering gaze, I felt a heat creep into my cheeks under the weight of his scrutiny. "What?" The word escaped me, laced with an unexpected shyness.

He shrugged casually, a teasing smile playing on his lips. "You fit well on my bike, Wildflower."

His comment made goose bumps spread across my skin, challenging me in a way I hadn't expected. I swiftly tried to deflect his comment. "So, what's a guy like you doing in our quiet town? You seem out of place in a local rodeo like Dust Devils."

His eyes lit up before a shadow briefly crossed his features. "Just passing through," he said vaguely, focusing back on his drink.

Unable to hold back my curiosity, I pressed, "Just passing through? That's a bit mysterious, don't you think?"

His laugh filled the air, a deep, rich sound. "Life's all about going where the wind takes you, right?"

His noncommittal charm was as irritating as it was intriguing. "I've lived here all my life," I admitted, taking another sip of the whiskey, feeling its heat course down my throat. "What about you?"

He shrugged again, a relaxed smile on his face. "I've lived all over."

My sigh slipped out, his dismissive attitude testing my patience. "Explains the RV," I conceded, feeling the liquid warmth spreading within me. "Do you travel for rodeo events? Or . . . something else . . . ?" I knew he was associated with the Dust Devils. I wondered if he was some sort of traveling drug dealer —or worse.

"I do a bit of odd jobs. I'm a contract hire," he affirmed, his voice unhurried. "But bull riding's been a part of me since childhood. My dad, he passed when I was twelve, but he taught me most of what I know." He paused, taking a sip of his whiskey before adding, "My mom, she's gone too."

The mention of his parents' death echoed a familiar pang of loss. "Oh." My voice softened, empathy coloring the single syllable. "I'm sorry to hear that."

Declan's gaze mellowed, momentarily letting his guard down. "Appreciated," he responded, a touch of frailty peeking through his tone. "Time doesn't really dull the pain."

Silently agreeing, I managed a soft, "I know." My words hovered in the air. "Grief, it leaves its mark."

His eyes met mine, reflecting a silent pact shared through loss. "Yes, it does," he replied, his voice resonating like the low strum of a guitar.

We were connected, two souls linked by past pains.

Our exchange carried a weight that seemed to quiet everything around us.

As the quiet lingered, I gathered my courage. "Bull riding, it's not my thing," I confessed, my voice edged with nervousness. "My dad died because of a ride, and my little sister is dead set on following in his footsteps."

Declan's face darkened, a mix of regret and comprehension in his eyes. "I'm sorry about your dad," he said, sincerity ringing in his voice. "This sport, it can be brutal."

Memories of my dad's accident surged back, pulling me into their current. "It's terrifying," I admitted, my voice shaky. "Watching someone you care about risk everything . . . it's a nightmare."

He nodded, seeming momentarily lost in thought. "No argument there," he said, his voice barely above a whisper. "But sometimes, you learn more from doing. And the more you're told no, the more enticing it becomes."

His words echoed my own thoughts about my sister. I wanted to shield her from the harsh reality of the rodeo, but I knew there was a draw she couldn't ignore. It was a tricky balance of wanting to protect her and knowing she had her own dreams to chase.

"You may be right," I conceded, a hint of resignation in my voice. "Maybe it's less about the risk and more about confronting our fears, finding bravery in the midst of the chaos."

Our eyes locked, a newfound respect in his. "Exactly," he said, his voice low and warm, stirring a whirlpool of feelings within me. "Risk is part of truly living life."

His words hung in the silence, escalating the connection between us. I was acutely aware of the uncertainty of our situation, the unspoken desires underpinning our conversation. It felt like something was pulling us closer, tempting us to explore the undefined boundaries of our attraction.

But Declan's involvement with the Dust Devils gang hung over us like an unspoken secret, a constant reminder of the potential problems surrounding him. I knew I had to keep my guard up to avoid the emotional rollercoaster that getting involved with him could trigger. "Seems like riding bulls doesn't really shake you up," I ventured.

"Hmm."

I took a sip of my whiskey, wrestling with the unease growing inside me. My aversion to bull riding was deeply ingrained, tied to painful memories and anxiety about Avery's future. My dad's accident cast a long, dark shadow, and yet Avery seemed determined to follow in his footsteps. "So, you ride for the Devils?" I pushed further, ignoring the discomfort of digging into this sensitive topic. I needed answers, but Declan was a vault of hidden truths.

"When they need me, I'm there," he replied nonchalantly.

"And do you do everything they ask?" I prodded softly, fearful of what his answer might be.

His gaze met mine, the power of it making my skin tingle. "As long as I'm in town, yeah."

His words were all the confirmation I needed. The harsh truth of our situation suddenly felt all too real. I couldn't deny my attraction to Declan, but I also knew pursuing anything more than friendship with him was a bad idea. Not only was he just passing through, but his ties to the infamous Dust Devils gang made him a troubling prospect. I couldn't afford to let myself fall for someone whose life was entrenched in unpre-dictability.

My mind raced as a heavy realization settled in. Understanding that Declan was a temporary figure in my life, not to mention his link to criminal activities, underscored the need to guard my heart from the potential pain and chaos that could follow.

"It's a shame you're a bull rider. We could have had fun," I said, forcing my tone to be lighthearted. I needed him to know that this was probably going to be the last time we saw one another. I needed to end this.

"We can still have fun," he replied.

"I don't have *fun* with bull riders that work for the Devils. After my father died, that sort of risk lost its appeal."

Declan's hand found its way onto mine, an unexpected gesture that caused a jolt of surprise. "Loss is hard," he began, his voice carrying a hint of an unspoken past. "When you lose someone, it feels like you could lose everyone else, too. Then, when you feel like you've lost everything, you start losing yourself. Sometimes, surviving means accepting who grief makes you."

I turned to look at him, a mix of surprise and curiosity bubbling within me. "Is it grief that got you tangled up with the Dust Devils?" I dared to ask, my words hushed in the dimly lit bar.

He shrugged, the corner of his mouth curving up slightly. "More like revenge," he responded, lifting his glass for a drink.

I held his gaze, feeling the charged tension that buzzed between us. I swallowed hard, a knot of uncertainty in my throat. "I should probably head over to Laura's place now . . ."

Declan signaled for the bartender, ordering another round of whiskey. He then turned back to me, his eyes filled with a familiar mischief. "You don't have to rush off," he murmured, his voice taking on a sultry tone. "Stay, have a drink with me. Unless you're afraid of what might happen if you do . . ."

His implicit challenge sparked a wave of both annoyance and curiosity in me. I wasn't one to be easily rattled, and his insinuation irked me. "I'm not scared," I shot back, matching his edge as I finished off my whiskey.

He inched closer, and his voice dropped to a whisper, his words laced with a tantalizing energy. "Maybe you should be."

The offhanded caution in his voice sent a jolt of apprehension through me. My heart thumped in my chest, and I found myself locked in the depths of his gaze. An enticing paradox of vulnerability and appeal, he was a puzzle I was afraid to solve, yet couldn't resist.

However, I maintained my defiant stance, matching his lingering gaze with my own unwavering one. The whiskey was a warm, spreading courage within me, nudging me to teeter at the edge of the precipice.

Ignoring the voice in my head screaming caution, I mirrored his posture, leaning in just a bit closer, my voice a mere whisper. "And what makes you think I should be?"

Declan's lips curled into a half-smile, his intense gaze holding mine captive. A charged silence hung in the air, pregnant with unspoken words and veiled promises. It wrapped around us, spinning a captivating web that quickened my breath. His hand reached out, fingertips barely brushing against mine in a gesture both audacious and subtle.

"Because, Wildflower," he murmured, his voice a gravelly whisper. A rush of exhilaration surged through me at the sound. "I'm not a man for half-measures."

His gaze, usually lively and playful, took on a heavier, more serious tone. The ferocity in his eyes added weight to his words, the unsaid as potent as what was spoken. "When I decide I want something," he continued, his voice dropping an octave, "I don't just dip my toe in to test the waters. I dive in headfirst. I'm all in, come hell or high water."

His words were a slow burn, a potent promise bundled with a cautionary note. The insinuation of his statement hung in the air, casting a shadow over the quiet camaraderie that had marked our evening.

His bold admission hung heavily between us, coaxing me to peel back layers of my own guarded heart. Emboldened by his openness, I found myself drawn into the conversation, our exchange evolving into a dance of vulnerability and revelation.

"I used to be like that too," I admitted, the taste of nostalgia bitter on my tongue. I found myself staring into the amber liquid of my drink, my thoughts lost in a time when I had been wilder, more reckless. "I was always the extreme one. Felt things more deeply, took greater risks . . . dove headfirst into life."

I paused, swallowing the lump of emotion that had welled up in my throat. "But then it all just . . . lost its shine, you know? The highs and the lows, the thrill of risk, even the feeling of the wind against my face on a fast ride . . . it just wasn't the same anymore."

Declan's gaze on me was patient, understanding, as if he was privy to a secret I hadn't yet discovered. "Maybe you're just looking for something to make you feel again," he suggested, his voice low and encouraging. "Something, or someone, to reignite that spark inside you."

A flutter of interest washed over me, despite my attempts at resistance. The allure of Declan was potent. His audacity promised an untamed adventure, and I couldn't deny the magnetic pull. "And Tara?" I found myself asking, regretting it the moment it slipped from my lips.

His brow furrowed, a picture of confusion. "Who?"

I cringed internally, having clearly stepped out of line. "The girl at your RV?" I tried to salvage.

A glint of amusement lit up his eyes. "Is that jealousy I detect, Clover?" His question sent a rush of heat to my cheeks.

I stumbled over my words, suddenly feeling defensive. "No, of course not."

"I don't mind jealousy," he responded, leaning closer, his voice a hushed whisper in my ear. "I can be a *very* jealous man. When someone's mine, I can be downright possessive."

The words lingered in the silence, expanding the tension between us. I fought back the blush creeping up my neck. "Is Tara yours then?"

He shook his head, a firm no. And then his gaze settled on me again, probing. "And you, Clover? Is there someone claiming you?"

Caught off guard, I found myself shaking my head, a strange blend of exhilaration and relief bubbling up. "No. I don't have someone like that."

A grin spread across his face, a daring promise twinkling in his gaze. "Good," he murmured. The force of his gaze was a jolt to my system, both daunting and enticing in equal measures. "Because, Wildflower, when I'm in, I'm all in."

"But you're not planning on sticking around," I challenged, searching for a semblance of sanity amid the frenzy of emotions.

He chuckled, a rich, deep sound. "True," he admitted, locking eyes with me once more. "But when I set my sights on something . . . or someone, I don't hold back."

His finger traced the rim of his whiskey glass, the movement slow, deliberate.

I swallowed. "Maybe I should just go—"

He leaned even closer, whispering into my ear. "It might be too late for that, Wildflower." His hand slid to my thigh, his touch sending sparks through my body.

I knew I should have pushed him away, should have stood up and walked out of the bar. But I was curious, and the thrill of the risk was too much to resist. I leaned in closer, my lips grazing his ear. "Oh?" I whispered back, feeling disbelief at my own audacity.

Declan's eyes flashed with desire as he stood up. He tossed some cash on the bar top, then took my hand and led me out of the bar.

What had I gotten myself into? But there was something about Declan that made me feel alive, made me forget about all the responsibilities and worries that weighed me down.

The night outside was a stark contrast to the buzzing energy within the bar, the cool air and the twinkling stars offering a tranquil setting to our charged encounter. Declan and I left the dimmed lights behind, his grip on my hand firm yet gentle. "Let me walk you to Laura's," he suggested, his voice barely more than a murmur.

A ripple of apprehension washed over me as we

approached his bike, a whisper of uncertainty tingling at the back of my mind. Yet, the idea of spending a few more moments with him was too enticing to pass up.

Just as I was about to agree, the intrusive chirping of his phone sliced through our intimate bubble. I felt him stiffen, the grip on my hand tightening momentarily. He cast a quick glance at the screen, his face contorting into a grimace, a visible storm brewing in his expression.

"I need to take this," he declared, his voice an edge harder than it had been moments ago. There was a finality to his tone that belied his earlier warmth.

"But . . . ," I started, confusion weaving through my surprise. The sudden shift in his demeanor was jarring.

He interrupted, his gaze locked on the phone. "It's important. I can't avoid this." His words were clipped, laced with an underlying frustration that was tangible. His hand slowly slipped away from mine, the loss of contact leaving me feeling hollow.

There was an urgent edge to his demeanor now, a far cry from the man who'd just promised to walk me to Laura's house. The tension from our conversation had given way to a different kind of pressure, the promise of our evening dissolving into a grim reality.

"Duty calls?" I threw at him, annoyance creeping into my tone. The connection we'd built was quickly being overshadowed by the specter of the Dust Devils and the reality of his other life.

His eyes met mine, a strange mix of regret and determination flickering in them. He reached out, pulling me closer to him. "Clover," he began, his voice low, intimate. "Believe me when I say I'd rather be here with you. I want . . . to see where this goes."

His words hung heavily between us, creating a heady atmosphere that sent a flutter of butterflies through my stomach. Yet, I couldn't completely quell the doubt creeping into my thoughts. He was just passing through town, after all.

"Declan, I don't want to be another nameless face in a town you're passing through," I confessed, my voice a mere whisper. "Another disappointment to add to my list."

He cupped my face with one hand, his touch sending sparks of electricity coursing through me. "Clover," he murmured, his gaze warm and sincere. "I can't make promises about the future, but right now, in this moment, there's nowhere I'd rather be than with you."

With that, he leaned in, capturing my lips with his in a kiss that was gentle yet insistent. It was a kiss that spoke volumes about his intentions, a clear testament to the electric charge that had been building between us. It was a kiss that, despite my skepticism, left me breathless and wanting more.

The kiss was fleeting, a ghost of a promise brushed against my lips. His touch was soft yet demanding, just a taste of what we could share. It was a tease, a moment that was over before it truly began, leaving a lingering warmth that beckoned for more.

Declan pulled back, his gaze dark and intense. The ghost of his touch hovered on my lips, leaving me with the desire to close the distance once more, to seek out the heat that his quick kiss had promised. "I'll take you to Laura's."

We hopped on his bike and he zipped down the block, practically skidding on the asphalt when he stopped. I quickly got off his bike and stared at him.

"Stay safe, Wildflower," he said. "Or don't. Seems I have a habit of saving you, and I'd love the opportunity to do it again." He winked at me before revving his motorcycle. The sound of his revving engine and the vision of his shadowed form disappearing in the night lingered in my mind long after he was gone.

CHAPTER 6
Wrangling Hearts

DECLAN

*A*s I moved toward the hidden rodeo, the remote sounds of the crowd and the snap of a whip reverberating through the balmy air gave me a sense of unease. The cool breeze of the night seemed to do little to soothe my jumbled thoughts.

As I wove through the bustling crowd, past shouting spectators and hardened gamblers, my mind was elsewhere. I was accustomed to the rush of the arena, the hum of adrenaline, but tonight, it was eclipsed by thoughts of Clover.

I found Hank leaning against the railings, eyes trained on the spectacle below. It wasn't until I stood beside him that he acknowledged my presence with a sidelong glance.

"Declan," he barely murmured above the din of the crowd, "I've been hearing . . . things."

A flicker of anger sparked within me, but I masked it with a neutral expression. "Things?" I asked, keeping my voice even, my gaze icy.

His eyes narrowed, adding weight to the silence between us. "You've been dawdling," he growled, an undercurrent of menace in his tone. "Tell me, Declan, have you found your mark yet? Remember, this is no optional task."

His question caught me off guard, but I forced my features to remain impassive. "I'm on it," I retorted. "You gave me four days."

Hank scoffed, shifting his gaze back to the bull riders as one of them was thrown off. "Patience isn't my virtue, Declan. And I don't offer second chances."

I clenched my fists, feeling the pressure of his words. I needed his intel, the name that could put an end to a lifelong vendetta. I was here to get it, even if it meant playing by his rules. So, I stood there, silent, bracing myself for the road ahead.

"Do we understand each other?" he growled, his voice a threatening whisper.

"I understand," I responded, my voice just as low, resolve fortifying my words.

He glanced at me then, his gaze hard to read in the dim light. "Remember, I'm the one with the information you want," he reminded, tapping his temple. In my mind's eye, I saw my blade piercing his skin.

A wordless threat lingered between us. As I watched the reckless riders, my mind filled with doubt. Was this revenge really worth it?

"I've been digging into your past," Hank said, his words breaking my train of thought.

"Oh?" I responded, my voice steady.

"You turned into a real hellion after your mom died. I get it. Your pa died when you were twelve. Your mom turned into a whore and died just three years later. You beat your foster parents, skipped school, joined a gang at fifteen."

My blood boiled. "I'll put up with a lot, Hank, but don't you fucking talk about my mother."

He threw his hands up in mock surrender. "I'm just saying. You've had a hard life, boy."

I acknowledged with a nod. "I did what I had to do. Survival."

A smirk spread across Hank's face. "I noticed something while looking at your record, Declan."

"What?" I asked, my voice sharp.

His grin expanded, exposing a row of discolored teeth. "You've always had issues with authority, Declan. Never the one to kneel before those who'd step over you."

"I don't kneel," I shot back, holding his gaze.

His features tightened, his eyes squinting. "That's the rule of life, Declan. To survive, you have to recognize when to relent and when to fight back. You need to understand who's above you and who's below."

"I didn't sign up for your pecking order, Hank. I was clear on that from the start."

His stare didn't waver. I could feel the heat rolling off of him as he moved closer, his cronies in tow. "That's why you'll fail," he stated, his voice chillingly cold. His disdain was like a slap to my face, inciting my anger.

"I won't fail," I retaliated, my rage barely controlled.

He smirked. "You already have. You've failed to deliver a head. There's plenty of people in this town that'll do. Take your pick. Take your kill. Show me you can do what needs to be done."

I felt my body tense, my hands quivering slightly. I was on a tightrope; one misstep could spell the end. Taking a deep breath, I voiced the risky promise: "I'll deliver."

He looked taken aback by my tone, but I wasn't backing down. Swallowing the lump in my throat, I added, "You want me to prove myself? I'll *more* than deliver. But remember this, Hank—you might wish you hadn't asked."

Hank's gaze hardened, his lips tightening. "Watch your tone," he warned, a threat lacing in his words.

I nodded without looking into his eyes. "And while we're at it, Hank," I said, turning to leave, "stop digging around in my past. It's irrelevant."

Hank let out a wheezing laugh. "Your past is the whole reason you're here, boy."

I ignored him and disappeared into the crowd, feeling the weight of his stare on my back. Anxiety gnawed at my insides, a familiar dread from days long past.

A quick survey of the busy rodeo grounds led my gaze to a solitary figure, firmly backed against a weathered arena pillar. I knew it was Avery, *my* wildflower's spitfire sister. She stood out, nervously glancing around as she waited her turn for the chute. It was easy to guess who she was because there weren't many women here willing to get on the back of a bull.

Her gaze, fervid and unwavering, met mine as I approached, halting just a few feet away.

"Hey," I said, my words floating above the clamor of the crowd. "My name is Declan. Gearing up for a ride tonight?"

She visibly relaxed, a glimmer of a smile playing at her lips. "I . . . yeah, I am."

"You're Avery, right? Clover's sister? She's mentioned you."

A spark of surprise danced in her eyes, followed by a hard swallow. "She did?"

"She sure did."

A slight shift in her stance and a downward gaze broke our connection. "My sister doesn't talk to rodeo men. Hell, she doesn't talk to anyone. Didn't think she knew you. *Or* would talk about me," she said, her voice faint but firm. "I've watched your rides, you know. You're a natural. I've been trying my hand at bull riding too, but you're leagues ahead. How long have you been at it?"

"Since I was a kid," I shared. "But I took it seriously after joining the Dust Devils."

"If I want to make a name for myself in this rodeo world, joining them might be a smart move," Avery countered, her bravado clearly a facade to mask her apprehension. "I've been thinking about initiating."

I chuckled, devoid of any humor. "You don't know what you're signing up for," I warned, my tone carrying an undertone of menace. But Avery held her ground, her gaze steady on mine, her spirit challenging. "Being a bull rider comes with its share of risk," I stated, my eyes burrowing into hers. "But can you live with the weight of taking another's life if it comes to it? Are you ready for the fallout? The rodeo is just a source of income for the Devils. If you joined, your life would become theirs." The silence that descended was potent, filled with unspoken questions and uncertain futures.

She flinched under my frankness but didn't back down. Despite her petite frame, up close, she radiated an inner strength that I recognized from my past, of protecting foster sisters from an unforgiving world. Her determination caught me off guard, giving me pause.

Defiantly, she held my gaze. "I can't answer for everyone else," she said, her voice rock steady, "but I'm not going down without a fight. I want this. I want to make a name for myself, show everyone they were wrong about me." Her declaration stood out against the cacophony of the crowd. "And my dad got his start here. Sponsors scooped him up. The same could happen for me."

I shook my head, a wry smile on my lips. "Hank won't make things easy for you," I said, breaking the tension. "He wants to keep you tethered to him, to control your dreams and shatter them whenever he wants. He'd have you desperate, perpetually chasing something just out of reach. And if the bulls don't kill you, Hank might."

Unfazed, Avery replied, "I can handle myself." Her voice resonated with steely determination.

I watched her, admiring her raw nerve. Clover had her work cut out for her. The task of reining in Avery's wild spirit seemed impossible.

"This is my chance," she finally murmured. "It's my way out. When I'm on that bull, I feel . . . free. I need to prove myself."

"Look, I'm not trying to be a hero or anything like that. Clover didn't send me here to talk you out of this," I hastened to add when Avery's mouth opened and closed like a fish. "It's just . . . Nightfall Rodeo has a way of making even the strongest of us feel like we're walking on eggshells."

Avery scoffed, crossing her arms. Disbelief was written all over her face. "You're like every other man in this sport—thinking that I can't handle myself."

I couldn't help but admire her tenacity and spirit, although misguided. "Alright," I said with a small chuckle, nodding my head in understanding. "But for what it's worth, it's not about being weak or strong— it's about being smart enough not to go alone."

With a determined nod, Avery turned and walked away. I watched her go, a strange mix of admiration and anxiety filling me up. As I did so, I caught sight of Hank watching us from the sidelines. His eyes were hard and unreadable as they followed Avery's retreating figure. He had been there the entire time, listening in on our conversation. He met my gaze before disappearing into the crowd again. Was he planning something?

As the night went on, the clamor of the rodeo continued to fill the air with an electric atmosphere that charged my veins with adrenaline. I couldn't help but keep a watchful eye on Avery as she stood at the edge of the arena, her wide eyes taking in every detail of the events as they unfolded before us.

I felt a strange sense of responsibility for her as I watched the cowboys and bull riders bravely battle each other, and I wondered what kind of future was waiting for any of us—Avery, Clover, or myself. I'd always been a protective bastard. I had a weak spot for women; some therapist once told me it resulted from failing my mother. She was murdered, so I felt the need to protect every woman that came across my path.

But this was different.

Avery was different.

Clover was very, very different. Even now I was feeling itchy, wondering if I should have taken her to the fucking hospital instead of that bar.

Soon enough, Avery's name was called. She took a step forward, striding confidently toward the chute with a look of determination on her face. I couldn't help but feel a surge of both pride and fear as she climbed onto the back of a massive, snorting bull. Its muscles seemed to ripple beneath its hide as she adjusted her grip on the rope tightly with one hand and signaled for the gate to swing open with another.

In an instant, the bull burst out of its confinement, bucking wildly to throw Avery off. My heart was pounding in my chest as I watched her fight to stay atop.

I held my breath as her body moved in sync with the powerful animal beneath her. Every twist, turn, and buck seemed to be met with equal force, Avery refusing to give up. The crowd roared with excitement, the energy in the arena reaching a fever pitch.

Avery's focus never wavered, and the seconds ticked by, each one feeling like an eternity. The bull kicked, twisted, and thrashed, but she held on, her strength and determination shining through.

The arena was deathly silent as the clock counted down the last few seconds of her ride. Finally, the buzzer sounded and Avery released the rope, jumping off the bull in one fluid motion. The crowd erupted in cheers that vibrated through the air as she landed safely on her feet.

Avery accepted the congratulations from her fellow riders, her face flush with victory. The announcer presented her with a pouch of prize money that she tucked into her pocket before scanning the stands for my face. When our eyes locked, she smiled wide and beaming, waves of pride radiating from every pore. I couldn't help but return it, proud of what she'd accomplished—but also knowing how hard it would be to turn away from this life when it's all said and done.

Avery's triumph was immediately cut short as a commotion erupted in the stands. In front of her sat a large man with skin red-hot with anger and veins that rose from his neck like tree roots. He clenched his fists and yelled at the spectators, accusing them of rigging the bets. His rage seemed to expand like a balloon, the fury visible on every inch of his face.

"That fucking bitch conned us all!" he screamed, shaking his fists in rage. Suddenly he lunged forward, his fists connecting with flesh with sickening thuds. The sound ricocheted through the air, fear rippling through the crowd like electricity. People scattered like cockroaches, pushing and shoving each other to get away from the brawl. Desperate to put an end to the chaos, I pushed my way through the maddened horde. He clearly had lost big on Avery's victory and was now casting around for someone to blame.

The man advanced forward, his fists curling into massive balls as he lunged at the nearest person. The sound of meaty fists connecting with flesh reverberated through the air.

The victim was already on the ground, and he had turned his attention to another hapless bystander when I stepped in, throwing myself between them. "That's enough," I growled through gritted teeth, my eyes blazing with fury.

He sneered contemptuously, unimpressed by my attempt at courage. "This ain't your fight, cowboy. Walk away while you still can," he taunted.

But I stood my ground. "You're causing trouble in *my* territory," I replied coldly. "It's my fight now."

With a roar of anger, the man swung at me. I sidestepped his attack and countered with a vicious right hook, my fist connecting with his jaw. He staggered backward, but quickly regained his footing, lunging at me once more.

We traded blows, each hit landing with brutal force. I felt my knuckles split open as they collided with his face, blood staining my hands. But I didn't let the pain slow me down. I ducked under another wild swing, driving my elbow into his gut and following up with a knee to his midsection.

The man doubled over, gasping for breath, but I could see the rage still burning in his eyes. He lunged at me again, but I was ready, grabbing his arm and twisting it behind his back. I applied pressure, feeling the tendons strain under my grip, and he cried out in pain.

"You're done," I growled in his ear, my voice cold and unforgiving. "Leave now, and I won't break your arm."

"Fuck you," he snapped.

He thought I was bluffing; I had warned him, though. Sighing, I reached for the damaged limb. Sweat beading on my forehead, I braced myself until bone cracked.

He screamed in agony, a high-pitched wail of horror and despair that echoed off the walls of the arena. His face contorted in anguish as I released my grip, and he slumped to the ground, cradling his broken arm against his chest. I watched without pity as the writhing figure was dragged out of the stands by security, and the crowd erupted into applause.

Breathing heavily, I looked around at the shocked faces of the spectators. I felt a mix of adrenaline and unease flowing through me, knowing that I had just made a very public statement about the lengths I would go to protect *my* territory, which apparently included anyone related to Clover now.

Fuck. I was seriously *fucked*.

As the crowd slowly dispersed, I caught Avery's eye. She looked at me with a mixture of gratitude and concern, her earlier triumph momentarily forgotten in the wake of the violent confrontation.

"I told you this was no place for you," I hissed, my voice rough from the fight.

With that, I turned away, leaving Avery to process the events of the night as I disappeared into the shadows.

CHAPTER 7
Stirrups and Secrets

CLOVER

I groaned as I opened my eyes, my head throbbing from the night before. I was on Laura's couch, and her son was poking my cheek. "Wake up, Clover!" he shouted, grinning mischievously.

I rubbed my eyes, trying to clear the fog from my brain. I remembered drinking with Declan at the bar.

Carson giggled while I yawned. "You're a sleepy-head." I grinned at him while forcing myself to wake up. Carson was a cute six-year-old with blond hair and bright blue eyes, and he could be a little devil when he wanted to be.

I sat up and rubbed my temples, still feeling the effects of the alcohol. "What time is it?" I asked groggily.

"Almost noon," Laura called out from the kitchen. "You want some coffee?"

I nodded, grateful for the offer. As I waited for the coffee, I tried to piece together the events of the night before. I remembered flirting with Declan and the way his kiss had made my skin tingle with desire. But then his phone rang, and he left in a hurry.

I shook my head, trying to clear the memories from my mind. I couldn't afford to get involved with a man like Declan, not with everything else that was going on in my life.

Laura walked into the living room, an apron wrapped around her waist and her fiery red hair up in a bun. She was seriously beautiful with her curves and her big brown eyes. As always, she looked completely put together despite the chaos of the house.

"So what happened last night, my love?" she asked, handing me the coffee cup.

I shook my head and took a sip of the coffee. "I hit a deer with my truck," I said.

Laura gasped. "Are you okay?"

I nodded. "Yeah, I'm fine. Declan—this guy I met at the Nightfall Rodeo—showed up and helped me deal with the mess. We ended up stopping at the bar by your house, but he got a phone call and left pretty abruptly."

Laura raised an eyebrow, a playful glint spreading

across her face. "Ooh, a cowboy came to your rescue. Tell me more."

I rolled my eyes, feeling my cheeks flush. "It's not like that. We just had a few drinks and talked."

"Uh-huh," Laura said, her tone skeptical. "And did anything else happen?"

I sighed, feeling a mix of frustration and arousal at the memories flooding back. "He flirted a bit," I admitted, taking another sip of the coffee.

Laura's eyes widened in surprise. "And?"

"And nothing. He had to go," I said, feeling a pang of disappointment. "He kissed me. Kind of. It was short and sweet. It doesn't matter, anyway. I can't get involved with him."

Laura placed a comforting hand on my arm. "Why not? You deserve to have some fun, Clover. And from what it sounds like, that cowboy could definitely show you a good time."

I couldn't deny the truth in her words, but I had a bad feeling about Declan. "He's a bull rider, Laura. And I'm pretty sure he's involved in some shady sh—" I looked at Carson. "Stuff with the *D-U-S-T D-E-V-I-L-S.*"

Carson interrupted. "I can spell, you know."

Laura tickled him. "You little devil. Go clean your room for a minute while I talk to Miss Clover, okay?"

He rolled his eyes. "Fine. But bull riders are cool, Clover."

"Go," Laura said with a laugh before turning back to me.

I took another sip of my coffee, and she eyed me for a moment before speaking again. "I think you should give him a chance," Laura said, her voice low and insistent. "As I was saying, you deserve to have some fun, and he could be just the thing to take your mind off of everything else going on in your life."

I shook my head, feeling a mix of desire and fear. "I don't know, Laura. He seems dangerous. And I can't afford to get involved with anyone right now."

Laura leaned in closer. "Sometimes, danger can be exciting. And maybe this is exactly what you need right now, Clover. A little bit of excitement and a whole lot of fun."

I couldn't deny the truth in her words, but I was still hesitant. "I just don't want to get hurt," I breathed.

Laura placed a hand on my shoulder. "I know, Clover. But life is short, and sometimes you have to take a chance. And if it doesn't work out, at least you'll get L-A-I-D. I'm not telling you to marry the man, just have some fun. You're working yourself to the bone, leading trails, watching your sister. I know you come over here to unwind, but I'm a boring mom with—"

"You're a fun friend and I love Carson. Believe me, hanging out at your house is the highlight of my week."

She looked around at the scattered Legos on the ground. "If dodging Legos is your idea of fun, then we seriously need to get you out more."

I giggled and tossed her the pillow I slept on. "Shut up. You're my best friend. Hanging out with you helps a lot. I don't need a man in my life."

"You have that impressive *D-I-L-D-O* I bought you for your twenty-third birthday last year."

Laura and I both laughed until tears streamed down our faces. It felt good to let loose and forget all of my problems, even if just for a moment. "Maybe you're right," I said, feeling an unexpected thrill at the thought of giving into my desires.

"Of course I'm right," Laura said with a wicked grin. "Oh. Avery called last night. She was worried you weren't home when she got there."

I frowned. "How late did she call?"

"Three. She didn't sound too drunk, though. Just riled up. Like she was on an adrenaline high."

"I bet she was bull riding again," I grumbled.

Laura grabbed my shoulder and squeezed. "Avery is eighteen now. You can't control everything she does." I sighed, feeling a mix of frustration and worry about Avery. She had a tendency to rebel, especially lately. I just hoped she wasn't putting herself in too much trouble.

Suddenly, my phone buzzed, interrupting my thoughts. I glanced at the screen and my heart skipped a beat. It was Avery.

"Speak of the devil," I muttered under my breath before answering the call. "Hello?"

"Hey, sis!" Avery shouted through the phone. "I'm sorry for calling so early, but I have big news!"

I fought back a yawn. "What kind of news?"

"I did it!" she exclaimed. "I rode Lightning Bolt for eight full seconds!"

My heart raced as excitement and fear coursed through me. "You did what? When?"

"Last night. Oh my gosh, Clover. It was incredible!" Avery said. "And the Dust Devils aren't so bad. A big fistfight broke out in the crowd, and Declan Wilder showed up and broke this guy's arm—"

"Avery!" I exclaimed, processing the fact that Declan disappeared to go to the rodeo. "A fist fight? Are you kidding me?" I shouted into the phone. "And did you just say Declan was there?"

Avery laughed, clearly unaware of my growing anger. "Yep. He talked to me, you know. He said he knew you. I didn't think he was your type, but I can see the appeal. He was kind of hot in his tight jeans and cowboy hat. And he helped break up the fight. He was annoying at first, trying to tell me to leave, but I guess he isn't so bad."

I felt a surge of jealousy and desire mixed together. "Avery, you need to be careful," I said sternly. "You can't just go around getting involved with dangerous men and bull riding. You could get seriously hurt."

"Relax, Clover. I'm fine," Avery said, sounding annoyed. "I just wanted to tell you about my big win."

I took a deep breath, trying to calm my nerves. "Fine. Congratulations on riding Lightning Bolt, Avery. But please be careful."

"I will. They invited me back to ride again. Apparently, they really like having a female rider. They want to support me, Clover. This is huge, I could make a name for myself and—"

"Avery. I'm worried about you," I whispered.

Laura reached out to pat my leg as Avery replied. "This is huge, Clover. I just want you to support me on this."

I eyed Laura, who stared expectantly at me. "Okay," I mumbled. "Tell me when the next ride is, and I'll be there to cheer you on."

Avery let out a squeal of excitement. "Really? You'll come?"

"Yeah, but only if you wear a helmet. And you promise not to get involved with the Dust Devils. Rodeo only, Avery. I mean it," I said firmly, glancing at Laura, who gave me a small nod of approval. "I don't trust them. Hank and his men are bad news."

Avery let out a laugh. "Oh, come on, Clover. They're not that bad. In fact, I think some of them are kind of hot. Declan certainly got my pulse racing."

I rolled my eyes, feeling a twinge of jealousy again. "Just be careful, Avery. And don't let him or anyone else pressure you into doing something you don't want to do."

"I won't," Avery replied before ending the call.

I let out a sigh, feeling a mix of excitement and worry about the upcoming bull riding event. I knew I had to be there to support Avery, but the thought of seeing Declan again made my heart race.

Laura placed a comforting hand on my arm. "If you're going, I'm going too."

"Really?" I asked, surprised.

Laura nodded. "You bet. My mama can watch Carson for a night. I don't want you going alone, plus, I need to meet this Declan character and see what all the fuss is about."

I smiled, feeling a wave of relief wash over me. I always wanted a big sister, and Laura did an admirable job of filling that role in my life. I was lucky to have her bright outlook and steady support.

"Okay," I said, taking a sip of my coffee.

~

My heart sank as I looked at the crumpled heap of metal that used to be my beloved truck. The tow had just delivered it, and now it was sitting in my driveway, where it would probably stay until I worked up the courage to sell it for scrap metal. It had been my faithful companion for years, taking me and my horses to countless trail rides and adventures. But now, after a freak accident, it was totaled. And with it, my hopes of saving enough money for a rainy day.

I took a deep breath and tried to shake off the sense of despair that was threatening to overtake me. I had to be strong for my horses' sake. They depended on me to take care of them, and I couldn't let them down.

With a heavy heart, I walked into the barn to start my daily routine of caring for my horses. As I went about my tasks, my mind kept drifting back to the financial burden that loomed over me. Hay prices were going up, and I didn't have enough of a cushion to weather the storm.

I knew I had to supplement my income, but I didn't know with what. Maybe a second job, but when would I find the time? My trail guide business was good, but it wasn't enough to cover unexpected expenses like a totaled truck.

I had a few trail rides scheduled for the week, a bachelor party and camp out the day after next, a birthday ride with one of the local judges and his wife in two weeks, and then a little girl's birthday party after that. I was a bit of an event planner, bringing picnics, tents, and all sorts of supplies to make the trips memorable. I'd grown in popularity over the years, but my goal was to buy some land and build some cabins with an event center to host weddings. That goal seemed further and further away.

Avery walked into the barn with a frown on her face. "Clover, you didn't tell me the truck was that bad. Are you okay?"

I had a bruise on my cheek from hitting the steering wheel and was a little sore, but it wasn't anything I couldn't handle.

"I'll be fine. Need to save up to buy a new truck, though. If you hear of anyone selling a used one, can you let me know?"

She frowned and walked up to me. "I got some cash for my ride," she whispered. "You can have it to help buy something new."

I shook my head and took a step back. "No, Avery, that's yours. You need to save up."

"But this is an emergency," Avery argued.

"No," I said firmly. "I won't take your money. You worked hard for this, and you should use it for yourself. I'll figure something out."

"You're always doing this," she seethed. "Always taking control and killing yourself to take care of everyone else. You did it when we were kids. You do it now. You don't have to do everything by yourself, Clover."

I put my arm around her and gave her a hug. "Thanks, Avery, but this isn't your problem. I'll find a way to get through this."

Avery gave me a sad look and shook her head. "But it's my problem too," she said. "You need a truck."

I smiled and nodded. "And I'll get one."

Avery walked away, but I could tell she was still trying to figure out the best way to help me. I glanced around the barn, realizing that without a truck, I couldn't take my horses out to do different trails around town. Most customers met me at the house to hit the trail that started on our land, but some preferred different routes.

As I finished up my morning chores, my mind kept turning over the problem of the truck. I knew I couldn't keep putting it off; I needed to start looking for a solution.

Suddenly, Avery strode into the barn, her eyes bright with excitement. "I just signed up for the next bull riding event," she said. "We will use the money I got for last night and next week's rodeo . . ." Her voice trailed off as she stared at me expectantly.

I studied my sister's face, realizing what she was suggesting. "Avery, I told you—"

"And I'm telling you!" she yelled, cutting me off. "I'm tired of you doing everything for me. I'm a grown ass woman, and if you're going to put your feelings aside to support my rodeo dreams, then I'm going to use my winnings to support you, too. We're a team, Clover."

I couldn't help but smile at Avery's determination. We always relied on each other, but I didn't want Avery putting herself at risk for my problems. I knew if we were going to do this, we had to do it together, and we had to do it right.

"Okay." I hugged Avery. "But we need to be smart about this. I don't want you getting hurt, and I don't want us getting involved with the Dust Devils."

"I know, Clover. But we need the money, and the rodeo is a surefire way to do it."

I nodded, knowing that Avery was right. It wasn't the first time we needed to rely on rodeo winnings to make ends meet—our father was always searching for the next champion winnings to keep our mortgage paid—but this time, the stakes felt higher. I had to be extra careful, and so did Avery.

"Fine," I said. "We'll train hard, and we won't let anyone else talk us into anything we don't want. Deal?"

Avery grinned and nodded. "Deal."

CHAPTER 8
Whiskey-soaked Love in the Neon Lights

DECLAN

I sat outside my RV, the dying sun casting long shadows across the barren landscape. Clover's face danced in my mind, her innocence a stark contrast to the darkness that consumed me. But there was no denying the twisted path I treaded.

I needed to kill someone for Hank. The faster I got this job done, the faster I got the name of Mom's killer.

A thought struck me like lightning. What if I asked Clover about any assholes bothering her lately? And what if I took it upon myself to make 'em vanish, one by one? A sick game, a deadly courtship where lust and murder mingled. I couldn't shake the idea out of my head. That would solve my problem with Hank. I could bring him someone giving her trouble.

Some guys bought their girls flowers.

I'd cut off some guy's dick and serve it to her on a silver platter.

My fingers fidgeted restlessly. This was my calling, after all. The space where I shone the brightest. I chuckled at the irony of it all. Being a killer made me realize what falling for someone felt like. How ironic.

Hank wanted me to bring him a fucking trophy— and sure, I'd bring him one.

But it wouldn't be for him. It was just another price. Another death. Another bullet in some unlucky motherfucker's skull.

It would be for the girl with a haunted smile and lips I wanted to sink my teeth into.

It had *killed* me to cut things short and leave her at her friend's. I wanted to see where the night took us, and maybe even the next morning. And the day after that . . .

I wasn't lying when I said I never did things half-assed. I dove full into my obsessions. It's why I became a contract killer. Torture wasn't enough. It's why I came here to find Hank and get the name of my mother's killer. I wasn't just a vengeful fucker. I was hell-bent on ripping someone's heart from their chest.

The trot of hooves stole my attention, and I looked up to see Clover approaching. She rode her mare with skill, her hips swaying, her light brown hair flowing behind her.

Fuck, those tight jeans were downright sinful. She was too damn beautiful.

I tucked the gun I was cleaning behind my chair and approached her.

"Wildflower, to what do I owe the pleasure?" I asked with a smirk as she got off her horse. She tugged on the straps of her backpack while approaching, cautious, like a rabbit sniffing out a wolf.

"I brought you something, to say thanks for helping me yesterday," she said with a nervous swallow before taking the backpack off and pulling out a gallon-sized bag of chocolate chip cookies.

"For me?" I asked while reaching for them.

"Don't get too excited," she said while I pulled one out and tore through it. It was delicious. "I got that premade dough. I'm not much of a baker."

"Thank you," I said before swallowing the treat. "But I thought we discussed how I would like you to show your appreciation."

Clover's cheeks flushed and her eyes widened in surprise. She took a step back, her hand reaching for her mare's reins. "I . . . I don't know what you mean," she stuttered out, her voice barely above a whisper.

"Oh, come on, Wildflower," I said with a chuckle. "You know exactly what I mean."

My hand shot out, gripping her wrist and yanking her toward me. Clover gasped as she stumbled, her back hitting the side of the RV. I leaned in close, my breath hot against her ear. "You owe me a kiss, remember?" I whispered. "And I've been thinking . . . maybe I could collect that."

Clover's eyes darted around, scanning the barren landscape for any sign of escape. I chuckled at her panicked expression and leaned in closer, pressing my body against hers. "Don't be scared, little wildflower," I murmured. "I promise I won't crush you."

Her eyes fluttered closed as I traced my lips along the line of her jaw, feeling her pulse quicken beneath my fingers. She tasted like the chocolate chips in the cookies she'd made, sweet and addictive. My hands wandered down to her waist, pulling her closer to me. She wrapped her arms around my neck, her fingers tangling in my hair. I moved back to her sweet lips, pushing her harder against the side of the RV. She moaned against my mouth, giving in to the kiss.

I moaned, pulling back to look at her flushed face. "You're so beautiful," I said, my fingers tracing the line of her cheek. "I want you, Wildflower."

The fear had dissipated from her eyes, replaced by a desire that matched mine. She nodded, her hand reaching for the hem of my shirt. I let her tug it off, my hands finding the curves of her body.

I knew what I was doing was wrong. I knew what I was capable of. But at this moment, with Clover, none of it mattered. Maybe I could find a little peace on my road trip to hell.

Clover's hands dragged down my chest as I pulled her even closer, my body throbbing with need. Her skin was soft and warm under my fingers, and I couldn't get enough of the way she looked and felt.

Our mouths met in a hot, urgent kiss that left us both gasping for air. Clover's hands roamed over my back, pulling me closer, and I gripped her hips tightly, lifting her up onto the RV's side.

"God, this is a problem," I whispered against her lips. "I shouldn't have kissed you. That was a *very* bad idea, Wildflower."

A flicker of doubt crossed her expression. "I'm sorry it wasn't up to your standards. I'm obviously not as experienced—"

I cut her off with another devouring kiss, nipping at her bottom lip until she moaned. Breaking the kiss, I shoved my leg between hers and smirked. "It was a bad idea because now I want more. In fact, there's no way you're getting away from me now." I kissed her neck. I was being fucking serious. Now that I had a taste, I felt that obsessiveness spurring to life. I was already thinking about getting her naked. Getting her into my bed. Keeping her. Stealing her. "I'm going to have you, Wildflower. And there's nothing you can do to stop me."

Clover stiffened as she processed my declaration, and I could practically feel the adrenaline pumping through her veins. She was scared, but there was something else there too—a spark of desire that made my own pulse race faster.

I leaned in close again, my mouth hovering just inches from hers. "You're not going anywhere," I repeated, my voice low and husky. "You're mine now, Wildflower."

She swallowed hard, her hands still gripping me tightly. "You're leaving. This is just . . . a fling," she said, her voice shaking slightly. "Just some fun."

I almost laughed. I'd had plenty of flings. Something about Clover demanded *more*.

"Some fun?" I asked.

She swallowed. "Yes. Nothing more. It doesn't have to mean anything."

But even as she spoke, I could feel her body responding to me—her heart beating faster, her breath coming in short gasps. I knew that she wanted this as much as I did.

I closed the distance between us again, my lips finding hers in another searing kiss. This time, I didn't hold back—I let my hunger for her take over, my hands roaming over her body. She moaned against my mouth.

"We can have fun," I said, my fingers trailing down her stomach. "But don't fucking tell me it won't mean anything, Wildflower. You're my new favorite obsession."

She trembled as my words sunk in, and a smirk crossed my face as I watched her reaction. She leaned into me, her hands wrapping around my neck as she whispered, "I want to feel for a little while."

"Baby, this means *everything*," I murmured before pressing my lips to hers once more.

Clover inhaled sharply as I slid my hands around her waist, tugging at the hem of her shirt. She nodded, her breathing ragged, and I slowly peeled it away from her body, leaving her exposed in the sunlight.

Her skin glowed, creamy and smooth with just enough freckles to make me want to kiss each one. My eyes roamed across her curves—every inch of hers perfectly made for me.

"That's better," I said softly, pushing a stray strand of hair behind her ear. "You were meant to be seen like this."

She shivered slightly, her body quivering beneath my touch. "Outside?" she asked breathlessly.

"Yes," I said firmly, wrapping my arms around her

waist. "Out here in the open. You belong to me—and I want the world to know it."

"I'm not looking for anything serious," she replied.

"Too late," I murmured.

I leaned in close, our foreheads touching. My hands splayed across her back, pressing her closer against me. I could feel the warmth of her skin radiating into mine, and all at once it felt like everything was perfect—that we had come home to each other after a long journey apart.

"Why'd you really come out here, Clover?" I asked while unclasping the button on her jeans.

"T-to say thank you. To bring you some cookies."

I laughed. She needed to be honest with herself if this was going to work. I was already losing myself to the madness. I always knew, when I found the woman I wanted, I wouldn't let her go. I had one of those compulsions that claimed. All or nothing.

"Tell the truth, and I'll reward you," I whispered while tugging her jeans down.

"I-I wanted to see you," she admitted.

"And?"

"I wanted to . . ." She stepped out of her jeans as I looped my fingers around the edge of her panties.

"Tell me," I groaned against her neck.

"I wanted to feel your hands on me," Clover whim-

104

pered. She was trembling with anticipation, waiting for me to do something, anything.

I kissed her neck softly, savoring the taste of her skin. "You want me to touch you, don't you?" I whispered as I slid my fingers into her panties.

Clover gasped as I began to trace circles around her clit. Slowly, gently, I rubbed and teased her, watching in fascination as her body responded to my touch. Goose bumps broke out across her skin, and her breathing grew ragged.

"Oh, God," she moaned, gripping me tightly. "Please don't stop."

I wasn't planning on it. My cock was already hard as a rock, and I knew I needed her just as much as she needed me. I slid two fingers inside her, curling them upward to hit that sweet spot deep within her. Clover cried out, her body arching to meet my movements as I increased the intensity. She was close, and I could feel her orgasm building.

"You're so responsive. Wound up tight like a little toy," I said while she rode my palm.

She bucked against me, her breathing coming in sharp gasps as she reached the peak. I held onto her tightly, not wanting to let go until she'd completely unraveled beneath me.

When she finally stopped trembling, I slowly withdrew my hand and kissed her gently on the forehead. "No one has ever made me feel like this before," Clover whispered.

"And no one ever will, Wildflower."

She shoved at my chest, but I didn't budge. "You're a Devil," she replied.

"I am."

"You're not staying."

"I'm not." *But that didn't mean she couldn't come with me.*

Where the hell had that thought come from? Oh well. I could steal her away if necessary. I was a possessive bastard and we were just getting started.

She glared at me. "This isn't permanent. Let's not pretend it is. Don't act all possessive. I don't want things to get confusing."

I shoved my finger inside her sensitive cunt once more, making her gasp. "Is this confusing, Wild-flower?" I asked, pressing my lips to her shoulder. "Are you confused when you come in my palm? Confused when you're wet for me? Confused when you *ache* for my cock? 'Cause I'm not. There's nothing confusing about how you respond to me."

She shuddered as I moved in and out faster, and I could feel her pussy gripping me harder with each thrust. "Fuck," she gasped.

"Good," I growled before surging forward one last

time and claiming her mouth in a passionate kiss. She tasted like pure bliss, and I never wanted to let go.

When we finally broke apart, she looked up at me, her eyes blazing with desire. "What do you want from me?" she asked, her voice barely a whisper.

I smiled. "I want everything," I replied, kissing her softly on the lips.

And I would have everything.

"I have to go," she choked out. "Sorry to leave you . . ." She eyed the outline of my hard cock through my jeans.

I laughed. "We have plenty of time for more of this."

"I think this might have been a one-time thing," she said before slipping away from me and quickly putting on her jeans.

I grabbed her wrist lightly before she could run away. "Are you sure about that?" I asked, my voice soft.

Clover stared at my hand and tugged it away. "I think it's for the best," she said before backing away.

I inclined my head, my gaze never leaving her. "I'm not so sure," I replied simply.

Clover paused and looked back at me, her face softening. After a moment, she nodded and walked away—leaving me standing there, my heart pounding, my mind spinning with possibilities.

Wildflowers were resilient. They grew against all odds.

And I'd fucking watch her bloom.

CHAPTER 9
The Devil's Lullaby

CLOVER

The desert basked in the late afternoon sun, its scorching heat radiating across the arid landscape. I wanted to stay in bed all day and think about Declan. His possessive words. His talented fingers. The way he made me come on his palm.

I quivered just thinking about it.

But this bachelor party booked me months ago, and I couldn't say no to the money, even though it made me nervous to do an overnight ride with a bunch of drunk guys.

As a trail guide, I had grown to appreciate the rugged beauty of this unforgiving terrain. But today was different. I found myself leading a lewd group of guys on a bachelor party trail ride, but they were quite the handful.

Their boisterous laughter and the pungent smell of alcohol hung heavy in the air, making it challenging to maintain composure. Riding ahead of the group, I kept a vigilant eye on the surroundings, searching for any potential hazards that could put a damper on our adventure. It was no easy task, but I was determined to ensure their safety and make sure we all made it back.

The men guzzled their drinks as we slowly trudged through the thicket. Their rowdy laughter filled the air, and they made crude comments that made my skin crawl. It was nothing like my usual peaceful excursions with a group of sober riders.

Suddenly one of them hollered, pointing at the rocky incline in front of us, "Watch this!"

Panic seized me. My heart felt like it was about to thud its way out of my chest. I knew these drunk wannabe cowboys could be risky, especially on horseback. The horses weren't some invincible mystical creatures—they were just regular desert breeds that could easily get hurt.

I held up my hands and yelled, "Whoa! That's enough of that! Let's just cool it before someone gets hurt."

The man sprinted up the rocky incline, his horse rapidly galloping, with wild whoops of joy bellowing from him. His friends egged him on, screaming and hollering like mad birds in flight.

I kicked my horse to keep up, gaining ground as I raced toward them. Fear and anger were pounding through me—these guys had no clue about this place. They were only here to have a good time.

I was too late.

The man was already halfway up the incline, his animal struggling to keep its footing on the unstable surface. The rest of the horses were whinnying and neighing, trying to escape the madness around them. I gasped in horror.

"Stop!" I shouted, my voice cracking with emotion. "You're going to get yourself and the horse killed!"

The man didn't listen, his eyes wild with excitement as he urged his horse higher and higher. It was a feat of incredible skill, but it was also incredibly dangerous.

Suddenly, the inevitable happened. The horse's hoof slipped on the rocks, and the man tumbled down to the ground. I could hear the sickening thud of his bones landing in the dirt as they hit the rocky terrain.

My heart felt like it had stopped beating. I urged my own horse forward, fear and dread sweeping through my veins. When I reached the fallen man— James—he lay there groaning in agony.

I dismounted and knelt by his side, my hands already shaking with anger. I checked him over as best I could, looking for signs of serious injury. "I think I hurt my upper thigh," he said. I ran my hands over his leg, trying to feel if anything was broken.

"Here?" I asked.

"Higher," he groaned.

I ran up his leg, already calculating how far we were from the nearest hospital and thinking about the release form they signed. I couldn't afford to be sued.

"I don't feel anything," I said.

He grabbed my hand and forced it over his cock, making a crude sound. "Right there, baby. Rub it up and down."

I snapped my hand back and scowled at him, making everyone else laugh. Thankfully, he seemed to be okay; he was just a total dick.

I scrambled to my feet, brushing the dirt from my jeans. Storm, the horse James had been riding, was thankfully unharmed but still trembling with fear. I reached out and ran a reassuring hand down his neck, speaking softly in an attempt to soothe him. His nostrils flared, his mane shook, he was still scared.

"Let's head to camp," James said, trying to be light-hearted after nearly killing my horse. He chuckled at his own joke, and some of the other men joined in. Fury coursed through me; I wanted to smack him right there for being careless with Storm.

We all got back on our horses and set off toward camp. Nerves had me nibbling my lip as I thought about what just happened and what the night could bring. I'd taken this job for the money, but now I felt foolish for trusting these drunken strangers out in the middle of nowhere.

"I feel free!" one of them—Grant—yelled.

"Grant, please slow down," I pleaded, but my warnings went unheard. He was too busy showing off to his friends, trying to impress them with his nonexistent horsemanship skills. I gritted my teeth, trying to control my anger at his recklessness. These men were endangering themselves and my horses, and it was up to me to keep them safe.

Another man—Thomas—laughed hysterically before taking a sip of his whiskey. "I feel like an old cowboy. Let's rob a bank." My patience was wearing thin as I heard Thomas's suggestion.

The men laughed, but I could tell that they were getting bored with the trail ride. I knew I had to come up with a way to keep them entertained and under control.

"Hey, guys, why don't we race to that spot over there?" I suggested, pointing to a nearby hilltop. "The last one there has to pour the first round of drinks at the campsite."

The offer piqued their interest, and soon they were urging their horses into a full gallop. I followed close behind, relieved that they were at least following my lead.

As we rode, I couldn't help but feel a sense of exhilaration. The wind whipped through my hair, and I felt the pounding of the horse's hooves beneath me. It was moments like these that made me appreciate the beauty of the land and its ability to make me feel alive.

This was the kind of experience I wanted to share with my guests—where I could teach them to respect and appreciate the wilderness, while still having a good time.

Our campsite was a secluded spot by a creek for the horses to drink. We were surrounded by jagged rocks and towering cacti. I dismounted from my horse and watched as the men stumbled off theirs, their laughter blaring through the quiet of the desert.

I set about the task of setting up supplies for dinner, trying to ignore the men's lewd comments and inappropriate behavior. But as the night wore on, their behavior only became more outrageous. They drank more and more, their voices growing louder and more slurred with each passing moment.

I built a fire and pulled out the food from my cooler. I typically made simple meals for the trails, stuff that could be easily packed and transported, but tonight, I had decided to go all out. I had brought steaks and potatoes. My mouth watered as I seasoned the meat with salt and pepper. They were a bunch of businessmen from Dallas and were willing to pay top dollar for a fun night—and I needed the cash.

I was hunched over the coal stove, grumbling under my breath while I cooked. My eyes caught glimpses of them out of the corner of my eye, their laughter grating on my nerves.

"Look at her," one of them snickered, winking at his friend. "She's a right beauty, ain't she?"

The comment made my stomach churn. No matter how hard I tried to ignore them, everywhere I turned, their lecherous gazes followed me like shadows.

Then James lurched toward me, his whiskey-scented breath making me recoil. "You look mighty fine, Clover." His hand shot out and grasped my arm.

My body ignited with rage as I ripped my arm away. "Dinner will be ready soon." My teeth ground together as I spat out the words. "You should go back and sit down with your friends."

James's eyes narrowed and he stumbled backward. A lump formed in my throat as I fought to keep from yelling. If I did, who knew what would happen?

So instead, I forced a smile onto my face and held it there until he returned to his seat. Cautiously turning away, I exhaled and resumed cooking.

Once dinner was ready, the men ate in a blur of laughter and toasts. I sat away from them, listening to their stories, their laughter like wheezing hisses in the darkness.

The orange flames pulsed and danced, lazily licking the underside of the night sky. The jeers and drunken cackles spilled up into the stars, riling my insides with unease. One by one, the men drifted off to slumber, their unconscious bodies sprawled across the soot-laden earth. I let out a breath of relief; my work was done for the night.

With great effort, I mustered what remained of my strength, determined to put an end to the chaotic scene before me. I diligently stamped down on each ember until only gray ash remained.

No more bachelor parties; it was too much work.

I dragged myself back to my tent, sinking heavily onto my sleeping bag. The darkness cocooned me in its cool embrace as I shut my eyes, content with the tranquility that wrapped around me. But as I teetered on the edge of conscious thought, whispers from outside my tent pulled me back to reality.

"I can't wait to feel her . . ."

My eyelids fluttered open at the sound of a zipper, the pitch darkness enveloping me in its embrace. I felt his presence move closer and closer, his oppressive aura smothering me as he neared. James's putrid breath filled my lungs as he stood over me, his tall frame was ominous in the tiny space.

He barreled toward me, his face a mask of steely determination. I tried to dodge him, standing on shaky legs until my feet slipped on the floor beneath me. He wrapped one large arm around my waist, and with one powerful movement flung me to the ground. His chest pressed into mine with so much force I couldn't move, my breathing coming in shallow gasps. I could smell the whiskey on his breath, feel the hardness of his body against mine.

I started to thrash against him, desperation and anger fueling my every movement. My hands flew through the air, slapping and pushing against him as hard as I could. I felt his hot skin beneath my fingers and knew he was trying to take what I wasn't willing to give.

I tried to fight back, but he was too strong. His fingers dug harshly into my skin with no mercy as he groped and grabbed me forcefully. I screamed out for help but could only hear the howling wind in answer. I suddenly worried that his friends may join him— maybe they'd all have a turn at me before killing me. Hot tears slid down my face as I fought with everything I had.

His movements never faltered, as if he were driven by some dark force beyond his control. He didn't feel pain. Only damning desire. And it wasn't lust. It was raw, predatory power. He wanted to claim me because he could.

"Stop fighting, bitch," he slurred drunkenly into my ear, hot breath on my skin sending chills down my spine. "Take my cock like a good little whore." Revulsion filled my stomach as nausea hit me like a punch. His weight increased with each passing moment, pushing me further into the floor of the tent.

Practically tearing my shorts from my quivering body, he threw them to the side. He pulled his cock out, the thin greasy thing full of veins and coated in sweat. It was like a knife between my thighs.

He'd already put a condom on.

As if he'd prepared for this.

"No!" I screamed. The muscles in his arms flexed as he forced his shaft toward my entrance, and I didn't even have time to stop him before he thrust deep inside me, filling me with pain I had never imagined.

It was like he was an expert at rape.

Had taken before.

Had forced before.

Like he knew exactly how to hold me down.

How to force my legs open.

How to thrust while I thrashed.

My body shook and tears poured down my face as he drove relentlessly into me. He grabbed a handful of my hair and pulled my head back as he taunted me, "I love it when they fight."

I screamed at the top of my lungs as I tried to fight him off, struggling against his brutal advance. His strength overpowered me, and I was pinned beneath his weight, defenseless and completely at his mercy.

My mind blanked out with pain as he sliced open a wound deeper than any I had ever felt before. My body convulsed and shook while my insides burned from his violent penetration.

Desperate for release, he thrust faster and faster, trying to come before I could fight him off. Grunting loudly with each stroke, he dug his nails into my shoulder and neck, drawing blood. His movements became more and more erratic, and I knew his control was slipping away.

Finally, he came with one last powerful thrust and collapsed onto my body, his full weight pressing against my sore and battered frame. "Your cunt felt so good," he muttered into my ear before slipping off me and zipping his trousers.

Utterly defeated and numb from the experience, I curled up into a ball, tears streaming from my eyes. I felt a hand on my shoulder and opened my eyes slightly to see him towering over me, gaze filled with drunken bliss.

At that moment, I knew my life had changed

forever. I had been violated and degraded in a way that I would never forget. Rage unlike anything I'd ever felt before filled me. He'd taken my body. My safety. My personal, vulnerable existence.

I crawled closer to him, noting my knife tucked in the corner of the tent. If only it had been within reach. Maybe I could have stopped this before . . .

"You want more, baby? Whores always want more. I could split your pussy in half and—"

I grabbed the knife and sliced at his thigh. It wasn't deep enough to really wound him but gave me the chance I needed to escape.

He roared in pain and surprise as he stumbled backward away from me. Taking advantage of the opportunity, I rolled out of the tent. As I ran toward the horses, the man stumbled after me, but he couldn't keep up with my speed. "You're fucking dead," he screamed.

My heart pounded in my chest like a wild, frantic drumbeat as I leaped onto the horse, my pulse racing in sync with the urgency of my thoughts. The rough, coarse hair of the animal scratched against my naked skin. But the coldness of the night air against my exposed body paled in comparison to the chilling terror that gripped me, gnawing at my very soul with its merciless fangs.

The lingering sensation of lube from the condom

oozed slowly down my leg, the sticky residue a chilling reminder of the horrors that had transpired just moments before. The splatters of blood on my arm were still warm, their metallic tang mingling with the acrid sweat that coated my skin. I tried to shake the memories from my mind, but they clung to me like a parasite, feeding off my fear and despair.

I drove my heels into the horse's sides, urging her to go faster, to carry me away from this nightmare. My breath came in ragged gasps as the powerful animal surged beneath me, her muscles rippling with every stride. My thighs clenched against the horse's sides, each hoofbeat sending a jolt of pain through my bruised and battered body. The wind roared in my ears, drowning out the screams that chimed in my mind.

Miles of desolate terrain stretched before us, an endless expanse of dirt and rock that seemed to swallow up the night. The darkness was a suffocating shroud, pressing in on me from all sides, threatening to smother the last remnants of my sanity. I could feel the anguish building within me, a boiling pot of fear and pain that threatened to overflow.

And then, as if to mock my torment, the first rays of the sun began to break over the horizon, bathing the barren landscape in a wash of warm golden light. The beauty of the sunrise was a cruel juxtaposition to the terror that had consumed me, and the sight of it brought fresh tears to my eyes.

The salty tears stung as they streamed down my cheeks, carving rivulets through the grime that coated my face. I choked on a sob, the sound lost in the howling wind, as the weight of my ordeal threatened to crush me. The golden light of dawn offered no solace, no relief from the torment that haunted me.

And yet, I clung to the faintest glimmer of hope that the sun's ascent might also mean my salvation. That it might guide me to safety, to a place where I could outrun the terror that had chased me through the darkness. But for now, I had no choice but to forge ahead, each galloping stride taking me further from what happened to me and closer to an uncertain future.

~

I rode until I spotted Declan's RV in the distance, and a flicker of hope ignited within me. I urged my horse on, my vision blurred by the tears streaming down my face. My body ached from the ordeal I had just endured, and fear clung to me like a second skin.

As I reached the RV, I dismounted and stumbled toward the door in a daze, my legs barely able to support my weight. I knocked on the door, my sobs coming in ragged gasps as I waited.

The door swung open, and Declan's concerned eyes met mine. He looked at my tears, my nakedness, the bruises on my thighs. His eyes drank it all in, and he pulled me close to him, his strong arms surrounding me with a sense of safety and security that I hadn't felt for what seemed like an eternity. The warmth of his embrace gradually thawed the icy fear that had encased my heart, sending a wave of peace through me that I hadn't known was possible.

"Who hurt you?" he demanded, his voice low.

I could barely choke out the words as I leaned against Declan's sturdy frame for support. "I-I led a trail ride, and one of the riders . . . he . . . he . . ." My voice trembled as I spoke, the memory of the attack still vivid and raw.

Declan's eyes blazed with a fierce, primal fury. It was like his protective instincts kicked into overdrive, as if some ancient alpha energy had awakened within him. He held me tighter, his growl reverberating through his chest. "Did he touch you?"

I nodded, too emotional to say the words out loud.

"Rape," I whispered, the word feeling like a heavy, bitter sore on my tongue. It was such a disgusting word, one that I'd always thought of as an abstract concept, something terrible and awful that had happened to *other* people but never to me. Saying it out loud felt like defeat, like admitting that I had been violated in the most intimate and brutal way possible.

I was struggling to make sense of what had happened to me and to come to terms with the fact that my sense of safety had been shattered.

It was foreign and raw, wrong and intimate all at once. My mind raced as I tried to come to terms with the fact that some monster had done this to me. I didn't want him to touch me, to leave his mark on me, but he had forced himself upon me regardless. The shame and fear threatened to overwhelm me, but Declan's unwavering presence kept me anchored in the present.

I wasn't in that fucking tent anymore.

As I confessed the unspeakable truth to Declan, I could feel his grip on me tighten, as if he could shield me from the horrors of my own memories just by holding me close. "Can I come in? I just want to bathe and . . ."

I wanted to feel clean. I wanted to feel new. I wanted to wash the stench of him from my body.

Declan grabbed a blanket, and I wrapped it around me as I focused on the inside of Declan's RV. Taking in my surroundings helped me not think of the warring thoughts in my mind. It was cozy and inviting, with warm wood paneling and soft lighting that gave the space a welcoming glow. The air was scented with a mixture of pine and cedar, creating a sense of relaxation and peace.

I had to focus on my surroundings. I wasn't in the tent anymore. I wasn't with James, I was safe.

As I stepped inside, my eyes were drawn to the comfortable-looking sofa that sat against the wall. The cushions were plump and inviting, and the soft throw blanket draped over the arm of the sofa looked incredibly tempting. The coffee table in front of the sofa was made of dark wood and was adorned with a vase of wildflowers that added a touch of color to the space.

I wasn't in the tent anymore.

I was here. I was in Declan's RV. I was safe.

To the right of the sofa was a small kitchen area, complete with a sink, a stove, and a refrigerator. The cabinets were made of the same warm wood as the walls, and were adorned with copper handles that added a touch of elegance to the space. A small dining table sat against the wall, with two chairs that looked well-worn and comfortable.

I wasn't in that fucking tent anymore.

I wasn't in that fucking tent anymore.

I wasn't in that fucking tent anymore.

I wasn't in that fucking tent anymore.

I wasn't in that fucking tent anymore.

To the left of the sofa was a small bedroom area,

with a queen-size bed that was covered in a soft white duvet. The walls were adorned with black-and-white photographs of the desert and its inhabitants, adding a touch of the wildness of the outdoors to the cozy space.

I wasn't in that fucking tent anymore.

I wasn't in that fucking tent anymore.

I wasn't in that fucking tent anymore.

I wasn't in that fucking tent anymore.

I wasn't in that fucking tent anymore.

Overall, the inside of Declan's RV was a perfect blend of comfort and ruggedness, a reflection of its owner's love for the outdoors and his appreciation for the simple things in life. I needed more things to look at. More things to focus on. I'd count the threads in his comforter. Lick specs of dust up from the floor and let them coat my raw throat. Point at ants on a hill. Anything to keep my fucking mind focused on something else.

I wasn't in that fucking tent anymore.

I wasn't in that fucking tent anymore.

I wasn't in that fucking tent anymore.

I wasn't in that fucking tent anymore.

I wasn't in that fucking tent anymore.

"Where are these bastards now, Wildflower?" he asked while picking up a gun from his table and checking the magazine. I wasn't in that fucking tent anymore.

I swallowed. "East of here, about twenty-five miles. We rode all day, so we got out pretty far. They're probably sleeping off their drunken night." It was still just thirty minutes past sunrise. I doubted they'd be moving anytime soon. I needed to find the strength to go back and get my horses.

I wasn't in that fucking tent anymore.

I wasn't in that fucking tent anymore.

I wasn't in that fucking tent anymore.

I wasn't in that fucking tent anymore.

"I was doing an overnight trail ride," I choked out while sitting on his couch. "They were all drunk, but one of the men . . . he . . . he got into my tent and . . ."

More tears streamed down my cheeks. I was so humiliated. Declan had now come to my rescue three times, and I was certain I looked a mess. Declan's eyes turned dark with anger as he listened to my story. He set the gun down on the table with a firm hand and sat down beside me, his arm around my shaking shoulders.

I wasn't in that fucking tent anymore.

I wasn't helpless anymore.

"That son of a bitch," he growled. "I'll make sure he never comes near you again."

For a moment, we sat in silence, the only sounds coming from my occasional sniffles.

"Can I take a shower? I feel so . . . dirty."

"Of course. Why don't you get cleaned up and rest?"

Declan gently led me into the bathroom, his arm around my shoulders, providing a comforting presence. He guided me to the shower, showing me how to adjust the water temperature and handed me a soft towel. As he left the room, he reassured me, "Take your time. I'll be right outside if you need anything."

The warm water cascaded down my body, enveloping me in a comforting embrace. I let it wash away the dirt, the sweat, and the remnants of the horrible ordeal I had just endured. With each passing minute, I could feel the trauma slowly dissolving, the water carrying it down the drain, taking with it some of the pain and fear.

I wasn't in that fucking tent anymore.

Tears mixed with the water as they streamed down my face, and I allowed myself to cry, the sobs wracking my body as I released the emotions I had been holding in. I lathered soap onto a washcloth, scrubbing my skin with a fierce determination, as if I could erase the memory of unwanted hands touching me.

I wasn't in that fucking tent anymore.

After what felt like an eternity, I turned off the water and wrapped myself in the soft towel Declan had provided. My body felt clean, but the emotional weight still clung to me. As I stepped out of the shower, I found Declan waiting outside the bathroom door with a clean change of clothes.

"Sorry I don't have anything your size," he whispered, his voice gentle and concerned. The clothes were clearly meant for him, but at that moment, the oversized garments felt like a cocoon of safety, wrapping me in warmth and protection.

I wasn't in that fucking tent anymore.

"No worries. Thank you," I said, grateful for his kindness. I slipped into the T-shirt he had given me and crawled into his bed, exhaustion hitting me like a ton of bricks. The soft, cozy sheets tucked me in as I drifted off into a deep sleep.

I wasn't in that fucking tent anymore.

CHAPTER 10
Riding with Shadows

DECLAN

*T*here she was, sprawled out, her hair a wild riot catching sunlight. Her damn beauty hit me like a sucker punch, driving me mad, making me lose my bearings.

She was something else, delicate, a twisted dream I didn't want to shake off. She snoozed without a care on my lousy bed, blissfully ignorant of the monster hovering over her. A raw, primal urge surged through me as I stood guard over her, like a crazed man.

My hand quivered, reaching out, fingers skimming the soft threads of her hair. I was itching to touch her, the warmth from her skin setting my blood on fire. The thrill, the wait, it was making me nauseous, drunk on the sight of her.

Today, I'd paint the ground a bloody red for her.

I'd tear the world apart for her.

I'd serve up vengeance on a silver platter for her.

I wasn't bullshitting when I said she was mine.

I had a thing for the delicate, the shattered. I liked to take them under my wing, give them a shine, a new lease on life, even if it meant taking on a bit of their brokenness.

The moment she came knocking, teetering on the edge of disaster, it was game over. Her fate was sealed.

My eyes bored into her resting form. A wild smirk spread across my face, my heart swelling like a balloon about to burst. She was mine, all mine—to shield, to look after, to keep out of harm's way.

The desert, now that was a son of a bitch, with the sun hammering down mercilessly in the day and a cold, heartless cosmos taking over the night. But today, ripping through its godforsaken sands on my bike, I had been grinning ear to ear. I was on a mission, driven by a thirst for blood that wouldn't be quenched until I had my fill.

It didn't take much to flip my murder switch. I was the kinda guy who relished the thrill of taking the reins, in the most messed up way possible.

It didn't take much to put me in a frenzy of murderous rage. I was the type of man who took pleasure in taking matters into my own twisted hands.

I was the type of man to make someone vanish without leaving a trace.

I wasn't a hero—I loved being the villain. I derived perverse pleasure in destroying lives and sowing chaos wherever I went.

My mission was clear. I protected people. No matter the cost. It had become an obsession. A compulsion. An itch I couldn't scratch.

My mother's death echoed in my mind.

She was why I protected.

Why it had to be me who did it, no matter how hard or how wrong it felt. I had to save them because no one saved *her*.

The world was a cruel and unforgiving place. There were no heroes, no saviors or guardians. Only villains driven to burn the world down for their own selfish reasons.

I was the villain.

Clover had become my reason.

So when someone like Clover came along, I couldn't resist. She was a lamb in the slaughterhouse, waiting to be gutted and dressed, and I wanted to try to save her. In my twisted mind, I convinced myself that it was all about protection. That no one had to suffer like my mother did.

But really, it was all for me.

The thrill of the hunt.

The thrill of possessing something so fragile and innocent.

The road became a blur as I sped away on my bike, the only thing keeping me focused on my destination —the campsite where Clover was attacked.

Maybe it was fucked up, but when she arrived at my door, covered in dirt and blood, I thought of my mother. How the men she dated used and abused her. How no one was there to save her. How I was a fucking coward.

Clover would have a fucked-up hero, even if my ghosts could not.

A cold, reckless rage whispered in my ear, promising twisted justice if I took its hand.

The campsite came into view as I rode my bike up the path. I parked a half mile away so I could sneak up on them. Dismounting my vehicle, I strode toward the tents with insane determination, wanting nothing more than to make sure I was the last thing they ever saw.

Every nerve in my body was on fire as I approached the campsite on foot, and I could hear the despicably vile voices of those who had hurt Clover.

Stooping behind a weathered rock, I spied on them with a poisonous eye—six men, each with their very own sins tucked away nicely in their souls. Every fiber of my being screamed to take action. But I waited . . .

and watched . . . as something dark and twisted began to churn within my psyche.

Hank wanted me to bring him a head to prove my loyalty.

Well, I'd bring him six.

They were laughing and joking like this was all some huge joke, but something about them made me incredibly uneasy. They were out here in broad daylight. Enjoying the aftermath of *my* girl's trauma.

I'd kill them all.

I'd fucking *ruin* them.

My eyes narrowed as I assessed them one by one. The tall one had strength on his side, but he also wasn't too agile or fast on his feet—an easy mark for someone like me. The scrawny one looked scrappy. They were all drunk or hungover, which meant they would be uncoordinated and tired.

It was almost too easy.

A bunch of businessmen on a trip.

A bunch of cowards pretending to be men.

They were gathered on the ground, their faces flushed and their laughter booming through the morning air. As I crept closer, I could hear their crude jokes and their brash boasts, each one trying to outdo the other in their stories of sexual conquest.

"I'm telling you, boys, my new secretary is a wild one," one of them slurred, his words barely comprehensible. "I had her up against a tree, screaming like a banshee."

The others hooted and hollered, egging him on.

"Come on, man, don't hold out on us," another one said. "You need to share your prizes with the rest of us."

The first man grinned, his eyes glittering with lust. "She was a real looker, let me tell you. Long brown hair, green eyes, and a body that just wouldn't quit. I'll bet she's still thinking about me right now. Sucks my wife made me fire her."

The others laughed, but I could feel my blood boiling with anger.

"I wish that fucking trail guide hadn't run off," another one said, his words slurring together. "I bet she's a real animal in the sack. She stabbed James—kinky whore."

"It was just a fucking flesh wound!" Another one—likely James—interjected. I stared at him, noting that he moved with a slight limp. Claw marks lined his neck.

The men laughed, but their words were like poison to me. I could feel my hands clenching into fists, my rage boiling over.

James was going to die. And he'd suffer the most.

"You should have woken us up and asked for help. We could have held her down," another one said.

Emerging from behind the rock, I sent the men into a drunken frenzy. I enjoyed the shock on their expressions. The confusion. Two of them even laughed, thinking I was a joke or a ghost.

I was a fucking nightmare.

"Hey, dude. Who are you?"

"Was looking for my wife. She's a trail guide," I said while rolling my shoulders back. "Have you seen her? She was supposed to call."

They exchanged wary looks. Probably shitting themselves. Men like this only respected women when they thought they belonged to another man.

Well, Clover *did* belong to me. But they'd learn the consequences of their actions soon enough.

"Haven't seen her," James choked out.

I cocked my head to the side and smirked. "Maybe I'll finally be rid of the bitch," I said with a fake laugh, disarming them.

They quickly joined in, relaxing some.

"Fuck yeah!" one of them shouted. "Women can be total cunts. If you're lucky, she'll get lost."

I smiled. Like this was a fucking joke. "Or maybe," I began with a laugh while picking up one of their beer bottles. "Some sorry fucker will rape her in the middle of nowhere."

They all stopped laughing and went completely silent. "What?" I began. "It's funny, right? We're all laughing. I mean, then, I could work out all this pent up frustration and kill a motherfucker. Let the vultures eat him. I've been dying for a reason to kill. Wouldn't it be *hilarious* if I crushed his balls? If I pissed on his corpse?"

One by one they stood up, squaring their shoulders at me as I tossed the bottle on the hard dirt, glass shattering everywhere.

James spoke up. "Hey, man, I don't know what lies that bitch told you—"

"I thought you hadn't seen her," I growled.

I charged toward them with a speed and agility that took them by surprise. Punching and kicking, I delivered blow after blow with a precision that was almost inhuman. I hit whoever was closest, fighting through all of them as they realized I was here for blood.

The men circled me and fought back, swinging wildly and stumbling in their drunkenness. One got me in the kidney. I broke his nose.

One of them was bigger than the rest. He looked like he could lift a car, but that didn't deter me. "Your bitch was asking for it," he spat.

Rage fueled me as I charged toward him, lifting my arm and delivering a sharp punch to his jaw. He stumbled back, shock etched on his face. "You really shouldn't touch what doesn't belong to you," I said, my tone sinister.

Suddenly, I felt a sharp pain in my side. One of the men had pulled out a knife and was now wielding it toward me. I narrowly dodged a second strike and kicked him in the stomach, causing him to double over in pain.

But I wasn't out of the woods yet. The other men were now closing in on me, and I knew that I had to act fast.

I bent down and swiped a nearby rock and sent it flying toward one of the men, hitting him square in the face. He staggered back, blood streaming from his nose. "Fucking hell!" he garbled as I spun around to grab the man charging for me. Five of them were down and trying to pull themselves off the ground. One remained.

The grand finale.

"You want to die for that bitch?" James asked while we circled one another. "She took my cock like a good girl. I loved the way she fought me off. I just wish I could have taken her ass before she escaped."

I couldn't wait to make him suffer.

My veins pulsed with rage.

"She was so tight. Almost like fucking a virgin," he added, the idiot.

With a snarl, I lunged forward with blazing eyes

and grabbed him by the neck, lifting him off the ground with my right hand. My muscles burned, but I was running off pure adrenaline. It was the same fucking power that roared through me when I rode bulls. It was the same protective rage that let women lift cars off of babies or let men in war dig deep to survive despite being battered with bullets.

He squirmed and screamed as he tried to break free, but it was no use. His strength was nothing compared to mine. "Please!" he mouthed.

"What? I can't hear you."

My grip tightened around his throat as I felt his life slipping away beneath my fingers. His screams grew quiet and soon he was still, all while I stared in determination at what I had done.

His body dropped to the ground like lead, and after a moment, he regained consciousness and gasped for air. I wasn't going to let him die that easily.

He needed to fucking suffer.

With a savage lunge, my iron-fisted grasp encircled his balls. I bore down, feeling the satisfying pop of his testicles beneath my clenched fingers. He howled in agony, quivering in maddening pain.

The men still struggling to pull themselves up and escape gasped, cringing while running toward the horses. I didn't have much time. They weren't going to stop me. They were trying to save themselves.

He thrashed and screamed, the desert air swallowing his agony whole.

I looked down and ripped up a cactus that was in the ground, letting the thorns stab me in the palm before jamming it down his throat. He screamed in agony as the thorns ripped through his flesh, blood pouring from his mouth. The other men looked on in horror, their bravado all but forgotten.

I glared at them with contempt while James writhed in pain amidst a pool of blood and tears.

Their fate had been sealed—today they would learn who was the true predator, and it sure as fuck wasn't them.

"Let's get out of here!" one of them screamed while limping toward Clover's horses, which were tied up and scared.

Not so fast.

I pulled out my gun.

Bullet in the skull.

Bullet to the spine.

The chest.

The neck.

And one between the eyes 'cause he was foolish enough to look back.

I hit them like perfect targets, and each of them fell in the dirt.

I cackled as I watched them fall, salivating for the

ultimate power trip. I pounced on James one more time with a feral ferocity, lifting him up with one hand around his throat. He was suffocating on his own blood. His balls squashed. His eyes bulged from their sockets, and he was gasping for breath—a desperate plea for mercy that did not come.

He moaned a plea, but the garbled hiss of his voice was barely understandable.

He spluttered helplessly as I forced myself upon him, enjoying my absolute dominion over his pathetic existence. The pleasure bubbled inside me as he writhed in anguish and terror, struggling against the inevitable with no hope for escape. His life ebbed away, and I felt his soul being dragged to eternal damnation, by my hands and at my will. I watched with a glee of psychotic delight until the final breath left his bloodied body.

"This is for Clover," I said just as he died.

I spat on his body because, even in death, he deserved to be humiliated. I slammed my boot on his skull. I cracked his ribs. I snapped his hand.

Standing over the lifeless body, I unzipped my jeans with a clink. His once-human form was now just a grotesque collection of battered flesh and splintered bone, and I felt a weird satisfaction.

My piss hit his body, making a low, almost silent splash. It soaked into his torn clothes, darkening the fabric. Droplets that missed him sunk instantly into the thirsty earth.

The morning sun was like a spotlight on the stream as it fell on his corpse, dribbling into his open wounds and pooling around his injuries.

The sharp stink of urine clashed with the metallic scent of blood, a grotesque mixture that filled the air. It was a harsh reminder of the messed-up situation.

It was a raw sight, my act of disrespect splattering on his broken body. A disgusting, final insult to his death. That was the full stop to his pathetic story.

I stood there, my chest heaving with exertion and my heart pounding with a sense of triumph. But even as I basked in my victory, I couldn't shake the feeling of unease that settled over me. The darkness that had fueled my rage was still there, simmering just beneath the surface.

It wasn't enough.

What if someone else hurt Clover? What if I couldn't protect her again?

I was done failing people.

I'd already failed my mother. I couldn't do it again. I wouldn't survive it.

As I stood there, looking down at the broken bodies of the men, a sense of confusion and dread washed over me like a dark wave. The ground around me was stained red with blood, the sun casting a blistering hot glow on the scene of violence that had just occurred. I could feel my heart pounding in my chest, my senses on high alert.

As I stood there, surrounded by the carnage, I felt something deep within me shift. I had crossed a line, and there was no going back. The bloodstains on the sand and the lifeless bodies lying before me were a testament to that. As the dust settled, a torrent of emotions surged through me. And in that moment, I knew.

She was mine.

Clover had awakened something within me—a force I could not comprehend nor control.

I would be her guardian, her sentinel, her avenger. I would be the shadow that lurked in the night, the blade that struck down her enemies, the shield that would protect her from all harm. I would be her strength when she faltered, her solace when she wept, her sanctuary when the world threatened to tear her apart.

As I stood there, the sun casting its punishing light upon the scene of my vengeance, I made a solemn vow.

For in the end, she was my salvation. And I would fight to the very last breath to keep her safe, to keep her close, and to keep her mine. Forever.

She just didn't know it yet.

CHAPTER 11

Scarlet Roses and Bullet Kisses

CLOVER

I stirred in my sleep, my dreams slowly receding as consciousness began to return. Blinking my eyes open, I gradually became aware that I was not in my own bed, nor in my own room.

As my gaze wandered, trying to make sense of my surroundings, I realized I was in an RV. The space was small but well-maintained, and there was a faint smell of leather and oil in the air. I felt a strange mixture of confusion and comfort, as though I was both out of place and yet somehow safe.

As I shifted, I felt Declan's unyielding stare pierce my skin. It was like he was sizing me up, examining each and every inch of me. What happened hit me like a punch, and I suddenly remembered everything that happened the night before.

The men.

The pain.

The fear.

The fucking tent.

"Hello," I stuttered, trying to mask the fear in my voice. I was still disoriented from last night and unnerved by his powerful stare. "Have you been sitting there all this time? How long did I sleep for?"

Declan shifted closer to me, his eyes never straying from mine. "You slept all day. About fourteen hours, actually. I had a few things to take care of, but you were out of it when I got back," he said finally, his voice low and dangerous. "But what's more important right now is how you're feeling."

With one quick movement, he snatched my hand into his own, squeezing it tightly. The possessiveness in his touch both frightened and exhilarated me.

I struggled to rise, my battered body aching from the torture. Before I could even gather my strength, Declan had already moved toward me in an instant. His strong arms supported me and pulled me against his chest with gentle care. Our eyes met, and there was a menacing strength that made me shudder.

"Thank you," I whispered softly, my voice quivering with appreciation and dread. "For everything."

Declan's piercing eyes softened at my words. "Don't thank me, Clover," he murmured possessively even as his thumb stroked my skin soothingly. "It should never have happened like this." His voice was gruff with apology, but it only served to ignite the fire inside me. He paused for a moment, the power returning to his eyes. "How are you feeling?"

I felt my heart skip a beat as I glanced at him, my throat suddenly dry. His presence filled the room with an almost obvious force, and I was acutely aware that he was lethal, volatile—yet his expression held me captive in a way I couldn't explain.

My mind wandered to what had happened yesterday, replaying the events until it began to feel like something out of a nightmare. I shouldn't even be looking at Declan. I'd experienced trauma, something dark and sickening that made my gut coil. Thank fuck he wore a condom. But what if I got pregnant? What if he gave me an STD? What if I was never the same? What if . . .

My horses were out there alone, and I needed to figure out what to do about the men. That was something I could focus on. I needed a task. Something to think about. Something to keep my mind busy.

"I'm . . . I'm alright," I managed to croak out, though my body quivered. "But I should go."

He looked at me intently, a deep fire burning behind his eyes.

"You're not going anywhere," he growled in warning. "You don't have to worry about your horses. I brought them back. They're safe."

I blinked in surprise, feeling a wave of relief wash over me. "What? How?"

Declan's eyes glinted, a smirk pulling at his lips as he regarded me. "Don't worry, I made sure that they were taken care of, no expense spared. Gathered them up and rode them back. Washed them off. Fed them. Gave them water."

"You went out to the campsite?" I asked.

"I did."

"Did you see them?"

"I did."

"And?"

He reached out, gently brushing away a tear that had escaped down my cheek. I gasped, feeling the warmth of his touch on my skin and a spark of awareness rushing through my veins. I tried to take a step away from him but found myself unable to break our connection.

"And I killed them, Wildflower."

I blinked. Did he say . . .

"Wh-what?"

I was frozen, his words pounding in my skull. My heart pounded against my ribs, fear and relief wrestling within me.

"K-killed?" I repeated, my voice barely a whisper. The reality of his confession stunned me.

His eyes never left mine. "Every single one of them," he confirmed, his voice steady as a rock, terrifyingly calm.

A cold shock ran down my spine. "You . . . you killed them?" The enormity of his actions began to sink in. The men from last night, the monster who had defiled me, were no longer of this world. Declan had seen to it.

"Yes, Clover," he affirmed, his voice grave. "They won't ever hurt you or anyone else again." His grip on my waist tightened, his presence almost stifling.

My mind was a whirl of emotions. Fear. Shock. Relief. Gratitude. Dread. I was shocked by the brutal justice that had been dealt, yet a part of me breathed easier knowing those men wouldn't be a threat anymore.

Tears pricked at my eyes, the events of the past twenty-four hours finally catching up to me. I collapsed against Declan, my body shaking with uncontrollable sobs. His arms enveloped me, holding me close against his solid frame.

"It's okay, Wildflower," he murmured into my hair, his voice a soothing balm against the chaos in my mind. "It's over. You're safe."

Declan's calmness amidst the storm was baffling. He was the eye of the hurricane, a beacon of control and resolution. The realization that he'd gone to such lengths to protect me made my head spin. His actions were extreme, but in his dark, twisted way, he'd taken care of me.

"Declan . . . ," I stuttered, my voice barely a whisper. He was a murderer. He had taken lives. My heart pounded in my chest, threatening to rip through my ribcage. "This is bad."

"Clover," his voice rang out, a warning and a challenge. "Do you wish I'd let them go? Allowed them to continue their lives as if nothing happened?"

"No, but . . ." I could barely form a coherent thought, my mind reeling.

"Do you trust in a justice system that turns a blind eye to women like you?" His words were heavy, piercing, relentless.

"But that doesn't justify . . ." I tried to argue, but my voice failed me.

"Sometimes, Clover," he said, his voice chillingly calm. "Sometimes, you have to take matters into your own hands."

A surge of fear consumed me, my breaths coming short and fast. Panic swept over me like a tidal wave. He had killed people. Declan, the one who'd saved me, was a cold-blooded murderer.

"No!" I screamed, the word ripping through the silence like a gunshot. The walls of the RV felt claustrophobic, closing in on me. "You killed them! You . . ."

His voice was a steady drum, unwavering amidst my storm of terror. The revelation that he'd willingly stained his hands with blood to protect me was too much to bear. It was horrifying.

The contrast was stark. His calm composure against my confusion and shock. His acceptance of his actions against my disbelief. He had done this in my name. I was safe because he had spilled blood. The lines between savior and murderer were smudged and distorted.

His actions were beyond extreme, beyond comprehension. And yet, in his warped, destructive way, he'd secured my safety. It was a punch to the gut, leaving me winded and scared.

"Listen, Clover," Declan began quietly. "I had hoped to make this easier for you, to make it less painful. Maybe even keep you safe from the horrors of who I really am and the things I have done. But now I have no choice but to show you just how dark things can get between us."

"Us?" I asked. There was no us.

His eyes flashed menacingly as he paused, as if considering whether he was ready to fully open himself up to me, for better or for worse.

"Us," he repeated. "You and me, Clover. Whether you like it or not, we're connected now."

"You're lying."

"I'm not."

"There were six men out there, Declan."

"And now there aren't."

"Why?" My voice was a mere breath in the silence. "Why did you do that?"

His answer was instantaneous, resolute. "They touched you, Clover." His words were sharp, raw. "You came to me, hurt. Ruined. It lit a fire in me, a thirst for blood."

He leaned in closer, his gaze holding mine hostage. "You walked through my door, and I knew. You were mine to guard, to claim." He paused, a grim smile curling his lips. "Something in me snapped, seeing you that way. It was rage. Pure, burning rage." His words hung in the air between us, a confession, a declaration. "I wanted them gone, Clover. Wiped out. No trace left." His eyes were flinty, unapologetic. "They hurt you, and for that, they paid."

I shook my head, trying to make sense of it all. Holy shit. He killed them? Literally. As in *ended their fucking lives.*

Declan killed them.

"Declan, murder? No, that's not . . . that can't be

right." The sane part of me was horrified, but there was power in his words. Vengeance. It was the deepest, darkest part of my soul. The part that felt warmed by his admission. That rapist was dead. He would never hurt me or another person again. I wouldn't have to wait for a failing court system. I wouldn't have to look over my shoulder. He was dead.

Still close to Declan, I didn't move back as he leaned into me. His eyes were dark and intense. "It's never about right or wrong, Clover. It's about protecting what you care for most—regardless of the cost. You don't have to understand it. . . You're just important to me."

My eyes welled up with tears, battling the truth of his actions that threatened to shatter my entire life. He had been my savior, and yet he could commit such a heinous act. I was at a loss for words, unable to comprehend what had just happened. I knew nothing would ever be the same again, as if an unbreakable chain had bound me to him for eternity; even if I wanted to run away, I wouldn't be able to escape his possessive grasp.

"You barely know me."

"I know enough," he replied with a shrug.

"You're insane."

"You're mine, Wildflower."

I shuddered, my breathing erratic. "Declan, I . . ." My voice trailed off helplessly as I tried to comprehend what he was suggesting. His words clung to me like a veil of steel, possessive and relentless. A daunting silence descended around us, thick with tension and unspoken danger. With a few simple sentences, he had claimed me as his own and made it clear that he would do whatever it took to protect me —even take lives if necessary. A thrill ran through me despite the fear his words provoked.

He looked deep into my eyes, his claws digging into my skin. "I know it's a lot to take in, Clover. You'll make peace with it soon."

My stomach churned with fear and excitement as I processed what he said. "This isn't something you just make peace with." I swallowed hard, my heart pumping ridiculously fast. "Am I . . . am I an accomplice to murder?" It was almost too much for me to handle.

His lips grazed my ear. "It's okay," he whispered. "I won't let anything bad happen to you. It's been taken care of." He spoke in a husky and commanding tone.

"What does that even mean?" I breathed, barely able to contain the fear and excitement rolling through me like thunder.

His fingers brushed my cheek.

"It means, Wildflower," he began, his voice

hypnotic and electric, "that I've made sure you won't be implicated in any way. I did it to protect you, and I'll continue to do whatever it takes to keep you safe— no matter what."

I pushed his hand away, my heart pounding with a mix of fear and confusion. "I can't be a part of something like this. I appreciate you saving me, but I can't condone murder. Holy shit, you killed them. Are you sure? I . . . I need some space to think."

His eyes darkened, and I could see the conflict within him. "You don't need space, you need breakfast. How does bacon sound?"

I blinked, taken aback by his sudden change of topic. This man was completely unhinged. Part of me wanted to argue and insist on having the space I needed, but another part of me recognized that he was a literal murderer and was supposedly *claiming* me. I wasn't even sure I could escape.

His proclamation was a stark reminder of the terrible situation I was in. Could I really argue with a man who had killed six people in cold blood?

"Breakfast sounds . . . good," I murmured, the words leaving my lips in a reluctant whisper. I wasn't in a position to argue, nor did I have the energy to. I felt like I was teetering on the edge of a cliff, one wrong move away from plunging into the abyss.

A small smile pulled at the corner of his lips, the

predatory glint never leaving his eyes. He moved away from me, leaving me to sit alone on the couch as he strode toward the small kitchenette. I watched him with wide eyes, my heart pounding erratically in my chest.

As he busied himself with cooking, I took the opportunity to collect my thoughts. The smell of bacon wafted through the air, but I barely noticed it. My mind was too preoccupied with the reality of my situation. The pain. The terror. The realization that Declan had murdered those men. His claim on me. His promise to protect me.

The fact that I was sitting in a small RV, far from my own home, with a man who was both my savior and my captor . . . Every fiber of my being screamed at me to run, but where could I go? The man I'd once trusted had turned out to be a ruthless killer. I was entirely at his mercy.

The smell of bacon growing stronger brought me out of my thoughts. Declan had set two plates on the small coffee table in front of the couch, each piled high with food. He moved to sit across from me, his gaze never leaving my face.

"Hope you like your eggs scrambled," he said, his voice unusually gentle.

I nodded, finding my voice suddenly deserting me. My mind was spinning, too overwhelmed to comprehend the sudden normalcy of the situation. Here I was, sharing breakfast with a man who was a killer. His possessiveness was terrifying. His conviction was chilling. And yet, despite all that, a part of me felt safer with him than I ever had before.

The rest of the breakfast passed in silence, the only sounds being the clink of cutlery against the plates. It was strange, surreal even. One moment we were discussing murder, the next we were sharing a meal. It was as if nothing had changed, as if the confession hadn't happened. But it had. The reality of it was a constant presence, a shadow that loomed over us.

When breakfast was over, Declan cleared our dishes while I sat there, lost in thought. His confession, his possessiveness, his care—it was all too much to take in. But one thing was clear—I was stuck with him. And whether I liked it or not, my fate was now intertwined with Declan's.

It wasn't until Declan settled down next to me that I realized I hadn't moved from my spot on the couch. I was frozen, paralyzed by fear and shock. He didn't say anything, just looked at me with those piercing eyes, as if he could see right through me.

"There's a lot to process," he said quietly. "But remember this, Clover. I won't let anything happen to you. I didn't save you just to let you go. You're mine now."

His words reverberated in my head, a chilling promise that had me trembling. Declan might have saved me from a horrific fate, but I couldn't ignore the fact that he was a killer. He was dangerous, and I was his. The thought was both terrifying and strangely comforting.

CHAPTER 12
Sins of the Saddle

DECLAN

G etting Clover tied up was a struggle. She was a fiery thing, her spirit unwavering even in the face of destruction. We'd had a pleasant meal, but I knew she was already planning her escape.

The moment she caught sight of the rope, her survival instincts kicked in. Her fists flew out, nails scratching my arms, her legs kicking out to try to fend me off.

"Calm down, Wildflower," I told her, my voice steady despite the chaos unfolding around us. She didn't seem to hear me, or if she did, she didn't care. Her fear fueled her, made her fight harder.

I had to use my weight to pin her down, holding her struggling form against the mattress. My knees pressed into the bed on either side of her, effectively trapping her. There was a wild look in her eyes, like a cornered animal. But she was more beautiful in that moment than I had ever seen her before, her cheeks flushed and eyes sparkling with defiance.

The proximity was difficult to ignore. Her writhing body under mine, the way her breasts pressed against my chest as she fought, the way her scent enveloped me. I felt a familiar stirring, a primal reaction that I did my best to suppress. It wasn't the time for that, not when she was scared and fighting.

Despite the situation, I couldn't ignore the jolt of desire that shot through me. The way her body felt against mine was electric. Her struggling form underneath me was an irresistible temptation.

"Stop squirming, Clover," I grunted, struggling to keep my voice level, the strain evident. I could feel my self-control slipping, and I needed her to stop moving.

It took all my willpower to shift my focus back to the task at hand. With considerable effort, I managed to secure her wrists with the rope, pulling it tight enough to prevent her escape but not enough to cut off circulation. As I worked, I tried my best to ignore the softness of her skin under my fingertips, the way her breath hitched when the rope bit into her flesh.

The struggle was over soon enough, with Clover tied up and me panting from the exertion. Despite the mad rush of adrenaline, I felt a twinge of regret for having to be so rough with her. But this was necessary. She needed to understand that I wouldn't let her go, that she was mine to protect.

She looked up at me, her chest heaving, the ropes contrasting sharply against her fair skin. She was breathtakingly beautiful, even with her eyes wide with terror and confusion. My cock twitched at the sight of her, a reaction I quickly squashed.

This wasn't about desire, I reminded myself. This was about keeping her safe, even if she didn't understand. But damn, if she didn't look irresistible all tied up and vulnerable. It was a sight that would haunt me, I was sure, but right now, I had other matters to attend to. I needed to step out and attend to business, leaving her here where she was safe and secure.

Safe and secure under my watch. And under my ropes.

Clover's panicked eyes were wide open, shimmering with unshed tears as she looked up at me, bound and helpless on my bed. I didn't take pleasure in her fear, but there was something oddly . . . satisfying in the way she looked, restrained and vulnerable.

"Why do I have to be tied up, Declan?" she asked, her voice barely above a whisper, her eyes pleading.

Her hair was a wild mess on the pillow. "I have business to take care of," I replied, my voice steady and impassive as I pulled the final knot tight. "I can't risk you leaving."

She flinched, sucking in a sharp breath as the reality of her situation set in. "You can't keep me here like this, Declan!" she protested, her voice laced with fear and confusion.

"I can, Clover, and I will," I stated flatly, my stare never leaving hers. There was a mad rush of adrenaline surging through me, a chilling excitement. The sight of her, so utterly terrified yet stunningly beautiful, set off a spark within me.

It was better this way. The more I thought about it, the more convinced I was. This was the only way I could ensure she was safe, the only way I could guarantee that she wouldn't run off and get herself into more trouble. The outside world was full of predators, and I wouldn't allow her to fall victim again.

"I can't trust that you won't try to escape, Wildflower," I confessed, my voice soft, almost regretful. "And I can't risk losing you."

Her eyes widened at my admission, the confusion evident on her face. "But I . . ."

I silenced her with a firm look. "No buts, Clover. It's for your own safety. Trust me."

"But . . . you're scaring me, Declan . . . ," she murmured, her eyes filling with tears. Her vulnerability stirred something within me, a tumultuous blend of protectiveness and possession.

"You have nothing to fear from me, Wildflower," I reassured her, moving to sit at the foot of the bed, close enough to keep an eye on her but far enough to give her space. "You're safe here."

"Safe? You've tied me up!" she cried, her voice choked with fear. She was desperate, struggling to make sense of the madness unfolding around her.

"Yes, and I won't apologize for it," I replied simply. "You'll understand someday, Clover. But for now, you need to stay here. For your own safety."

I stood up then, moving toward the door, casting one final glance back at her. I knew she was scared. I knew she didn't understand. But she didn't need to. Not now.

Her safety was paramount, and I would do anything to ensure it. I had crossed a line tonight, a line I could never walk back from. But I didn't regret it.

As I left the room, Clover's hysterical cries hit me, pulling at something deep within me. A part of me hated to see her in such a state, but the larger part, the part that was cold and ruthless, was satisfied. Because I knew, with absolute certainty, that while she was here, tied up in my bed, she was safe.

I sauntered into the Dust Devils' compound, six heads heavier than when I left. The desert sun had hardened the blood on the burlap sacks I carried, a metallic scent wafting from them with each step. A sly grin crept across my face, the thrill of the hunt still lingering.

I had been tasked with proving my worth to Hank by delivering the head of some sorry fucker in town. But, always one to exceed expectations, I'd brought Hank a half dozen.

The compound was teeming with life, its inhabitants engaged in their daily grind—gun running, drug dealing, and whatever other illicit activities the Dust Devils were involved in. I strode through the camp with my head held high, basking in the feeling of accomplishment.

Finally, I reached the epicenter of the operation—Hank's office. The dark, foreboding doors seemed to beckon me inside. As I pushed them aside, I was met with the furious glare of Hank, the Dust Devils' leader. His hulking frame cast a long shadow across the office, and his hands clenched into fists as he glared at my offering.

"What the hell do you think you're doing, Wilder?" Hank snarled, his voice low and menacing. "I asked for one kill, one head as proof of your loyalty. Not six!"

"Well then, I suppose I proved myself in excess, Hank," I said while dropping the burlap sack on the floor and strolling over to his bar cart and pouring myself a whiskey.

He stomped his boot. "You put six hearts on my doorstep."

I swallowed the burning drink. "I also buried body parts all over your property. You can try to find them, but I hid them pretty well."

"What?" he stammered. "How the fuck did you pull that off?"

I spun around to face him. "Borrowed some horses and hauled them to the Devils' compound. An arm here. A leg there. I'll give you a hint. One of their dicks is in your mailbox."

Hank's eyes narrowed at my words, but I could tell part of him was impressed with my ingenuity. Still, he wasn't one to be toyed with.

But I suppose neither was I.

"You think this is a game, Wilder?" he growled. "You think you can go above my head and do whatever the hell you please?"

"I think you are confused about who is in charge," I snapped back. "You hired me. You need me. I don't like being threatened, Hank. And now I've got something over your head. You try to hurt me, you try to go against me, and I'll have the FBI at your door with a search warrant and a map to all the bodies you forced me to hide."

Hank was furious, and it made me happy to see him squirm. He'd been in a position of power for too long.

"You need me," he growled. "You need the information I have about your mother."

I smiled. "And you're going to give it to me. Or I'll kill every last one of your men and make it look like you were some asshole cult leader that cut off their heads. Don't test me, Hank."

He stammered. "You wouldn't."

I walked up to him and crossed my arms against my chest. "Try me. We both know what I'm capable of. We both know the resources at my disposal. I didn't become a skilled assassin by sitting around on my ass and letting everyone else do the heavy lifting. I have connections you wouldn't even dream of. We both know the only reason you're still alive is because you have information I need, and I'm willing to work with you to get it. You can either stop throwing your weight around and cooperate or you can die, Hank. Either way, I'll get the answers I'm searching for. One way or another."

He sat in his seat, huffing and puffing like a tired old man. "Are you still going to kill the judge for me?"

"I'm a man of my word, Hank. But it'll be on my terms. When the dust settles, you'll tell me the truth."

I turned around and walked out of the room, leaving behind a frightened and angry Hank. I had made my point, and I had no doubt he would comply.

I had become the one thing I had always strived to be.

The one they feared.

CHAPTER 13
Vengeful Hearts, Vicious Rides

CLOVER

*C*onsciousness crept back slowly, a stealthy, creeping cat padding over the cool tiles of my mind. I was lying on something firm yet not completely uncomfortable. The sharp aroma of cleaning solution tinged with something . . . rusty, maybe, filled my nostrils. I squirmed, only to have the rough bite of rope chafe my wrists.

My eyes flew open.

"Easy there, Clover."

The voice was soft, dangerously soft, like the murmur of water just before it tumbles down a fall. I craned my neck to find the source of the voice. Declan. He was sitting on a chair, casually sipping from a steaming mug, watching me with a fire that was both unsettling and oddly captivating.

His dark hair caught the dim light filtering through the closed blinds of the RV. His chiseled jaw was relaxed, stubble shadowing the strong lines of his face. But it was his eyes, those ocean-hued eyes, that drew my attention. They were filled with a strange brew of amusement, mania, and something else I couldn't quite place—was it concern?

"Why . . . why am I still tied up?" My voice emerged as a croak, my throat dry and scratchy. I'd been angry when he tied me up. Furious. I fought so hard against the restraints that I wore myself out and fell asleep.

He placed his mug on a small table nearby and stood. The movement was fluid, panther-like. His broad shoulders filled out his shirt perfectly, muscles shifting under the fabric as he walked toward me. He looked . . . good. Disturbingly good.

No. I couldn't think like that. This man was insane. A murderer. He was keeping me tied up here.

"I can't have you running off now, can I?" he replied, a humorless smile tugging at the corner of his lips.

Despite the insane circumstances, a perverse part of me fluttered at his words. It was twisted, it was wrong, but it was there. I was terrified, but I was also drawn to him. Something about his protective insanity was compelling, in a twisted, upside-down sort of way.

But I had to remember what was at stake, even as my traitorous body responded to his nearness.

"I won't run," I lied, looking straight into his eyes, hoping he'd believe me.

His stare lingered on me for a moment, silence stretching between us like a taut rubber band. Then, he let out a soft chuckle, the sound vibrating through the compact space.

"Even if I were to believe that, Clover, I can't risk it." Declan's voice was soft, almost tender, yet there was an undercurrent of a promise in it, something solid and unyielding.

I tugged at the ropes, the fibers digging into my skin, a sharp reminder of the reality of my situation. Fear slithered around my chest, squeezing it tight. I had to get out of here, I had to . . .

"Your horses are okay," Declan's voice interrupted my frenzied thoughts. He was watching me, eyes softer now, less manic. "I fed them. Gave them fresh water."

My breath caught in my throat. He had taken care of my horses? A wave of relief washed over me, swiftly followed by a tide of confusion. What kind of deranged man was he? A murderer who made sure my horses were fed?

"And Avery?" My voice trembled as I spoke. Avery,

my sweet little sister. What had happened to her? Would he hurt her? Was she worried about me?

"Avery is safe." The words were gentle, soothing almost. "Hope you don't mind, but I found your phone at the campsite and texted her. She thinks you're staying the night with Laura. She doesn't know anything."

A part of me, a very small part, wanted to believe him. I wanted to trust those ocean eyes, the easy way he had talked about feeding my horses, how he said my sister's name. But I couldn't afford to trust him. I couldn't afford to let my guard down.

"I want to see her," I blurted out. "I want to see Avery."

A smile, sad and fleeting, crossed his face. "I know, Wildflower. But not yet. I have some things to settle first."

The hope that had sparked in my chest flickered out. I closed my eyes, pushing back the tears. I had to be strong. I had to fight. But oh, it was so hard when the enemy was this confusing . . . this alluring.

A strangled laugh bubbled from his lips. "You know, there's something so . . . tempting about seeing you tied up like this." Declan's voice was low and gravelly. He leaned in closer, the scent of him—clean soap and something uniquely masculine—flooded my senses, making me lightheaded. "You're so beautiful, Clover. Even more so now, with your spirit still defiant, still fighting."

Defiance and dread warred within me, and I swallowed hard, holding his stare. I would not show him fear, not when he seemed to feed off it. But his next words sent a jolt of raw panic through me.

"It bothers me, you know," he began, his thumb tracing the contour of my jaw, his touch surprisingly gentle for a man who'd just tied me up. "Thinking about the man who touched you. Can't seem to get it out of my mind."

He continued, his eyes never leaving mine. "I want to erase him, Clover. I want to erase the touch of any man who's ever had his hands on you."

Fear turned to ice in my veins. I tugged at my restraints, desperate to put distance between us, but the ropes held fast. His face was so close to mine I could see the flecks of silver in his eyes and could feel the warmth of his breath.

He withdrew slightly, reaching into his pocket. The sound of metal clicking open was deafening in the silence. My eyes dropped to the pocket knife he held in his hand, the sharp blade glinting ominously in the dim light.

"Declan," I whispered, my voice shaky. I needed to

keep him talking, keep him distracted. I didn't know what he was planning, but I knew I had to stop him. Somehow, I had to get out of this. I just had to figure out how.

I held my breath as the blade descended, the cool metal a ghost of a touch against the skin of my arm. It was a delicate brush, dancing on the edge of danger. My pulse hammered in my chest, each beat a frantic plea for this madness to stop. But Declan was lost in his own world, his eyes dark and wild, focused intently on the path the blade was carving.

He moved lower, drawing the knife across the fabric covering my chest. I could feel the edge against me, skating over the soft curves with a precision that was horrifying. It was a promise, a threat, a chilling hint of what he could do, what he was capable of.

"All the men who've ever touched you . . . ," he murmured, his voice a rumble that echoed in the confined space. "I'll make them disappear, Clover. I'll erase them. And you . . ." He paused, his stare flicking up to meet mine. "You'll only know my touch."

A chill swept over me, freezing me to the core. What did he mean? Did he want to hurt the people from my past? Or did he mean he would overwrite their memories with his own? Either way, it sounded like a threat, a promise of something dark and terrifying.

"I don't want to hurt you, Clover," he continued, his voice softer now, almost tender. "I want to take the pain away. I want to fill you . . . with me. Erase them all, until there's only me."

The words hung in the air, a chilling premonition of what was to come. I was torn between fear and a strange fascination, a twisted attraction toward the man that saved me. I was repulsed and captivated, petrified and fascinated. The man was a monster, a deranged murderer. And yet, part of me couldn't help but be drawn to his protective madness, to the intensity in his gaze.

Even though terror gnawed at me, there was also this crazy buzz that hummed in response to his words. It felt wrong, warped, but it was there, clawing for attention.

Before I could fully grasp the situation, the icy sharpness of the blade slipped gently under the edge of my shirt. His actions were measured, deliberate, completely at odds with the unhinged sparkle in his eyes. He sliced the fabric away, slow and almost worshiping. A pang of panic stabbed me, my fingers pulling futilely at the ropes binding my hands.

But they held tight.

Then, I felt a strange stirring. It was not just fear— it was something more, something I rarely let myself feel. The realization hit me hard: this was a kind of twisted awakening. I was always the one in control, the one making decisions. But here, in this moment, having that control stripped away felt . . . freeing. It was a scary yet oddly exhilarating feeling. Was I attracted to the danger, to his dominance, and to the strange release of surrendering control? Maybe. It didn't mean it was right, but it was a part of me that I was just now discovering.

But this situation was far from the terror I experienced in the tent. Back then, control was ripped away from me by a man who only wanted to hurt and dominate, a nightmare I never wanted to revisit.

But this . . . this was different. He was different.

He wasn't a predator preying on my vulnerability; he was a protector, someone I trusted with my life. And for the first time, I found myself willingly surrendering control. Strangely enough, I wasn't just accepting it; I was reveling in it. The contrast was startling, but the realization was more so. I was no longer a victim, but a participant, exploring the contours of my desires.

"Declan, stop!" Even as I begged, I didn't want him to stop. My plea howled through the small space, but he seemed to pay no mind. He just continued, the knife gliding through the material as if it were nothing more than butter. My pulse pounded a frenzied rhythm in my chest. I closed my eyes, refusing to see the look on his face as he cut the last of my shirt.

I felt the cool air of the RV against my skin as my shirt fell open, leaving me exposed. My breath caught in my throat, my body trembling. He paused, the silence in the small space deafening. I could hear the ragged sound of my own breathing, feel the cold sweat beading on my forehead.

I risked a glance at Declan. His eyes were dark, focused on the task at hand, and there was a look of grim determination on his face. He looked up at me, and for a moment, our eyes locked.

"Declan, please . . ." I tried again, my voice barely above a whisper. The ropes chafed against my skin as I tugged on them again, but it was futile.

"Hush, Clover," he murmured, his voice soft but firm. The knife was back at work, now at the waistband of my sweats. I closed my eyes again, despair washing over me.

As my sweats were cut away, I felt the cool air caress my bare legs, the vulnerability of my situation hitting me with a new wave of dread. But Declan didn't stop, his gaze on me never wavering as he discarded the remains of my clothing.

His eyes fell on my thighs, and I watched his face darken, a fierce rage replacing the cool detachment.

The bruises.

The ones left by James.

I remembered the unwanted touches.

His fingers ghosted over the discolored skin, his touch featherlight but still enough to make me flinch. He let out a string of curses under his breath, his fingers clenching into a tight fist before he regained control of himself.

With a sudden, chilling calmness, he picked up the knife again. He trailed the flat side of the blade over my bruises, his movements gentle, almost caring, the sharp edge a vivid contradiction to his soft touch.

"I'd cut his touch out of you if I could, Wildflower," he muttered, his voice a low growl. He looked at me, his eyes dark, the manic energy I'd seen earlier now replaced with a cold, ruthless determination.

I swallowed hard, my throat dry and scratchy. My mind raced as I searched for a way out of this situation. His words were a twisted lullaby that filled me with a horrifying mix of fear and beguilement. I was at his mercy, and I could only hope that his bizarre fascination with me would not lead to something worse.

The blade was at my neck now, a cold, sharp caress that made me tense up. Panic surged, pushing at the edges of my consciousness, and I struggled against my restraints, the ropes digging painfully into my skin.

Yet, amidst the fear, there was another sensation bubbling up. One that was completely out of place, unexpected.

I was trembling, not solely from the threat of the blade at my throat, but from something else. Something that came unbidden, stirring in the pit of my stomach and spreading warmth through my veins. Arousal. I fluttered, confused and a little horrified at my own response. Was something wrong with me?

Declan's ocean eyes bore into mine. "Admit it," he demanded, his voice dropping to a rough whisper. The blade stayed steady at my throat, its cold presence a stark contrast to the heat blooming within me. "You want me to erase him for you. Erase him from your body."

His words stole the air from my lungs. I gaped at him, too shocked to formulate a response. Did I want that? To erase the man, his touch, his violation, from my body? The thought was horrifying, repulsive . . . and a tiny, traitorous part of me whispered, *yes*.

I stayed silent. Declan's fierce look didn't waver, his eyes studying me, evaluating me, challenging me. The weight of his stare was like a physical touch. There was something about his passion, his single-minded obsession, that had me both frightened and entranced.

"I . . ." My voice trailed off. What could I say? What did he want to hear? I was playing a treacherous game, and I didn't know the rules. I felt lost, adrift in the ocean of his madness, fear and desire churning inside me like stormy waves. I was scared of him, of what he could do, but I was also inexplicably drawn to him, to his dark passion.

He leaned in closer, so close that I could feel his breath fanning my lips, a tantalizing tease. His scent, a heady mix of pine and something uniquely Declan, flooded my senses, making my head spin. My heart pounded in my chest like a drum, every beat echoing his name. Declan. Declan. Declan.

"Admit it," he said again, a soft demand that carried an undercurrent of anticipation. "Say it, Clover, and I'll reward you. I'll make those memories vanish. I'll replace them with *me*."

I was teetering on the edge, caught between wanting to give in to the strange, forbidden allure he presented and resisting his commands. I was scared, petrified even, but that tiny spark, that perverse part of me, craved him. Craved the oblivion he offered.

Was it the fear? The adrenaline? Or was it something more? Something about Declan, with his menacing yet protective demeanor, his madness wrapped around an odd sort of tenderness, struck a chord deep within me. I was drawn to the fire in his eyes, the promise of an escape, however temporary, from the terror that haunted me.

I licked my lips, caught in the fine line between fear and anticipation. My skin buzzed as I met his stare, drowning in the depths of his eyes. The silence stretched on, each second ticking by like a countdown to an unknown fate.

And then, in a voice barely above a whisper, I said it.

"Yes."

The word was out before I could swallow it back, a soft admittance of my hidden desires. I watched as his eyes darkened, the corner of his lips curving into a satisfied smirk.

"Good girl," he said, a soft purr of approval that sent a rush of heat down my spine. The madness in his eyes flared brighter, yet there was an odd sense of relief there, too. As if he had been waiting, anticipating my submission.

With that one word, I had stepped into his world, a place where fear and desire walked hand in hand. I didn't know what lay ahead, but I knew one thing for certain—there was no turning back now.

Still keeping his eyes locked with mine, Declan began to strip. He pulled his shirt over his head, the fabric catching for a moment on the stubble lining his jaw. The sight of his chest, broad and dusted with dark hair, sent a strange flutter through my stomach. His muscles were well defined, the lines of his body hard and unyielding.

I had expected him to be fit, but the sight of him bare-chested was still a surprise. Declan was built like a warrior, strong and powerful. There was an intimidating rawness about him, an undeniable masculinity that was both terrifying and oddly appealing.

He dropped his shirt onto the floor, not breaking eye contact. His penetrating stare was hungry, as if he were drinking in my reactions, feeding off my fear and curiosity. I could see a strange satisfaction in his eyes, like he enjoyed the way I was studying him.

Next, he unbuttoned his jeans, the sound of the material parting seeming deafening in the otherwise silent room. He pushed the jeans down his legs, revealing powerful thighs and a glimpse of his lower abdomen.

Declan kicked off his boots, then stepped out of his jeans, leaving him in nothing but a pair of dark boxer briefs. His body was an interplay of light and shadow, each muscle standing out in sharp relief. The sight was almost hypnotic, like a siren song that promised both satisfaction and pain.

The room was filled with a heavy tension, each second ticking by with the weight of a thousand unspoken words. There was a strange pull between us, a magnetism that I couldn't deny. I was apprehensive, yes, but I was also drawn in by the enthralling promise of what could be.

Declan stood there for a moment, letting me take in the sight of him. Then he slowly started moving toward me, a predator closing in on his prey. His eyes were on me, watching every shift of emotion on my face, every hitch in my breath.

And I, regardless of the ropes, could do nothing but watch him approach, transfixed and anxious about what would come next.

He came to stand beside the bed, his body taut with anticipation. His eyes never left mine as he reached for his boxers and slowly began to slide them down. The fabric clung briefly to his hips before falling away, revealing the hard lines of his body beneath. His skin seemed to glow in the faint light of the room. His cock was hard and thick, long enough to make me part my lips in surprise.

I felt a strange ache deep in my core as I looked at him. He was beautiful but in a wild way that made me fear him even more. With one step forward, he brought himself close enough to touch me—and then he did something that I wasn't expecting.

He leaned down and kissed me deeply on the lips, setting my whole body ablaze with ecstasy.

He continued to kiss me, moving slowly from my

mouth to my throat and finally lower onto my chest. His lips were like velvet against my skin, soft and gentle yet filled with an undeniable passion. I could feel the heat radiating off his body as he moved along my skin, the sheer strength of his presence overpowering me in the best possible way.

And then, finally, he got on top of me on the bed. My limbs were bound with rope, and I felt completely powerless beneath his touch. But at the same time, something inside of me was also warming with anticipation—this was exciting and dangerous all at once, a thrilling combination that had me trembling in eagerness for what would come next.

Declan continued his slow assault on my senses with featherlight kisses across my collarbone and shoulders before finally coming back up to meet my eyes again. His stare was hungry yet controlled at the same time. "Sweet, sweet Wildflower."

The way he said those two words, like he was savoring each syllable, sent a shiver of bliss through me. I felt a strange spark of electricity between us, and in that moment, I knew that something inside me had shifted.

And then, finally, he moved between my legs and pushed himself inside me. His thrust was hard—almost violent—but at the same time incredibly satisfying. I gasped as delight radiated through me, pleasure that only increased with every stroke of his hips.

My whole body lit up with sensation as Declan plunged into me, each thrust making me full.

Fuller.

Full of him.

Full of release.

Full of control that didn't belong to me.

Full of freedom to feel pleasure and not be responsible for it.

Every inch of him seemed to have been made just for me, fitting together in a perfect mixture of passion and desire. "No one will ever have you like this, Clover. Never again."

His words were a whispered promise in my ear, and I clung to them as I felt the force of his movements increase. He started fucking harder, driving himself deep into me with every stroke. The RV rocked with each movement, and soon the sound of skin meeting skin was like a beat that seemed to take me higher and higher. It was bliss on the verge of pain, like he wanted to fuse all of his cells with my own.

And then, suddenly, it was over—an explosion of sensation coursing through us both until we lay in a breathless heap on the bed, our bodies tangled together in exhaustion. As Declan's breathing slowed down and his grip around me relaxed, I felt a strange warmth fill my chest—something I couldn't quite place or understand.

Something wrong.

Something terrifying.

But also, something I wanted to experience again.

My fucked-up brain *enjoyed* it.

CHAPTER 14

Midnight Desperados and Velvet Hearts

DECLAN

I pretended to sleep, feigning heavy, slow breaths while she went to work on her bindings. The small, secret smile that had taken up residence on my face was the only giveaway to my true alertness, should anyone have been watching. But no one was watching. Just me. Just her.

I felt her shift, the way the mattress beneath us gave slightly under us, subtle though it was. She was being careful, so careful, her movements small and measured as she reached for the knife I'd carelessly left in her reach. She was a lot of things, Clover, but careless wasn't one of them.

A chuckle bubbled up from within me, unbidden and unwelcome. I had to suppress it, my body shaking slightly with the effort. This was too good, too damn enjoyable. It wasn't often that I was surprised by a person, not often that I found amusement in the face of someone else's defiance. But this woman . . . Clover was a different breed altogether.

It was like trying to break in a wild horse. The harder they bucked, the more satisfying it was to finally have them under your control, to finally break them and bend them to your will. And I could tell, Clover was going to buck hard. It was a challenge I looked forward to.

And when she broke, I'd take care of her. I'd treat her like a fucking queen.

I allowed my eyes to flutter open, barely a crack, and watched as she sawed through her bindings with the knife. Her brow was furrowed in concentration, lips pressed into a determined line. It was almost endearing, her resolute focus and unwavering determination.

In that moment, I realized that to fully control her, I had to understand her. Understand her spirit, her fight, her resolve. Only by witnessing the lengths she would go to in order to escape, only by measuring her will, could I begin to comprehend who she was.

With a final tug, the rope fell away from her wrists. The look of triumph in her eyes was almost beautiful, a sight to behold. But it was fleeting. Soon it would be replaced with fear, confusion, and finally, submission. I couldn't wait.

But for now, I let her revel in her victory, let her think she was escaping. I wanted to see how far she'd get, how hard she would fight. It was all part of the process, breaking her in. So I lay still, a predator hidden in the shadows, watching his prey unknowingly walk into his trap.

I had to admit, I was looking forward to what came next. Because no matter how hard she fought, no matter how far she got, she was still mine. Clover was mine to break, mine to tame. And I wouldn't have it any other way.

I watched her, or rather listened, as she shuffled to find some clothes. Every small rustle, every tiny exhale, became a soundtrack of anticipation. Then, right on cue, I stirred. It wasn't an overly dramatic movement, just a soft grunt, a slight shift, enough to inspire fear.

Her breath hitched. Even without seeing, I knew what expression crossed her face. Fear, likely mixed with resolve. She was a stubborn one, my Clover, an attribute I found endearing in its own twisted way.

Her fear was my pleasure, an adrenaline rush that eclipsed any traditional thrill. It was intoxicating, this cat and mouse game. It made me feel alive, powerful.

The soft creak of the RV door followed by a rush of

cool air signaled her departure. I didn't have to see to know she was gone. The absence of her, the silence she left in her wake, was loud enough.

An unhurried smile tugged at the corners of my lips. There was no rush. She wouldn't get far, not from me. I was her captor, yes, but more importantly, I was her observer. I understood her in ways she likely didn't understand herself.

So I lay there, a predator relishing in the thrill of the chase. Her fear, her flight, it was all part of the dance. I let the silence stretch, savored the calm before the storm, before finally pushing myself off the bed.

She had a head start, but that was all part of the fun. I looked forward to the chase, to seeing the surprise and fear in her eyes when she realized escape was a delusion.

And so, with her scent still lingering in the air and her fear echoing in the silence, I went after my wild-flower, ready to enjoy the hunt.

$\sim$

J was grinning like a damn fool, hiding in the undergrowth, my face hit by the night air. There she was, Clover, changing her locks like that could keep me out. It was laughable, really.

She was a runner, that much was clear. Those long

legs of hers, squeezed into tight jeans, looked ready to sprint a marathon. But against me? She wouldn't stand a chance. Her moves, graceful as a damn ballet, were not lost on me. I was watching, always watching.

Her hair, long and flowing, was a beacon in the night. I could almost feel it slipping through my fingers, pulling her close. And her lips, man, those lips. Red. Full. Inviting. They were something I was ready to savor.

But those eyes. Damn, those brown eyes. Bright with life and smarts, and something else. Fire. And I was ready to snuff it out. Ready to replace it with me, with need. It was a drug I was willing to mainline.

My blood pumped faster with every move she made. I was itching to claim her, to make her mine in every way. The thought of her under me, giving in, had my skin prickling with anticipation. The night held a promise, a promise of her.

She went inside. Avery's car was nowhere to be seen, which meant Clover was alone. Probably armed, but I wasn't worried. Disarming her? Piece of cake. Let the fun begin.

I'd had more lead aimed at me than any man had a right to survive. Yet, here I was. I savored the fight, the struggle, and especially the win.

The night fell heavier, the shadows lengthening, and the world hushed down. I slipped from my hideout, heartbeat quickening as I stalked closer to her place. I was a shadow, unseen, unheard.

A window left open.

The drone of an air conditioning unit covered any noise I might make. The joke was on her. Quiet as a cat, I was inside, all smooth moves and practice. Her place was cast in a moonlit haze. My boots, silent, moved me closer. The thrill of the hunt was everything, every damn time.

I prowled through her home, pausing at each door to listen for her breath. When I finally heard it, a thrill shot through me. There she was, lying in her bed, a picture of peace.

I was about to unleash a storm.

Every step was measured, noiseless, not wanting to wake her just yet. I was so close. Her body, barely concealed under the thin blanket, fueled me further. Ignorance is bliss, they say. For her, ignorance was about to end.

I could feel my cock hardening, and I ran my palm over it, twitching at the pleasure I felt. I yearned to feel the warmth of her body as it melted against my own.

Need boiling in my veins, I quickly pulled out my cock and grasped my shaft with both hands before pumping it feverishly. My muscles clenched as pleasure surged through me, shaking my core. The desire to feel her soft skin against mine burned within me, filling the air around us with an undeniable potency.

Her eyes were closed, blissfully unaware of the lustful thoughts rushing through my mind. I wanted so badly to wake her up, to make her witness this moment between us. To feel the heat radiating off my body and experience a mutual surge of passion like we'd never felt before. Ecstasy erupted from every cell in my body, flooding all my senses with raging satisfaction until I shot my load, coating my hands. Panting, I allowed myself to sink back into reality, feeling blissfully content.

I cleaned off with her yoga pants that were sitting on the floor, hating that I couldn't shove every drop inside her pretty pussy.

Inhaling deeply, I approached her bed, checking if she was still asleep. As I watched her sleep, it hit me. She was perfect for me, in ways she didn't understand yet. I'd studied her, knew her better than she knew herself. I knew she was mine, even if she didn't.

The curve of her hip, the arch of her neck, her rhythmic breathing, it was all too much. My fingers longed to feel her, to claim her. She shifted in her sleep, moaning softly. My pulse pounded. I couldn't hold back.

My hand found her shoulder, and the shock of

contact sparked something in me. I whispered, "You're mine, Clover. You just don't know it yet."

Some might say it's fucked up, showing up so soon after . . . When she was tied up in my bed, I hadn't planned on taking her. Claiming her. But we both needed to get rid of that fucker's stain on her body.

But I was here to protect, to care. I wasn't a saint, but my obsession with her? That was real. I wanted her thoughts, her flesh, her future.

Her body tensed at my touch, even in sleep. The thrill of it, of knowing I affected her, was addictive. There was a pull, a connection, I could feel it. She was meant for me, and me for her.

The night wrapped around us, the sound of her breath filling the space. We were destined, I knew it. I'd show her, make her see that we were meant to be. She was mine, no question about it.

With the confidence of a cat, I stripped and slid into bed with her. She stirred, snuggling against me, not even awake. Her arms held me close, her body warm and soft. A smile on her lips.

I pulled her to me, her body fitting against mine like it was made for me. And the reality of it hit me, right in the gut. For tonight, she was mine. The woman I'd been chasing, the woman I'd claimed in my mind, was here, in my arms. The thought sent a jolt of satisfaction through me.

Her hair fanned across my chest, tickling my skin. Her soft snores filled the silence of the room. I closed my eyes, relishing the feel of her against me. I wrapped my arm around her, pulling her closer, letting her warmth seep into me.

It wasn't enough. It would never be enough. I craved her, needed her. The mere thought of her with anyone else was unbearable. She was mine, and soon, she'd know it too.

CHAPTER 15
Gunslingers and Lipstick Stains

CLOVER

I awoke to a strange sensation; it felt like a thousand tiny butterflies dancing along my inner thigh. The room was dimly lit, but I could see the gentle curve of a shoulder and feel the tender touch of fingertips tracing my skin.

As consciousness slowly crept over me, I realized the sensation came from soft, warm lips pressing tender kisses along my skin. I struggled to process this sudden intimacy. My body was alive with tingling sensations, and I could feel a warmth pooling deep within me.

"Wha. . . ?" I murmured, my voice barely audible. The kisses paused momentarily, and I heard a chuckle that made my heart race.

"Good morning, Wildflower," a familiar voice

whispered, and I suddenly recognized the person responsible for my early morning surprise.

I stiffened immediately, shocked that Declan was in my house.

In my bedroom.

In my bed.

My entire body went stiff.

"Oh, but you were so open before. Pry your creamy thighs so I can taste you."

I moved the comforter and saw his tumbling black hair and electric eyes as he peered up at me, his mouth rimmed with scruffy hair poised just over my center.

I was frozen with fear and arousal, my instincts at war with one another. I wanted to run. I wanted to feel him.

"What the fuck are you doing here?"

"Waking you up," he murmured before using his strong hands to pry my thighs open even further. I watched him.

I watched him even though I knew I should have been horrified.

I watched him even though I knew I shouldn't let him control my body like this.

I watched him and my mind raged. My body ached. My clit begged to be licked.

"I like that you don't wear panties to bed, Wildflower. Makes it so much easier to see your pretty pink pussy."

"Declan. How did you get in? How did you know where I live?" I asked, because that was what I was supposed to ask. Because I'd always been the sensible one.

I was supposed to be the fucking sensible one.

He chuckled. "You think I left that knife out by accident? I wanted to see you fight, Wildflower. I followed you. And the new locks on your door are cute, but you should make sure your windows are shut."

In a moment of sanity, I pushed on his head, trying to get him away, but it was like shoving a brick wall. A shudder of revulsion traveled down my spine. For a moment, it wasn't Declan between my thighs. It was James, the asshole that violated me. My breaths turned shallow. My vision blurred.

"Stay with me, Wildflower. Tell me who's about to taste you," Declan said.

I shook my head, my pulse racing with phantom adrenaline, reminding me of the horrific thing I'd endured. I was still fucked in the head about it. Still devastated. Still dealing with everything.

I thought about how I ran to Declan. How he killed those men. How he tied me up. How he made me feel things I shouldn't have felt so soon after being . . . fuck, I hated that word. I didn't want to say it.

But I was raped.

I was fucking raped, and then right after, Declan did something that felt a whole fucking lot like rape but maybe wasn't.

And then I couldn't go to the cops. Because there were six men dead, and I was now technically an accomplice.

How I couldn't tell my sister because I didn't want to put her in harm's way.

How I spent all night trying and failing to figure out what the hell to do. I even packed a suitcase, prepared to run, but I couldn't leave Avery or my horses, and I didn't have a truck.

"Tell me who I am," he whispered. "Stay here with me. Chase those nightmares away, baby."

I swallowed. "Declan."

"Good girl. You want to know what I'm going to do?"

I was still too scared to speak. This was fucked up on every level.

"I'm going to make you feel good. That dead bastard that hurt you was all about *his* pleasure. But you know what, Wildflower? All I want to do is make *you* feel good."

"It's too soon," I choked out.

"Says who?" he asked.

Says probably any decent psychiatrist.

"It's wrong."

Declan leaned in closer, his warm breath fanning my skin before his tongue began to lap at my center. I gasped as bliss surged through me, unfamiliar sensations washing over my body. "Take your power back, Wildflower." His hands were firm as they gripped my thighs, pressing them open wider and giving him access to all of me. He took his time exploring and tasting me, his tongue slipping inside and then flicking against my most sensitive spots until I was all but trembling with desire.

My protests had faded away as I was lost in a sea of satisfaction. Every lick and every caress sent a wave of delight through me, and soon my body was swaying and moving to meet his lips.

Maybe it was fucked up.

Maybe I should have been nursing my wounds.

Maybe Declan made me feel fucking powerful. Like choosing to submit was my way of fighting back.

Maybe I didn't know what I needed anymore, and maybe I was damaged past the point of no return. But I wanted this. I wanted to feel good.

I finally grasped his head in my hands, wrapping my fingers in his hair and pushing him deeper into me. His mouth moved over me in a way that felt like pure ecstasy, pushing me higher and higher until I was practically screaming out. He growled low in his throat, the sound vibrating through me and amplifying the feeling of his stroking tongue. Just when I thought I couldn't take it any longer, he pulled away, leaving me panting and wanting more.

His teeth gently grazed across my swollen flesh as he increased the power, sending sparks of pleasure shooting through me with every touch. And then it happened; a delicious heat pooled deep within me as Declan drove me closer and closer to the edge with expert precision.

Just as I thought I could take no more, his fingers joined in, and it felt like every nerve ending in my body was on fire.

"I'm going to make you come," he promised before increasing the pressure of each stroke until I was on the brink of tumbling over the edge. With one final flick of his tongue, I broke apart into pieces beneath him, wave after wave crashing over me until I lay spent.

He shifted up, pressing soft kisses along my inner thighs before slowly crawling up beside me in bed. "You need to leave," I croaked.

"Well, that's not nice," he teased. "And no."

Our eyes were locked in a fierce battle of wills. The

tension between us was palpable, like the charged air before a storm.

"Declan," I said, rolling my eyes and crossing my arms defiantly. "This is really fucked up."

He smirked, a mischievous glint in his eyes. "Well, Wildflower, sometimes fucked-up things are fun," he taunted, leaning closer, the heat of his body radiating toward me.

I felt my face grow warm, but I refused to back down. "You tied me up," I retorted. "I escaped and now you're here . . . here . . ."

"Eating your pussy? I thought you liked that." Declan chuckled, leaning in so close that I could feel his breath on my ear. "You say no now, but I bet you'd change your tune if you knew what I had planned for you," he whispered, his voice dripping with seductive intent.

I swallowed hard as I fought to keep my composure. I refused to let him see how much his words affected me. "Oh, really?" I challenged, raising an eyebrow and meeting his searching eyes with all the confidence I could muster. "And what would that be?"

He grinned, his eyes darkening with desire. "That, my dear Clover, is something you'll have to discover for yourself," he replied, his fingers lightly brushing against my arm, and my heart skipped a beat. "Once you stop fighting me, I'll make you feel so good."

I sucked in a harsh breath, fortifying myself against his provocative gaze. "Don't mistake lust for affection," I bit out, attempting to hide the storm of conflicting emotions within me. "I won't be manipulated by you, Declan. We can't simply ignore the fact that you're a murderer."

His eyes danced with a potent blend of tenacity and mirth. "All loose ends are tied, darling," he purred, his voice resonating with an ominous assurance. "No one will come looking."

A distant clatter from the kitchen pierced through my spiraling thoughts. Avery. Panic gripped me, the stark reality of Declan's life suffocating my playful demeanor. My protective instincts flared to life.

"Declan, you have to go," I demanded, my tone steeped in urgency. "Avery is here. You showing up unannounced is a risk I can't afford."

His brow furrowed, a grimace of disappointment tainting his features. "What if I just stayed for breakfast? Your sister won't be in danger. Neither will you."

"No, Declan. Your assurances aren't enough. Get out before she notices," I implored, desperation creeping into my voice.

Ignoring my pleas, Declan got up from the bed, his signature smirk returning. He began to dress, and for a fleeting moment, I allowed relief to wash over me. However, instead of making his exit, he sauntered toward the kitchen, his audacity leaving me breathless. As quickly as I could, I pulled on my robe and trailed after him, apprehension gnawing at me.

"Declan, I'm not joking. Get out!" I spat, attempting to push him back toward the entrance without attracting Avery's attention.

With a dismissive chuckle, he shrugged me off. "Just want a meal, Clover. Then, I'm gone."

My fists clenched, fury sweeping through me at his blatant disregard. "This is not okay, Declan!"

Before I could further argue, Avery's surprised gasp made me flinch, her keen eyes falling on Declan. "Clover, why is Declan here?"

I opened my mouth, fumbling for a plausible explanation, but Declan was quicker. "Spent the night. Going to be a regular thing."

Avery's gaze shifted back and forth between us, confusion etched on her face. I forced a smile, attempting to mollify her. "He was just . . . leaving."

"Sure, after breakfast," he countered, settling at the table like he owned the place.

"And Avery," he continued, a devilish grin plastered on his face, "Clover and I . . . we're together now. Maybe even planning a wedding."

Avery's brow furrowed, her eyes darting between us, seeking clarification. "Is this . . . true?"

I vehemently denied it, my face burning. "No, Avery! Declan is . . . misunderstanding things."

But Declan wasn't fazed. "Admit it, Clover," he chimed, his tone laced with a possessive dare. "We're meant for each other."

My temper flared. "Enough, Declan! Get out!"

He reclined comfortably in his chair, a smug grin curling his lips. "I'll leave . . . once you confess you crave me just as much as I crave you."

Avery, stuck in the crossfire, looked like she'd stumbled into a foreign film with no subtitles. I locked eyes with Declan, a silent plea for him to cut the act. The last thing I needed was for Avery to get sucked into this terrible whirlpool.

A pulse of uncertainty passed before I bit the bullet. "Say it and you're out?" The only thought running through my mind was getting Declan out the door, away from Avery, even if it meant playing his dirty game.

His smirk was the edge of a blade, too close for comfort. "You're my bride-to-be. Say it."

Avery, thrown in the deep end, was struggling to swim. "Clover? What's this all about? Why is he talking like that?"

I glanced at my sister, then back at Declan. Backed into a corner. Out of choices. "Alright, Declan. If it sends you packing and keeps Avery safe, I'll . . . I'll say

I'm your . . . fiancée." The words tasted like poison on my tongue.

Avery looked like she'd just been slapped with a cold fish, her mouth opening and closing in shock. But I shot her a look, a silent SOS.

Declan's grin was the victory of a conqueror, reveling in his spoils. "That's my girl," he purred, giving the last word an extra twist of the knife. He rose from the table, stretching languidly, like a cat in the sun.

Sick as it made me, I'd given him what he wanted to keep Avery safe. This was just an act. A lie. I didn't know this man. I wasn't going to fucking *marry* him.

Declan moved to me, like a shark closing in on its prey. His hands cradled my face, and before I could react, his lips claimed mine, marking his territory. The thunder of my heart was drowned out by the taste of me on his lips, a violent reminder of our earlier encounter.

His kiss was a declaration of power, a brutal dance of possession. He drew me in, his body a furnace that consumed my resistance. Despite everything, the pull was magnetic.

It was hard to keep up the fight when his tongue coaxed me open, inviting him in. I let him, surrendering to the wildfire of his kiss.

Beneath the raw passion was a sense of dread that

hung over us like a guillotine, ready to fall. I couldn't lose sight of the stakes.

When he finally pulled back, both of us gasping, his look was one of self-assured victory.

"You're mine, Clover." His voice was gravel, hard and sure. "Remember that."

I found myself wishing he wouldn't leave as he finally moved toward the exit.

It was a crazy thought, to want him to say.

My words kept denying him, but my body begged for more. My soul begged to be claimed and controlled.

Fucked up. I was so fucking fucked up. Fuck.

But my mind was a storm of turmoil. What had I done? How deep was I in Declan's twisted game?

Why did I like it?

What the hell was wrong with me for wanting more?

Once he'd disappeared, Avery shattered the silence. "What the hell just happened?" she choked out.

My heart felt heavy, my body numb. "Call Laura," I murmured. "We have a lot to discuss."

CHAPTER 16

Vixens of the Dust

CLOVER

*I*n the dim lighting of Laura's living room, I sank deeper into the cushions of the couch, my best friend on one side, my sister Avery on the other. The recounting of my story echoed hollowly in the quiet room. I'd just revealed the truth, Declan's brutal act of retaliation against my attackers, his strange, possessive claim over me. The silence was heavy, their faces pale and drawn in shock and fear.

"Clover," Laura said, her voice a frail whisper, "I can't . . . I can't begin to understand what you went through."

I shook my head, words caught in my throat. I was still grappling with the terror of the incident, the grotesque rape. The fear was still so tangible, so close.

Avery's knuckles whitened, her hand clenched into

a fist. "Declan's off his rocker, but I wish I'd been there, could have given them what they deserved—"

"I think Declan did that," I replied, my voice a hoarse whisper. I tried to shrug off the cold sensation skittering along my senses. The brutality of Declan's actions and my strange, conflicting emotions were a storm inside me.

Laura's response was a quiet nod. She was tough, always had been. Avery, though younger than me, had the same fierce protective streak. I knew I could trust them with my fears, my secrets. But could I trust them with the impossible situation we were now entangled in?

Laura broke the silence again. "What do you need, Clover? How can we help?"

"I . . . I don't know," I confessed, my voice barely a whisper. I should have been in mourning, healing, not succumbing to Declan's touch like a moth to a flame. His cruelty was undeniable, but my body sang a different tune. The memory of pleasure clouded my judgment, leaving me in a state of tumultuous confusion.

Avery's gaze hardened, her eyes darting toward me. "Clover, you . . . you didn't . . . this morning . . . with Declan . . . he didn't . . ."

I shook my head, a lump forming in my throat. "No, he didn't hurt me. But he . . . we . . ." My voice trailed off. How could I explain the irrational pleasure in the wake of such horror?

My mind was a whirlwind of tormenting images and emotions. Feeling a need to speak, to voice the terror I'd been bottling up, I took a deep breath.

"That night . . . it was . . . it was so awful," I began, my voice shaky. "James . . . he took me in my tent. I was so scared, more than I've ever been."

Avery reached out, her hand grasping mine in a comforting squeeze. "You don't have to share if you're not ready, Clover."

"No, I need to," I insisted. "I need to face it, not hide from it."

Laura nodded in understanding. "Whatever you're comfortable with, Clover."

With another deep breath, I dove into the memory. "I barely managed to escape . . . I was naked from the waist down, bruised and terrified. All I could think of was reaching safety. I rode Ginny bareback all the way to Declan's."

Avery's face paled at my recounting, her hand tightening around mine. "Jesus, Clover . . . That's . . . that's just . . ."

"I was horrified, Avery," I admitted. "Every shadow, every rustle . . . I thought they were behind me. Chasing me."

"And then you got to Declan's . . . ," Laura prompted, a question unspoken in her words.

I nodded. "Yes, and he . . . he took care of me. Despite his own violence, he was gentle with me. Protective."

The room fell silent again as I finished my story, my emotions poured out in a hushed whisper. Both Laura and Avery seemed to be processing my words, their eyes reflecting a mix of anger, fear, and profound sadness. But, amidst those feelings, I also saw determination—a promise to support me, to help me navigate this storm. Despite the horror of the situation, I wasn't alone.

Avery was quiet, staring at her tightly clenched hands in her lap. Her fingers were knotted together, her knuckles pale. There was a tension in her, a restlessness that contrasted with the stillness of the room.

Finally, she spoke, her voice so quiet that it barely disturbed the silence. "I feel . . . I feel like it's my fault."

Laura and I turned to look at her, surprise written on our faces. "Avery . . . ," Laura began, her tone gentle.

But Avery cut her off, her words coming out in a rush. "If I could've done more, if I could've helped . . . you wouldn't have had to work so hard, Clover. You wouldn't have had to take that job."

Her words hung in the air, an apparent regret that seemed to thicken the silence around us.

"Avery," I started, my voice shaking slightly, "You can't blame yourself for this. None of us could've seen this coming."

"But you're always working so hard for us," Avery continued, her voice growing stronger. "I feel like I'm not pulling my weight. I don't help pay for things around the house. I don't support your trail ride business. If I had been there, maybe this wouldn't have happened."

I reached out, gripping her shoulder firmly. "Avery, look at me." When she finally lifted her tear-filled eyes to meet mine, I spoke again, with all the sincerity I could muster. "This is not your fault. The only one to blame is the man who did this, and he paid for his crimes. You're my family, and I would do anything for you. Don't blame yourself for what happened."

She nodded slowly, taking in my words. We sat there, connected by our hands and shared pain. The night was young, and there were still countless words to be spoken. But for now, we sat together, finding comfort in the solidarity and support we provided each other. The road to healing was long and winding, but we would walk it together.

Avery, her expression troubled, glanced over at the flat-screen television mounted on the wall. "We should check the news. See if the Devils have already started their cover-up."

Laura nodded in agreement. "Good idea. Something like this . . . six men dying after a bachelor party . . . it's bound to make headlines, even if the Devils try to manipulate the story."

A jolt of fear surged through me. The prospect of seeing the incident splashed across the news was both terrifying and oddly comforting. If the news was already out, then it meant the Devils had moved swiftly to control the narrative, which gave us some idea of their game plan.

Avery reached for the remote and switched on the TV, flipping to a twenty-four-hour news station. Images flashed across the screen, but there was no immediate coverage of the incident. An undercurrent of dread pooled in my stomach as we scrolled through channels, anxiously waiting for any snippet of news related to the events of that night.

Finally, we found a brief mention on a local station. The reporter talked about a tragic gas explosion at a private bachelor party on the outskirts of town, killing six men. The preliminary reports suggested all victims were from out of town, celebrating a bachelor party.

"Gas explosion?" Avery scoffed, throwing the remote onto the coffee table. "That's their story?"

"It's plausible, easy to swallow," Laura said grimly. "For the general public, it's just a tragic accident."

I felt a knot tighten in my stomach. The cover-up

had begun, and the Devils were playing their hand. It was horrifying to see the ease with which they manipulated the truth, turning a brutal act of violence into a tragic accident. But it also confirmed what Laura had warned us about. The Devils had power and influence, and they were going to use it to protect their interests.

Laura leaned back, her face pale, her eyes thoughtful. "If they're going to these lengths . . . it means Declan is neck-deep in their operations. He's not some fringe member."

"More than that," she added after a pause, her voice low, "they're covering up multiple homicides committed by one man. It suggests . . . it suggests he does this often."

Fear and revulsion danced across my skin at the implication. Could Declan really be a frequent executioner for the Devils? The quiet man who lived on the outskirts of the town, the man who had been my sanctuary in the storm, was he really a hired killer?

"Declan, a . . . a killer?" I asked, the words tasting bitter and foreign on my tongue. The man who had held me gently, who had made me feel pleasure in the wake of horror, had also dealt out death without blinking.

Avery's face was stricken, her eyes wide. "That means . . . he . . . he must be their enforcer. That's . . . oh God, Clover."

Their words were a cold shock to my system. It was one thing to see Declan's violence in person, quite another to consider that it was not an isolated incident. That he might kill again, that he had probably killed before.

"Yes," Laura said, her tone grave. "Clover, you're tangled up in something risky. But we'll figure this out. Together."

Despite the terrible revelation, I felt a thread of warmth at her words. At least I wasn't alone in this. I had my sister and my best friend. Together, we might be able to navigate this impossible situation.

But the shadow of Declan, of the man he truly was, loomed over us all.

In the gloom of the room, I tried to shake off the chilling revelation. "Maybe we should just . . . leave. Start over somewhere else."

But even as I spoke, the thought of my horses, the ranch, our home filled with memories of simpler times, it made my heart ache. How could I leave all that behind? Avery's next words, however, caused me to shake with dread.

"Clover," she said quietly, her face serious, "Declan . . . he's obsessive about you. We saw it ourselves. If we run . . . he might find you. Track you down."

Her words mirrored my own fears. The Declan I'd witnessed that night, his possessive declaration, his violent actions . . . there was a sense of dangerous obsession in it all. Could we truly escape his clutches? Would he let us go so easily?

"But we can't stay either," Laura added, her face taut with worry. "It's too risky."

I let out a deep, shuddering breath. Caught between a rock and a hard place, my mind raced to find a solution but came up empty. The reality of our predicament loomed large before us, the possible outcomes weighing me down.

A thought pierced through the uncertainty, causing my heart to jolt. "What about Carson?" I looked at Laura, her face reflecting the worry I felt. "You can't just uproot him. His life is here."

Laura sighed deeply, her expression distant. "But I don't want him growing up in a town run by the Devils. I won't risk him getting caught up in all this. We're all in this together."

We sat in silence for a while, lost in thought. It was Avery who broke the quiet, her voice quivering with a hint of hope.

"We could . . . sell the horses. To Mr. O'Riley. He's always been asking about them." Her words hung in the air, carrying the weight of a potential solution.

A pang of grief stabbed through me at the thought. Those horses were more than just animals to me. They were part of my family, part of me. But . . . they could also be our ticket out.

"And my lease is up in two months," Laura added, her voice barely audible. "We could . . . leave. Never look back. Put your house up for sale."

The idea felt so foreign, so unthinkable. Yet, it also offered a glimmer of hope, a possible escape from the madness that had become our lives. It was a desperate plan, one fraught with uncertainty and risk. But perhaps it was the only plan we had.

"But what do we do in the meantime?" I asked, looking between them, the gravity of our situation sinking in further.

Avery bit her lip, her intense stare meeting mine. "You . . . you should go along with Declan. Pretend . . . for all our sakes."

Laura nodded in agreement. "It might be the safest option for now. If we poke the bear . . ."

My whole body tingled with anticipation at the thought of continuing the charade with Declan. But I understood their point. We were playing a dangerous game, and one wrong move could tip everything into chaos.

Swallowing my apprehension, I nodded. "Alright, I'll . . . I'll be with him. Pretend that everything is normal."

"Then when the time's right," Laura added, her

stare firm and resolute, "we leave. All of us. Together." Laura cleared her throat, a thoughtful look on her face. "I have a friend, she lives in New Mexico . . . She has some land and a guest house. Her husband is a cop. We could go there, lay low for a while until we figure out our next steps."

New Mexico. The thought seemed distant and unreal, yet it sparked a tiny flame of hope within me. A sanctuary, a safe haven amidst the storm.

"But . . . Laura," I began, my voice wavering, "I don't want to drag you and Carson into this. It's—"

"No, Clover." Laura cut me off, her tone firm. "We're in this together. You're not dragging us anywhere. We are choosing this. Choosing to stick with you."

I swallowed hard, feeling a rush of gratitude for these women, my pillars of strength. Their determination fortified my resolve, despite the daunting journey that lay ahead. We would face this storm, and we would survive. Together.

CHAPTER 17

Blood on the Roses

DECLAN

Climbing out of my new truck, I paused, pocketing my keys and glancing at the dilapidated farmhouse. A weighty piece of metal pressed against my thigh inside my pocket, a constant reminder of why I was there. The ring. A little something I bought last night.

I bought a truck to haul Clover's horses around. I knew she needed one, and my bike was fun for feeling her hot body pressed against mine, but we needed something more practical.

Money was never a problem. It hadn't been for a while. Killing paid well. But it wasn't about the money. Not anymore. It was about providing for her, giving her the life she deserved.

My eyes swept over the property, taking in the

cracked wooden siding of the house, the rusty, half-collapsed barn. The place was a shambles, but I could see its potential. I could fix it, make it a home, a real home for both of us. I thought about the barn, her horses. I knew how much she loved them; I bet she dreamt of transforming that run-down barn into a proper stable.

I fished the ring out of my pocket, studying the glittering diamond. It was a simple design, nothing flashy. Just like Clover. She wasn't the kind to be swayed by shiny things, but I wanted her to have it, to know my intentions were serious.

Time was a bullshit construct. We didn't know each other for long, but we'd already been through a lot. I didn't need a year or two to decide she was mine. I was already calling her Mrs. Wilder in my mind.

Taking a deep breath, I pushed away my musings and made my way toward the house. Today, I was going to change everything. For her, for us. I just hoped she'd see that too.

The creak of the front door breaking the stillness snapped me back to reality. Avery stood there, her slender arms crossed over her chest and a deep scowl etched into her features.

"Declan," she said, her voice steely. The defiance in her penetrating eyes was like a cold bucket of water.

I'd expected this, but confrontation always set me on edge.

She looked me over for a long, hard moment before speaking. "I know what you did . . . for Clover."

The barest acknowledgement of gratitude peeked through her tough exterior. I just nodded, not knowing what to say.

Avery took a breath, then stepped down from the porch. "Just so we're clear," she said, her voice tense, "Clover is all I have. You hurt her . . . I swear, Declan, I'll—"

"I won't," I interjected, holding her gaze. It was a promise I intended to keep.

"I wanted to be there for her," Avery admitted, her voice wavering. "To protect her from . . . from everything. But I wasn't." There was a bitter twist to her words, a tangled knot of regret and fury.

"I know," I replied, the raspy undertone of my voice bouncing off the stillness of the quiet morning. I couldn't tell her it wasn't her fault, because she wouldn't have listened, wouldn't have believed it.

As Avery's words rang in the air, I wasn't surprised. No, not really. The sister bond between Avery and Clover was something sacred, unbreakable. Of course Clover would've confided in her.

A bitter taste lined the back of my mouth as I understood the weight of my own decisions. Every choice I made was now entwined with Clover's life, Avery's life, and all the countless threads that wove their world together.

"I take it she told you everything?" I asked, my tone laced with an understanding that came from knowing the bond of family, of blood.

Avery nodded, her eyes never leaving mine. "She did."

I felt a gnawing pit in my stomach as I warned her, "You understand, Avery, that no one else can know?"

She looked at me, eyes flinty, resolve steeling her face. "You think I'd do anything to hurt Clover? I might not like you, Declan, but I won't jeopardize my sister. She's all I have."

"I know. And I won't hurt her either. In fact, I'm here to talk to both of you," I replied.

Avery hesitated, the muscles in her jaw twitching with the conflict that brewed on her face. After a beat, she moved aside, gesturing with a tilt of her head for me to enter.

Inside, I found Clover at the kitchen table. Her eyes were trained on a pile of crumpled papers—bills, invoices, numbers that told a story of struggle and hardship. Her fingers anxiously bit at the nails of her free hand, each harsh nibble hissing in the room's silence.

She looked up as I walked in, her eyes wide and

startled, like a deer caught in a headlight. I took in the dark circles under her eyes, the lines of worry etched into her face, and a surge of anger rose in me. This was no way for her to live.

"Evening, Clover," I said, trying to keep my tone neutral.

She seemed to snap out of her reverie, blinking at me before giving a weak nod.

"We need to talk," I began, my fixed stare switching between the sisters. My fingers brushed over the ring in my pocket. This wasn't the time for that. Not yet. "There's a rodeo event coming up. Avery, you're expected to be there."

Avery raised her eyebrows but didn't argue. Clover looked back down at the pile of bills, a slight frown creasing her forehead. I knew that look—she was calculating, figuring, worrying. I needed to get her out of that, and fast.

This was the first step. Everything that needed to happen, would. I'd ensure it. For her.

Clover's eyes met mine, a hint of fear fluttering in their depths. "I . . . I don't know, Declan. The rodeo . . . it just feels too soon. I'm worried about Avery going out there."

I gave her a steady look, the importance of my words settling into the room like a heavy fog. "Clover, we need to make sure everything seems normal. The

Devils can't know you're aware of what happened . . . not yet."

Avery, who had been silent, piped up then, her voice barely above a whisper. "I've wanted this for a long time, Clover. To get on the back of a bull . . . It's been my dream. If I cancel now, it will look suspicious."

I nodded, my gaze still locked on Clover. It was crucial that she understood this. We were in uncertain territory now, walking a thin line. The slightest misstep could have dire consequences. For all of us.

Clover seemed resigned, but she nodded in agreement nonetheless. As Avery excused herself, presumably to get ready for the upcoming rodeo, I found myself alone with Clover.

"You're not as feisty as usual," I said, approaching her cautiously. I had expected her to order me out of her house, like she had before. Instead, she just scowled, and there was something off about her response.

"There's no point kicking you out. You'll just appear anyway," she shot back, her words carrying an edge.

I smirked at her retort, but something was nagging at me, a feeling that she was hiding something. I decided to push a bit further. "How are you doing, Clover?"

"I'm . . . just focused on some work that's piled up," she replied, her eyes skirting away from mine.

I wasn't convinced. I reached out, taking her hand in mine and giving it a reassuring squeeze. I leaned forward, my eyes locking onto hers. "How are you really doing, Clover?" I asked, my voice soft but firm. This time, I was looking for the truth.

Her glare hardened and then her palm came crashing down onto the table, a loud thud that sliced through the tense silence. "I'm not okay, Declan," she burst out, her voice a trembling mixture of anger and fear. "Something fucking terrible happened to me. I knocked on your door because I was looking for safety. But instead, I found a killer."

Her words cut me, but I kept my face impassive, letting her vent out her pent-up frustrations.

"Now, I'm an accomplice to murder. I'm dancing this fine line with the Devils," she continued, her voice wavering. "My sister, Laura . . . they're all involved—"

"Does Laura know?" I interrupted, my heart hammering in my chest. Shit. I didn't think she'd involve anyone else. I'd made a mess of things, and Clover was stuck in the middle of it all.

Clover looked horrified, as though she didn't mean to reveal Laura's involvement. "Laura has a young kid. I don't want her involved," she whispered, her voice barely audible. "I shouldn't have said anything, but . . . but I have shit to process, too. When you tied me up and . . . and we did what we did . . . I was still coming to terms with what happened to me."

Her words hung heavily in the air, echoing the trauma she'd been through, the tumult she was still grappling with.

"Do you want me to apologize for what we did?" I asked, my voice steady.

She swallowed deeply, a tremor passing through her. Slowly, she shook her head. No, she didn't want an apology. The tension between us shifted, became something darker, richer. I leaned in, my stare locked with hers, an unspoken challenge hanging between us.

"Did you like it, Clover?" I probed, watching her reaction closely.

She looked away, uncertainty shadowing her face. "I . . . I don't know how to answer that."

I could see the conflict in her expression, the struggle between desire and guilt. "You don't feel like you should enjoy being with me, do you?" I murmured, stating the truth we both knew.

Her silence was the only answer I needed.

"It's okay to process your trauma, Clover," I told her, my voice a soothing rumble. "I won't force you to do anything you're not ready for."

I was a killer, not a comforter. I wasn't supposed to

be gentle; I wasn't supposed to care. But for her, I'd be both.

"I asked you if it's what you wanted. I'm always going to ask."

She remained silent, her chest rising and falling with heavy breaths. The tension was palpable, a live wire sizzling between us.

"I'll balance your need on the edge of a blade," I promised, my voice raspy. "Give you control at the precipice. I'll push you right to the edge . . . and then I'll ask your permission before we both tumble over."

Her eyes widened at my words, but she didn't pull away, didn't retreat. There was fear in her expression, but also curiosity . . . and something more. Something that set my blood on fire.

Pulling the ring out of my pocket, I set it down gently on the table. Its diamond caught the dim light, scattering it across the worn wood. She stared at it.

"We're engaged," I stated simply, my voice a deep rumble.

Her head snapped up. "What?"

"I meant what I said, Clover. You're mine." The words came out as a growl, my eyes never leaving hers. "And this"—I pointed at the ring—"this is the proof."

A horde of emotions raced across her face: surprise, confusion, disbelief, and an inkling of something I couldn't quite read. Was it fear? Or was it something closer to acceptance? Only time would tell.

Clover's words stung. "If I don't have a choice, then it isn't real," she said.

I clenched my jaw, my mind unwillingly pulled back to that night, the sight of Clover, broken and haunted. James. That bastard. My knuckles whitened as my hands tightened into fists. I forced myself to take a deep breath, to rein in the fury threatening to explode.

"I want it to be real, Clover," I said, the words gruff but sincere. "I want you to have a choice. And . . . I want you to choose me."

Her laugh filled the room, sounding hollow and bitter. "You're insane. Who proposes to someone they barely know?"

I shrugged, unfazed by her comment. "Who said I'm pretending to be sane?"

She tilted her head, studying me. "Why are you so obsessive? How did you . . . how did you become a murderer?"

I sighed, sinking into the chair opposite her. I'd never spoken about this before, not to anyone. But I wanted her to understand, to see the twisted path that had led me here. "I grew up on a ranch a few towns over," I started. "We were a happy family. Then it was just me and my mom, after dad passed away."

I could see her body stiffen, her stare unblinking. "She started dating, trying to find someone to fill the hole my dad left. I guess you can't really call it dating. She slept around with anyone willing to give her attention. One night, she went on a date with a new guy. I didn't get his name. She didn't come home. They found her body in the river by our house."

I looked down, focusing on the ring I'd placed on the table between us. "I got thrown into foster care after that."

Her voice was a whisper when she asked, "Is that why you're so protective?"

I nodded. "I couldn't save my mom. But I did what I could to protect the girls in the foster home."

I reached over, my hand shaking slightly as I gently touched her cheek. "I couldn't kill the man who killed her. But I did what I could to protect others from people like him. Gangbangers, criminals. It's not pretty, Clover, but it's the truth."

"Yeah, it's not pretty," she agreed, her voice barely above a whisper. She looked down at the ring, her brow furrowed in thought. Then, she asked the question I'd been expecting, "Why me, Declan? Why are you so obsessive about . . . this?"

My chuckle was dry, devoid of humor. "Clover, you have this way of getting under my skin. From that first rodeo to the car accident, to the night of the trail ride . . . You're stubborn, fearless. You don't back down."

"But I don't need saving," she insisted, her eyes flashing defiantly.

"I disagree. You've been dealt a tough hand, darlin'. You've been fighting all your life, haven't you? Trying to keep Avery safe, to keep this house together . . . I can see it in your eyes. You're tired. You stepped up when your mom walked out. Took care of everything when your dad died. Who takes care of you?"

Clover stayed silent, her scrutiny flicking between my eyes and the ring. There was a vulnerability in her expression that made my chest tighten. "I take care of myself."

"I'm not trying to swoop in and play the hero, Clover," I admitted, my voice gentle. "But I am offering to stand by your side. To help carry the weight that's been burdening you."

She looked up at me, her eyes brimming with unshed tears. "Why would you do that?"

"Because I want to, Clover," I replied, the truth of the words resonating in the air between us. "Because I've seen you fight and I admire your spirit. And because when I save you, I feel like maybe . . . just maybe . . . I'm saving a part of myself too."

Clover let out a frustrated sigh, "You're infuriating, you know that? Why can't you just be . . . normal?"

I laughed, the sound dark and husky. "Darlin', *normal* isn't a term I've ever been familiar with. And if I was 'normal,' I might not have been able to save you."

Clover's defiant eyes softened slightly, a flicker of confusion and perhaps even understanding passing over her face. She pressed her lips together, her fingers idly tracing the edges of the ring.

"Okay, cowboy," she finally replied, an odd note of resignation in her voice. "What now?"

I reached for her hand, tangling our fingers together, "Now, we play along, Clover. For your sake, for Avery's, for Laura's. We act like everything's normal, even if it's far from it."

"And if I can't do it? If I can't pretend?" Clover's voice was barely a whisper, the reality of our situation beginning to set in.

"Then you lean on me, Wildflower. We're in this together now. Whether you like it or not." My gaze never left hers, my promise hanging heavily in the air between us.

CHAPTER 18
Scarlet Embers

CLOVER

The Nightfall Rodeo was a whirlwind. People shouted. Music played. Hooves thumped against dirt. But I wasn't there for any of it. My mind was elsewhere, my heart still thudding with the beat of a trauma that was all too fresh.

I moved through it all, my fingers wrapped around a piece of Declan's jacket. It was like holding onto a lifeline. He was there, a steady presence by my side as we wove through the sea of people.

"Nervous?" he asked, his voice barely rising above the noise.

"Terrified," I admitted. No point in lying. His grip tightened, a simple gesture that spoke volumes.

Everywhere I looked, there were reminders. Men.

Noise. Unwanted attention. It was a sensory overload that had my skin prickling with unease. I tried to focus on Avery, to channel her excitement, her nerves. This was a big day for her. She was finally accepted as a regular for bull riding. But even her joy felt distant, muted.

Declan stayed by my side, a solid force amidst the chaos. There was an undeniable comfort in his presence. It didn't wipe away the fear, but it made it bearable. Which was really fucking confusing. I should have been scared of him, but at least he was the Devil I knew.

Avery squeezed my arm, her eyes sparkling with nervous anticipation. "I'm off to get ready for my ride," she declared, her voice steady despite the adrenaline that was surely hitting her hard.

She disappeared into the throng of competitors, leaving Declan and me alone. "You should go with her," I suggested while watching Avery's retreating figure.

He shook his head. "She's strong, Clover. She needs to do this on her own."

My heart thrummed with nervous energy, and I suddenly felt an overwhelming concern. Not just for Avery, but for Declan too. "Aren't you riding tonight?" I asked, forcing myself to look back at him.

"No, not tonight," he answered, meeting my stare with an unwavering ferocity.

I was momentarily surprised by the relief that washed over me. It was odd, this new protective instinct I was feeling for Declan. He was the strong one. Yet, I realized, beneath it all, I worried about him too.

As the bustling crowd of the rodeo continued around us, I stood there, mulling over what Declan had shared earlier. The revelation about his past was still fresh, a sobering reminder of the man standing beside me.

His words about his mother echoed in my mind, the memory of her brutal end something that clearly haunted him. It explained his urge to protect, to keep those around him safe even at a terrible cost.

Despite the cruelty he was capable of, there was a nobility in his actions too. He was molded by pain and loss, but used that to shield others from experiencing the same. This was the complexity of Declan—a man who killed yet sought to preserve life.

I looked up at him, his silhouette stark against the bright lights of the rodeo. He was trouble, yes, but he was also a protector. In some strange, twisted way, he had become *my* protector, and I couldn't help but feel a grudging sense of comfort in that.

Declan and I positioned ourselves at the edge of the arena, eyes firmly set on Avery as she prepared for her ride. "Are the Devils here tonight?" I asked, my voice barely rising above a whisper.

He scanned the crowd, looking as intense as a hawk. "Yeah," he confirmed quietly, "but they probably won't bother us."

"Is it safe for us to be together?" I questioned, the words tasting like fear in my mouth. At this, Declan coughed, seeming slightly uneasy.

"It's not unusual for me to be seen with a pretty woman," he said, trying to lighten the mood.

His comment made me squirm uncomfortable, and I couldn't help but picture Tara's flirty smile in my mind. I couldn't stop thinking about the wild romantic life he led before supposedly becoming *obsessed* with me. He had a long line of one-night-stands and flings. How could I be sure this means anything to him? And here I was, inextricably tied to him, fighting off feelings of jealousy that seemed to come out of nowhere.

Declan must have caught the change in my expression, because his lips tugged up into a wicked grin. His dark eyes sparkled with mischief as he leaned in closer.

"Are you jealous, Clover?" he asked, a teasing lilt in his voice. The corners of his mouth were twitching, fighting to contain the laughter that was bubbling up within him.

"No," I denied a little too quickly, a bit more defensively than I'd intended. I shook my head for emphasis, as if the motion would solidify my words. But the uncertain tremor in my voice betrayed my denial.

A hearty chuckle escaped from him then, a sound that was as warm as it was infuriating. I crossed my arms defensively, but he only leaned in closer, his grin never leaving his face.

"Now why don't I believe that?" he murmured, his voice dropping an octave. His fingers traced a path up my arm, sending shivers of anticipation through me. The heat in his expression made me feel exposed, seen, and despite my earlier protests, I knew I wasn't fooling him one bit.

His amusement at my expense was annoyingly endearing, and I found myself helplessly caught in the dark allure of his humor. This was a side of Declan I liked from the start, one that was lighthearted and playfully affectionate, and it only added to the confusing mess of emotions I was dealing with.

"I'm not . . ." I started again, trying to reclaim some semblance of control, but he cut me off with a gentle squeeze of my hand.

"Relax, Clover," he reassured, his voice soft, almost

tender. "You've got nothing to be jealous of." Despite my better judgment, I found myself believing him. And, much to my surprise, I felt a slight pang of disappointment in myself at my response to his reassurance.

I shouldn't care.

I should be running the hell away from this man.

The announcer's voice filled the arena, booming over the loudspeakers. "Next up, we have the Devil's very own female rider. She'll bust your balls and ride you hard. Give it up for Avery Matthews!!" I felt my heart hammer in my chest as my sister moved into the spotlight.

My hands gripped the railing, knuckles turning white. I was never good at watching Avery ride, too many memories of our father getting thrown. Knowing that the Devils were lurking in the crowd somewhere, my anxiety was on high alert. Declan noticed the change in my demeanor.

"You okay?" he asked, concern etching his handsome features. I nodded, but the tightness in my throat gave me away.

The gate burst open, and Avery exploded out on the back of a monstrous bull. The crowd roared, a surge of excitement and anticipation. Declan didn't let his gaze waver from me, even with my sister on the bull. He knew I couldn't bear to watch, not with the dangerous dance my sister was in.

"Tell me a story, Clover," he said, his voice a firm command yet gentle, understanding. "Something to distract you."

Nodding, I latched onto the first memory that popped into my head. "I was seven the first time I rode a horse," I started, trying to focus on the memory rather than Avery's ride. "She was an old mare named Daisy. Gentle and patient, perfect for an excited little girl."

As I dove into the memory, I could hear the crowd's reaction to Avery's ride, each cheer and gasp acting as a terrible reminder of what was happening just a few feet away. But Declan's hand was a grounding force, his thumb tracing comforting circles on the back of my hand.

"Daisy was a beautiful chestnut color, with a white blaze down her nose," I continued, my voice shaking slightly. "I remember being terrified, but the moment I was on her back, it felt . . . right. Like I was meant to be there."

Throughout my story, Declan's hand never left mine. His steady presence served as an anchor, helping me get through Avery's ride. I could hear the cheers grow louder, signaling the end of her ride. My heart pounded in my chest as I waited for the dust to settle, my story forgotten, replaced by the fear of what might have happened to my sister.

And then she was there, standing in front of us, all dusted up, panting, and grinning from ear to ear. Avery had been thrown, that was clear from the state of her, but she was standing. She was okay.

"Didn't stick the landing, but hell, was that a ride or what?" she exclaimed, her chest heaving with exertion. She doubled over, trying to catch her breath, but the excitement in her eyes was unmistakable.

Despite the whirl of emotions streaming through me—relief, fear, anger—a laugh bubbled up from within me. It was shaky, teetering on the edge of hysteria, but it was a laugh all the same.

"You scared the life out of me, you reckless cowgirl," I managed to choke out between bouts of laughter.

My sister just winked at me, her face glowing with pride and adrenaline. "But you should've seen me, Clo. I was practically flying."

The terror I'd felt moments ago started to ebb away, replaced with relief and a begrudging admiration for my sister's fearlessness. I glanced at Declan, ready to share a relieved laugh, but found him staring at me instead.

His eyes were soft, thoughtful, his thumb still tracing gentle circles on my hand. He looked like he wanted to say something, but instead, he gave my hand a reassuring squeeze and turned to Avery.

"Sure gave us a show there, Avery," he said, his voice steady and strong. "You did good."

His simple words, spoken with such sincerity, were like a balm to the chaos of the evening. For a moment, it felt like we were just regular folks at a rodeo, not a group of people hovering over the edge of disaster. It was a comforting illusion, one I allowed myself to get lost in, if only for a little while.

Then Hank and his crew materialized out of the crowd. He was a mobster in a cowboy hat. The smell of smoke and whiskey lingered around him like a cloud. He walked over to Avery, clapping her on the shoulder.

"Good job, girl," he growled, his voice rough like gravel. He shoved a wad of cash into her hand. Then he turned to me, his gaze lingering curiously. "I remember you. The worried sister. How'd you end up here with Declan?"

My blood turned to ice. I swallowed hard, looking over at Declan, searching for some kind of sign. But he was cool as a cucumber, his confidence masking any hint of concern.

He chuckled, reaching around to slap my butt. "She's a fun piece of ass for the night," he said with a shrug.

I squeaked in surprise, forcing out a nervous giggle. Inside, I was screaming, my mind racing. How had things spiraled so out of control? The danger we were in felt obvious, and all I could do was giggle and play along, hoping that we would somehow make it through this night.

Hank lingered, his expression taking on a perverse gleam. "Is that so?" he drawled, looking me up and down. "Well, missy, you're more than welcome to come to our rodeo anytime you like."

His smile was all teeth as he looked from me to Avery. "It's nice having two beautiful women here," he continued, his stare settling on Avery. "I want to see you at every event, darling. You've got talent. It would be a shame to waste it."

The words were sugarcoated, but the threat underneath was clear as day. He was telling Avery she didn't have a choice. And with his look still fixed on her, I knew he was serious. I felt Declan tense beside me.

With a gruff, raspy chuckle, Hank turned away, leaving us alone. The moment he was gone, a surge of panic washed over me, constricting my chest. I forced a shaky smile at Declan, hiding the fear in my eyes. Without a word, he steered me away from the arena, toward the parking lot.

My mind was already racing, formulating a plan. As much as I cared for Declan, as much as he stirred something inside me, I knew I couldn't stay here. I glanced over at him, the man who had saved me and placed me in harm's way all at once. He wouldn't understand. No matter what, I knew what I had to do.

We had to leave this town for good.

CHAPTER 19
Stilettos and Steel Spurs

DECLAN

*W*alking into Hank's lair was always a unique experience. The smell of cigars and the undercurrent of fear that clung to the men who served him was a cocktail that drove the point home—this was Hank's world and we were just living in it.

I was living in it until I could flip the switch and burn it all down.

Fucking bastard.

"Declan!" Hank boomed as I entered, his husky laughter scratching my nerves as he toasted with one of his goons. The stench of whiskey was heavy in the air, adding another layer to the perfume of power and debauchery. His shark eyes pinned me with a grin, full of unspoken threats and challenges.

"Hank," I greeted, my tone casual, a smirk teasing at the corners of my mouth. His eyes narrowed ever so slightly at my nonchalance, but the grin didn't fade. Oh, he loved this game of ours. The power play, the show of dominance. It was what he lived for.

"You look like a man with a plan," he stated, a spark of amusement in his eyes as he took another swig from his glass.

"I've been thinking," I started, my voice calm, controlled. "The horse trail gig . . . it's too public. Too predictable. A cabin, on the other hand . . ." I trailed off, letting the implication hang in the air.

Hank's eyes sparked with interest. "A cabin, you say?"

"They rented one for the wife's birthday weekend. It's remote, secluded. A much better spot for a . . . quiet conversation." I offered a hint of a devilish smirk tugging at the corner of my lips.

Hank chuckled, a sound that scraped at my nerves. "And I suppose the trail guide wouldn't need to be there, would she?"

I shrugged. "Wouldn't make much sense, would it?"

Hank leaned back in his chair, studying me with those ice-cold eyes of his. Then, out of the blue, he chuckled. "Wasn't the trail guide the hot piece of ass you had at the rodeo two nights ago?"

A jolt shot through me, my cool facade momentarily faltering. He'd been watching me, watching us. My grip on my emotions tightened, refusing to give him the satisfaction of seeing my surprise.

"What can I say, Hank? I've got good taste."

His laughter filled the room, a chilling sound that bounced off the walls. "Oh, I bet. Seems like you've got more than just a *taste* for her."

My expression hardened, frost creeping into my voice. "What's that supposed to mean?"

Hank shrugged, feigning innocence. "Nothing at all, Declan. It's just . . . I looked into those six men you killed. Apparently, they were on a trail ride of their own. A bachelor party."

I swallowed. "What a coincidence," I lied.

"I see. And the trail guide, would she know about these six men you killed?"

Fuck. I should have known Hank would figure it out. "Nope," I lied. "Caught them at the end of their ride while they were heading into town for drinks."

"I had to blow up one of my bars to make it look convincing, Declan. I lost a lot of money because of you. I covered it up because you're going to kill that judge for me, but make no mistake, you work for *me*. If I ask for *one* body, I mean *one*. I won't punish you for being ambitious, but it wasn't easy covering it up. We're lucky they were all known for being stupid drunks that like to party."

I gritted my teeth.

"That being said, Declan," Hank continued, his eyes never leaving mine, "we're sticking to the plan. The judge dies on the trail."

I raised an eyebrow, my heart pounding in my chest. "I thought the cabin was a good idea."

"Your ideas aren't what I pay you for," Hank spat, leaning forward, resting his elbows on his mahogany desk, his icy eyes boring into mine. "You execute my orders, and right now, my orders are for the judge to take his last breath under the open sky."

I fought back the urge to retaliate, to tell him where he could shove his orders. But there was something bigger at stake. Something that Hank held over me, something that I needed from him.

"And remember," Hank added, his voice a low growl, "no witnesses. I don't need any more loose ends."

His words were a clear threat. Not just to me, but to Clover too. I nodded, hiding the fury in my eyes behind a mask of compliance.

"I've got it, Hank. The judge dies on the trail. No witnesses."

"Good." Hank smirked, leaning back in his chair, satisfied. "Remember, Declan, you work for me. You follow my rules, my plans. If you want that name, you'll do as I say."

The name. The one piece of information that kept me tethered to this monstrous man. The name of the bastard who had killed my mother. The main reason I was still in this hellhole, still playing Hank's twisted games.

"I remember, Hank," I replied, my voice laced with grit. "I've always been good at following orders."

Hank's smirk widened, his eyes glinting with cruel satisfaction. "That's what I like to hear, Declan. Now get out of my sight."

I nodded curtly, turning on my heel and heading for the door, Hank's laughter was a chilling reminder of the power he held. But power shifts, and I knew, sooner or later, the tables would turn in my favor. After all, every dog has his day.

～

The moon was high in the sky when I arrived at Clover's small ranch house, the quiet of the night making the task ahead even more daunting. Avery, Clover's sister, was out with friends, her absence a small mercy. I didn't want to have to lie to her too.

My hands were steady as I slipped the thin strip of metal into the lock of the front door, an old skill from my foster days. The lock yielded with a faint click, and

I pushed the door open, the creak of the hinges sounding unnaturally loud in the silence.

Clover's bedroom was at the end of the short hallway, the door slightly ajar. I paused at the threshold, my heart pounding in my chest. I was crossing lines when we'd made so much progress at the rodeo. But right now, I didn't give a damn.

As quietly as possible, I stripped down to my boxers and slid into bed next to her. Clover woke with a start, her eyes flying open and darting around the dark room until they landed on me.

"Declan?" she asked, her voice groggy with sleep, confusion marring her features. "What . . . what's wrong?"

How could I tell her? How could I say that Hank knew about her, about us? That he might use her as leverage, might hurt her to get to me? How did I tell her that he wanted me to *kill* her? I wouldn't but it was yet another obstacle. The thought was a weight in my chest, a poison seeping into every vein.

"I just . . . needed to be with you," I said instead, my voice barely above a whisper. The bed shifted as she turned to face me, her eyes searching mine in the dim light filtering through the window.

"Declan, you're scaring me," she admitted softly, her hand coming up to rest against my cheek. I closed my eyes, leaning into her touch. It grounded me, provided a small comfort in the havoc that was raging within.

"I don't mean to, Clover," I murmured, my hand finding hers and entwining our fingers together. "I never want to scare you."

A silence fell over us, my confession hanging heavy in the air. It was the truth, yes, but it was only part of it, a fraction of the storm that was coming. And as much as I wanted to protect her from it, I couldn't help but feel that I was dragging her right into my mess.

I drew in a deep breath, steeled my nerves. "Hank knows," I admitted, my voice a low rasp in the silence. "He knows everything."

The shock on her face cut me deep. I could see her mind working in overdrive, connecting the dots, grappling with the implications. "He . . . what? What does that mean, Declan?"

"It means he wants me to do something, Clover," I continued, my words slow, deliberate. "And it's something that puts you at risk."

Her hand squeezed mine, her breath hitching in her throat. "What is it, Declan?" she asked, her voice trembling. "What does he want you to do?"

"That doesn't matter," I said, shaking my head. "What matters is that I'm going to make sure you're safe. No matter what."

"Why . . . why do you work for him, Declan?" Clover asked, the question hanging in the air like an unspoken accusation.

The truth was ugly. It was a raw, open wound, one that I'd carried around for years. I was a mercenary, drifting from gang to gang, my only loyalty to the highest bidder. But Hank, he offered more than just money.

"I'm usually a contract hire, floating from one job to the next," I admitted. "But Hank . . . Hank has something else. Information about the man who killed my mother."

Clover's eyes widened. "Your mother?" she echoed, her voice barely a whisper.

I nodded, my throat tight. "Yeah. Apparently, the man who did it was a rodeo rider who used to work for Hank. He's the only one who might know who he is."

The revelation hung between us, a dark and bitter truth. But it was out now, exposed and undeniable. We were caught in Hank's dangerous game, our fate intertwined with the brutal whims of a mobster cowboy.

"But that doesn't mean I'll let him hurt you," I declared, my stare holding hers, my words a promise, a vow. "I won't let anything happen to you, Clover. Not now, not ever."

The fear in her eyes didn't dissipate, but there was a new look there, one of understanding, of acceptance.

She knew the threats we faced; she understood the stakes. But she was still here, still with me. As if to affirm that, she reached up, her fingers trailing a path up my arm, over my shoulder, her touch lighting up my skin.

And then she was leaning in, her eyes holding mine captive as she bridged the gap between us. Her lips met mine in a soft, desperate kiss, an intimate collision that sent shockwaves through my entire body.

It was a carefully calibrated dance, a skillful negotiation of teeth and lips, tongues seeking and finding in a rhythm that was all our own. I tasted the sweetness of her breath, felt the gentle press of her tongue against mine, a teasing invitation that I was all too willing to accept.

Her hands found their way to the back of my neck, pulling me closer, deepening the kiss, while mine settled on her waist, pulling her flush against me. I could feel the heat of her body searing through the thin fabric of her clothes, could sense the rapid beat of her heart matching pace with mine.

We broke apart after a long moment, both of us panting and starry-eyed. My eyes fell on her, taking in the flushed cheeks, the slightly swollen lips, the glint of satisfaction in her eyes. She was beautiful, a vision of strength and vulnerability that brought me to my knees.

A moment of confusion washed over me. "Clover," I asked, my brow furrowing, "what was that for?" I was caught off guard. She'd always been so reserved, so careful with her feelings. But this . . . this was different.

Her eyes, glazed over with a sheen of unshed tears, met mine. There was something in her expression, a turmoil that reflected the chaotic whirlpool of emotions I was feeling.

"I just . . . I just wanted to kiss you," she said simply, her voice trembling. But the simplicity of her words didn't mask the depth of the sentiment behind them.

And then, before I could react, she was pulling me in again. This time, the kiss was different. It was slower, more deliberate, filled with a sad kind of urgency that resonated with the fear lurking at the back of my mind.

Her fingers tangled in my hair as she kissed me with an enthusiasm that took my breath away. There was a hint of desperation in the way her lips moved against mine, a silent plea that sent a pang of guilt through my chest. This kiss tasted of longing and farewell, of unspoken fears and unfulfilled desires.

It was a goodbye of sorts, a premonition of pain that we both wanted to ignore in the moment. And so, for a few minutes more, we let ourselves be swept away by the power of the kiss. We explored each other's mouths with greedy fingers and tongues, tasting and savoring all there was between us.

And then her hands were moving lower, trailing down my chest and abdomen until they reached their destination. She dipped below the waistband of my boxers and pulled out my cock. The feel of her soft hand wrapped around me felt so good I couldn't help but moan softly in pleasure as she stroked me slow and steady. My heart was racing as she pumped her hand up and down my shaft, making it swell.

A crackle of electricity filled the air, expanding with each passing second. My desperate hands clawed at her clothing as I dragged her body close to me. Her movements were liquid gold, melting my heart and sending flutters of anticipation coursing through my veins. My cock throbbed hungrily as she lowered herself onto it inch by agonizing inch.

A gasp escaped her lips as her tight warmth engulfed me. I grasped her hips, steadying them as she rode out the carnal pleasure that overwhelmed us both. I felt like I was being consumed by a wild inferno, awareness of time and place evaporating in the overwhelmingness of our passion. Her hips rolled against mine, a steady rhythm coaxing me ever closer to ecstasy.

Our bodies moved together in such perfect harmony it felt almost spiritual, until we were both swept away in a tidal wave of rapture so thrilling it threatened to shatter us into a million pieces.

We collapsed into each other, our ragged breathing slowly easing to a steady rhythm. As I ran my hands lazily over her body, I whispered something in her ear.

"No matter what happens, I want you to know I'll always be here for you, Clover," I said. "I'll always protect you."

Suddenly, I noticed her hand rise, swiping at her eye in a quick, almost imperceptible motion. A tear.

"Clover?" I asked, the concern evident in my voice.

But she just rolled over, her back to me, her shoulders hunched in a defensive posture. My hand reached out, hovering just above her, unsure if I should offer comfort or respect her need for space.

"Clover," I said again, but this time she didn't respond.

The silence that ensued was deafening. It filled the room, pushing against the walls, seeming to close in around me. Suddenly, the room felt smaller, colder. I could still feel her, her warmth seeping into my skin, but the connection felt distant, like it was slipping through my fingers.

Something was wrong. The realization hit me hard, churning my stomach. I could tell from her silence, from her unusual response, that something was deeply, deeply wrong. But what? And more importantly, what could I do to fix it?

As these thoughts whirled through my mind, I stared at the back of her head, the dim light casting a soft glow on her hair. I wanted to reach out, to comfort her, to reassure her. But I was frozen, trapped in my own uncertainty and worry.

"Clover . . . ," I whispered one last time, but the silence remained. And with it, a sinking feeling of dread.

CHAPTER 20
Glamour, Guns, and Guilty Pleasures

CLOVER

*W*hen I woke up, the house was quiet, a stark contrast to the turmoil that filled my mind. I sat up, my heart hammering in my chest. The sheets were cool next to me, the emptiness mimicking the hollow feeling in my stomach.

I looked around the room, my heart aching as I took in the familiar sights. The morning light streamed in through the windows, casting a warm glow over everything. It was comforting, normal, everything my life was not. The walls felt like they were closing in on me, the space too confined to contain the whirlwind of emotions threatening to overwhelm me.

Avery. I needed to call Avery.

Scrambling out of bed, I grabbed my phone, my

hands shaking as I dialed Avery's number. She had spent the night at a friend's house, a last-minute sleepover that had been a welcome distraction from everything that was going on. But now, it felt like a blessing, a small reprieve from the storm that was about to hit.

"Avery," I whispered into the phone when she picked up, my voice hoarse from the knot in my throat. "You need to go to Laura's house. I'll meet you there."

"What?" she sputtered, clearly confused. "Clover, what's going on?"

"I can't explain right now," I rushed, my words tumbling over each other in my haste. "Just promise me you'll go. We have to leave today."

"But—"

"Just do it, Avery," I cut her off, my voice pleading. "Please."

There was a pause, then a quiet sigh. "Okay," she said finally. "I'll go. But Clover . . . what's going on?"

"Hank knows," I admitted, the words leaving a bitter taste in my mouth. "He knows everything."

The line went quiet. And then, "Okay, Clover. I'll go."

I hung up, my heart pounding in my ears. This was it. The beginning of the end.

I quickly typed a text to Mr. O'Riley, our friendly neighbor and a horse lover, telling him he could have our horses for free. "Please take good care of them," I added before hitting send.

Heart pounding, I dashed to my closet. I yanked out the emergency backpack Avery and I had packed when we first realized we might need to run. It was a mishmash of essentials—clothes, money, toiletries. We'd briefly planned for this day, but now that it was here, it felt surreal, like I was living in a bad dream.

Time was slipping through my fingers like sand. I needed to move, and fast. But I didn't have a car. I observed my old bicycle leaning against the side of the house. It wasn't ideal, but it would have to do.

I grabbed a few more things, stuffing them into the backpack. A photo of dad. Avery's favorite book. Things that couldn't be replaced.

I took a deep breath, trying to steady my racing heart. I glanced one last time at the home that had been my safe haven for so long, the walls that had heard my laughter and seen my tears, the house that was about to become just a memory.

But there was no time for sentiment. I had to get to Laura's. Once we were together, we could drive away in her old Toyota, heading for New Mexico. That was the plan, anyway.

Shouldering the backpack, I headed for the door. The house felt unnaturally quiet, like it was holding its breath. I paused, took a last, lingering look around, then stepped out into the bright morning light.

Before I could force myself onto the bike, my eyes were drawn to the stables. An overwhelming urge to say goodbye to the horses hit me hard. I dropped the backpack and ran toward the stables, my feet pounding on the ground.

"Ginny," I called out as I approached the first stall. The beautiful chestnut mare whinnied, recognizing my voice. Tears blurred my vision as I reached out to stroke her velvety snout. She nudged my hand, her warm breath puffing against my skin, causing a fresh wave of tears to spill over.

"I'm so sorry, girl," I sobbed, burying my face into her mane. "I didn't want it to be like this. I didn't want to leave you."

Ginny snorted softly, as if understanding my turmoil. I stayed there for a few more minutes, my tears soaking her mane, the rhythm of her breathing providing a small amount of comfort.

Eventually, I forced myself to move. There were the others to say goodbye to—Dusty, Comet, Storm, Filo, and Rose. I went from stall to stall, murmuring soft goodbyes and promising that Mr. O'Riley would take good care of them.

I managed to gather myself enough to feed them one last time, my hands shaking as I poured the feed into their troughs. They whinnied and nuzzled me, oblivious to the heartbreak that filled me.

When I'd finally said my goodbyes, I took one last look at the stables. "I love you all," I whispered, a fresh set of tears rolling down my cheeks. Then, with a heavy heart, I turned away and walked back toward the house.

The backpack felt heavier when I picked it up again, the reality of the situation pressing down on me. But I couldn't afford to break down now. I needed to get to Laura's. For Avery. For myself.

Each pump of my legs on the bike pedals was met with a harsh gust of West Texas wind, its heat tugging at my hair and whipping it around my face in a frenzied dance. Sweat trickled down my temple, my heart pounding in my chest like a wild drum.

There was a momentary calm—a deceiving respite in the incessant howling of the wind. And then I heard it, the distant growl of a motorcycle engine. An all-too-familiar sound that sent icy tendrils of fear spiraling through my veins.

Declan.

My grip tightened on the handlebars, my knuckles turning white. I had to think fast.

The roar of the engine was getting closer, blasting ominously through the barren landscape. The dusty road stretched out before me, an endless path leading me away from the life I'd known. The only cover was the sparse underbrush lining the sides of the road.

With a sudden burst of adrenaline, I swerved off the road, jumping off the bike and throwing myself into the prickly underbrush. I crouched low, the bike concealed behind the brambles.

The distant roar of the motorcycle grew louder, closer, its echoes a thunderous symphony of fear in the quiet morning. The sound filled the arid hills, a tangible presence that shook me to my core.

I held my breath, my heart hammering in my chest, the roar of the motorcycle now deafening. I could almost feel the heat of it, the vibrations of the engine shaking the ground beneath me.

And then, he was there. The motorcycle thundered past my hiding spot, the wind of its passage whipping through the brush. I squeezed my eyes shut, fear coiling in my stomach like a venomous snake.

I was trapped, prey in the desert, a helpless lamb caught in the trap of a predator. My heartbeat was a drum against my ribcage, its rhythm punctuating the silence of the deserted West Texas road. Fear coursed through me like a rogue river, threatening to tear me apart.

In the distance, the low growl of Declan's motorcycle reverberated through the open expanse. Every nerve in my body screamed at me to disappear, to meld into the landscape that surrounded me.

The motorcycle pulled up beside my discarded bike, the plume of dust following its trail like a ghost of my dashed hopes. Declan dismounted, his boots crunching against the gravel of the deserted road, his ice-blue eyes zeroing in on my hiding spot.

"Clover," he called, his voice a whip cutting through the stillness of the desert. He approached with an air of a predator, steps measured and determined.

Panic welled up within me. Without a second thought, I scrambled out from my hiding spot, my heart pounding like a wild horse in my chest. The sparse desert vegetation offered little cover, my movements betrayed by the swirling dust.

Before I could make my escape, Declan was on me. His arms coiled around me like a vise, halting my progress. His body was a wall of unyielding muscle against my back. I stilled, my body quaking with fear, adrenaline, and a desperate desire to escape.

"Don't," he hissed, his hot breath stirring the loose strands of my hair. His voice was low, almost a whisper, yet it boomed like a thunderclap in my ears.

His grip tightened, trapping me in his formidable embrace. His words were more than just a threat. They were a promise, a vow.

"You're never leaving me, Clover," he murmured, the harsh certainty in his tone ricocheting through the tense silence. The land bore silent witness to his words, his oath. "Not ever."

~

The Texas sun was unrelenting, hammering the dry earth without mercy. The farmhouse, old and sturdy, stood out against the barren landscape. I was held captive on its porch steps, forced to reckon with my betrayal.

The man I'd said goodbye to with my body.

The man I'd tried to flee.

Now, Declan was at my side, his proximity overwhelming, a human furnace in an already scorching day. He'd started a fire in the yard, a jarring sight amidst the baking dirt and heat. Flames jumped and snapped, a violent burst of life in the drought-weathered terrain.

Declan broke the stifling silence, his voice grating against the midday lull. "You know, Clover," he began, his tone deceptively casual. "People always leave me."

His words hung in the heat, like dust particles caught in a shaft of sunlight. He prodded the fire with a piece of wood, sending a shower of sparks toward the ruthless blue sky.

"Been abandoned, discarded, thrown away like a piece of trash," he continued, his gaze fixated on the unnatural dance of the flames. "My father left me. My mother. My foster parents passed me around like trading cards."

His profile was enhanced by the vivid backdrop of the afternoon, his normally calm demeanor twisted into a portrait of desperation and obsession. His eyes flickered to me, a spark of mania igniting within them.

"But not you, Clover," he asserted, his voice hard and determined. "You're not leaving me. You can't."

His words bore into me, their weight heavier than the suffocating Texas heat. They wound around us, binding tighter than any physical restraint. I was entrapped, not just by his physical presence, but by the sheer energy of his emotions. His possessiveness. His manic determination.

"I won't let you," he murmured, his declaration barely audible over the crackling fire. His stare held mine, a promise and a threat entwined in the deep blue of his eyes.

I sat there, stunned into silence, the scorching heat of the fire battling against the chill that had taken root within me. The bright Texas day had taken a dark turn, and I found myself trapped under Declan's fierce declaration and the relentless weight of the midday sun.

"Declan, this is too much. Maybe we should talk about this—"

He cut me off. "You want to know how serious I am about this? Come here. Let me show you."

Declan had started a fire, a wild, fervent thing that crackled and popped in the midday heat. He'd taken hold of my wrist, his touch both gentle and firm, guiding me closer to the blaze. I was caught in the spectacle of the fire and the magnetic pull of the man beside me.

His grip slackened, and he moved toward his motorcycle, rummaging in the saddle bag with an intent I couldn't fathom. A coil of unease began to unspool within me, curiosity and apprehension vying for dominance. Was this another power play, another means to bind me tighter to him?

Yet despite my fears, an unfamiliar anticipation stirred within me. A vulnerable curiosity, a morbid fascination with the man who oscillated between tender lover and ruthless captor. As I watched the fire, its hypnotic dance mirrored the chaotic whirling of my thoughts.

Returning to the fire, Declan held something behind his back, his demeanor suggesting a hint of playfulness that was as mesmerizing as it was unsettling. "What do you have?" I asked, my voice barely above a whisper.

His reply came in a growl, as raw as the wind whipping across the Texan plains. "Strip, Wildflower."

Confusion washed over me, and I instinctively stepped back, taken aback by his command. He set something down on the ground. I stuttered, the word a mere puff of air escaping my lips, "Wh-what?"

"Strip, baby. Let me see your creamy skin," he insisted, his voice layered with a possessiveness that sent a tingle running down my spine, a chilling counterpoint to the oppressive heat of the day.

I paused, caught in the crosshairs of his intense stare, his command lingering in my mind. His words were a challenge, a threat, and a promise, all at once.

"Why?" My question emerged as a choked whisper, caught in the dry desert air.

His answer was swift and brutal. "Because if you don't, I'll tear your clothes off anyway. You can be in control, or I can. Your choice. Run, and I'll chase you. I'd love nothing more than to chase you down, Wildflower."

My breath hitched, and I could feel my pulse pounding in my veins, a staccato rhythm of fear and exhilaration. The rational part of me screamed to flee, but a wild, reckless desire held me in place, tantalized by the man before me and the thrill of his demand.

Summoning a bravery I barely felt, I inhaled deeply, my hands trembling as I began to shed my clothes. With each piece that fell to the ground, Declan's eyes left mine, tracing the path of my undress, his eyes a searing caress that branded my skin.

"Breathtaking," he whispered, his fingertips lightly tracing the curve of my hip, causing a jolt of electricity to spark along my skin. I held my breath, shivering under the weight of his stare, his reverence making me feel cherished and desired in equal measure.

Declan stepped closer, his presence filling my senses, his shadow merging with mine under the harsh Texas sun. His hands found their way to me, exploring the contours of my body with a deliberate slowness that seemed to both respect and claim every inch of me. His touch was both gentle and firm, a silent declaration of possession that made my breath hitch. "What are you going to do to me?" The words emerged as a ragged whisper.

His response was simple, but it sent a ripple of anticipation spreading through me. "I'm going to make you feel good, Wildflower."

Before I had a chance to process his words, Declan's weight was on me, pushing me to the ground, my wrists held captive on either side of my head. I gasped, a mix of shock and fear quickening my heartbeat. He leaned over me, his voice a low murmur in my ear. "And then, you'll understand why you can't leave."

The crackle of the nearby fire seemed to grow louder as he unfastened his jeans. I squirmed, my attempts to free myself met with a stronger restraint. His eyes held a glint of mischief, an unspoken challenge. His lips found mine, sparking a rush of electricity that buzzed in my chest as our tongues danced an intimate tango. His fingers traced paths of fire over my skin, eliciting responses I didn't know I was capable of.

I teetered on the edge of surrender, craving the sweet oblivion of losing myself in his touch. But I held back, fear knotting my insides. Vulnerability was a terrifying concept, even more so with a man like Declan. I wasn't just any girl willing to share her body with anyone. I craved more than fleeting contact. I craved a connection. I wanted love.

But as Declan continued to sweep me away with his passionate kisses and caresses, I couldn't help but start to let my walls down piece by piece. I felt myself softening under his touch.

He flipped me over and plunged inside of me. I gasped as my body adjusted to the sensation of him filling me up—it felt like nothing I had ever experienced before. His skin was slick with sweat, a sign of how much he wanted me.

The fire crackled beside us as if in harmony to the rhythm we had created together.

He tossed something in the flames but forced me to turn my head and look away while fucking me. The sensation of Declan's body against mine was intoxicating. Every thrust sent waves of pleasure through my veins.

He kissed my neck and grabbed onto my hips, grinding himself deeper inside of me as I felt myself beginning to unravel with each passing moment. I moaned louder and louder until Declan suddenly leaned back.

He paused for a moment, his eyes filled with a tenderness that sent a flutter through my chest. "You're not leaving," he whispered, his lips brushing against mine.

And then he spanked me hard while he continued thrusting inside of me. I screamed out in pleasure as the sensations became almost too much to bear. My body swayed back and forth beneath him as his hands moved up and down my body in an almost tantric rhythm.

As Declan and I grew closer, our bodies entwined and our hearts beating in unison, he slowed his thrusts and began to speak softly in my ear, his words like a seductive caress. "You know, when I grew up on a ranch, just like this one," he murmured, his breath hot against my skin. "One of my jobs was to brand the animals. It was important, you see, because the animals could get lost or hurt otherwise. The brand was like a promise, a symbol of belonging and protection." His voice grew tender, almost nostalgic, as if he were sharing a treasured secret.

Then he started pounding into me harder. Breathing faster. Stroking the deepest parts of me with his cock.

Declan's grip on me tightened as his powerful strokes filled me completely. I felt overwhelmed, consumed by the dynamic of our connection. With every thrust, the heat between us grew, the fire inside me burning brighter and brighter.

The edge of pleasure was a precipice, a cliff's edge that Declan's masterful touch pushed me toward. Breathless, gasping, my body taut as a bowstring, I was on the verge of release.

And then I felt the rush of my orgasm.

And then . . .

Then . . .

Out of nowhere, a searing pain tore through the haze of pleasure. It was like a white-hot blade cutting deep into my shoulder. A hot iron brand, the smell of my own burning flesh punching through the heady mix of sweat and fear. The pain was raw, visceral, a violent intrusion that yanked me back from the edge, my cry of pleasure morphing into a strangled scream of pure agony.

Declan had seized a branding iron from the fire. He brought it down on my bare shoulder in that pinnacle of sensation, the white-hot iron sizzling against my skin. It was like molten lava being poured onto my flesh. Yet, paradoxically, the ensuing pleasure of my climax magnified it, morphing the pain into something almost transcendent.

As he pulled the iron away, Declan whispered into my ear, his voice a gentle murmur against the backdrop of my whimpers. "Good girl." Each word was steeped in reverence. "You're mine."

The sensation was like nothing I had ever experienced before—a dizzying, disorienting mix of pleasure and pain that left me breathless and trembling. I felt as though I were being torn apart and stitched back together, the boundaries between our bodies and souls dissolving in the heat of our passion.

I had never felt more alive.

I had never felt more destroyed.

More owned.

More devastated.

More . . . more . . . more . . .

I recoiled from Declan, a surge of hot, pulsating pain radiating from the seared flesh on my shoulder. My body was wracked with sobs, guttural and primal, as the nauseating scent of my own burning flesh filled my nostrils. Salty tears carved rivulets down my cheeks, blurring my vision as I turned to look at him. A fog of bewilderment and betrayal clouded my eyes.

"Why . . . why would you do this?" I managed to stammer, each word hitching with the rhythm of my sobs. My gaze darted between the fading glow of the branding iron and Declan's hardened expression, struggling to reconcile the man who had promised to protect me with the one who had marked me with such calculated brutality.

He looked back at me, his eyes a mix of passion and something softer, almost tender. "It's important to know who you belong to," he said simply. With that, he tossed the branding iron back into the fire, the flames greedily consuming it.

Another wave of sobs tore through me, each one underscored by the gnawing burn from my shoulder. The pain was a brutal, unending echo of what he'd just done to me. Arms clutching my sides in a futile effort to comfort myself, I was a rough and open wound in the aftermath of his savage act.

The stark reality of his betrayal had not fully sunk in yet; his actions were a labyrinth of confusion and hurt I couldn't navigate. He'd branded me like cattle, an act of possessiveness that was as painful as it was inexplicable. The "why" ricocheted around in my head like a bullet, each impact leaving me more disoriented and scared.

Declan's fingers moved to the buttons of his shirt, tugging them free one by one with an efficiency that was both frightening and entrancing. The material fell away, revealing the canvas of his torso—a landscape of rugged muscle and scarred skin.

I was drawn to the scars, those imperfect patches that interrupted the smooth flow of his flesh. Each one was a cryptic tale written into his skin, of battles won and lost. His muscles were the product of a life lived on the edge, shaped and hardened by demanding physical labor.

The expanse of his chest was commanding, a fortress of muscle veined with dark hair that emphasized the unrestrained strength lying just beneath the surface.

"Sit tight." Declan's command sliced through the tension in the air, delivered in a tone that brooked no argument. He bore my scrutiny without a hint of discomfort, his stance betraying a familiarity with being under a critical stare.

His eyes locked with mine as they traced over the raw scars littering his torso, provoking a deep sigh from him. "Legacy of one of my foster dads," he divulged, honesty seeping into his usually guarded tone. It was a crack in his usual stoic front, offering a fleeting glimpse into a history he often kept shrouded.

Even as the blistering pain of my new brand throbbed in rhythm with my heartbeat, his admission kindled an odd sense of connection. Our pasts had branded us, although in very different ways, molding us into who we stood as today. His words hung in the air, heavy with the weight of shared pain. "And now you're going to mark me too," he breathed, his words a mere whisper, carried away by the Texas wind. "Brand me, Wildflower."

I stiffened, my breath hitching in the cool air. A wave of pure dread rolled through me, dark and overwhelming, as the meaning of his words sank in. He wanted me to mark him like he had done to me. The violent memory of searing pain was still too fresh, the scorching sting of the brand on my skin a constant reminder.

"No," I muttered, instinctively recoiling from him, my voice shaky. "I won't do it."

Declan's demeanor shifted, a strange gentleness replacing his earlier harshness. He closed the gap between us, his strong hands enclosing mine. The warmth of his skin seemed to pulse against mine, his expression almost tender.

"You're gonna take some of the power back," he stated gruffly, a glimmer of vulnerability in his expression. "I've marked you, now it's your turn to mark me, to own me, just like I own you."

"I don't want to own you, Declan," I responded, the words slipping out amidst the whirlwind of emotions. He was so close, his energy so potent, it was hard to think. I needed a doctor to look at the agonizing brand on my skin. The pain was too real, too present.

His lips curved into a wicked grin, his grip on my hands tightening. "Too damn bad, Wildflower," he said, "because you're stuck with me. I'm yours just as much as you're mine."

Declan's hand moved with purpose, seizing the branding iron still alive with a harsh, fiery glow. Its heat was a palpable, radiating energy, a searing reminder of the savage moment in which we were suspended. His hard eyes locked onto mine, a mix of fervor and resolve swirling within their depths.

Wordlessly, he pressed the burning iron onto his bare chest, the hiss of searing flesh piercing the tense silence. A guttural grunt escaped his lips, but no cry of pain, no tears; his ironclad resilience was as mesmerizing as it was chilling. I was drawn in, captivated by the gruesome spectacle, my gaze unwavering as he finished branding his skin.

The scent of charred flesh hung heavy in the air, a stomach-churning stench that had me fighting the urge to gag. Still, Declan remained stoic, enduring the self-inflicted agony with an eerie level of composure.

As he set down the branding iron, he turned to me, a triumphant grin splitting his face. The sweltering mark on his chest matched the one on my shoulder, a gruesome testament to our twisted bond.

"We're connected now, Wildflower," he murmured, his voice softer now, a strange, unsettling kind of affection emanating from him. "For better or worse."

CHAPTER 21
Devilish Desires and Bedazzled Revolvers

DECLAN

*J*sat on the porch, my eyes fixed on the dusty road stretching out from the farm-house. A heat haze shimmered in the distance, but there was no sign of Laura's beat-up Toyota nor Avery's silhouette in the passenger seat. The farm was quiet save for the steady buzz of insects and the occasional bird call. The silence was heavy with anticipation.

I knew they'd come looking for Clover.

And I was ready to set them straight.

Inside, Clover was resting. After the branding, after I'd pressed the hot iron against her flawless skin and marked her as mine, I'd done everything I could to ease her pain. I'd disinfected the raw, angry mark, smeared it with a thick layer of cooling cream, and bandaged it carefully, all the while making sure to keep my touch light. She was mine, yes, but that didn't mean I would let her suffer.

I'd managed to find some pain pills in the medicine cabinet, and they seemed to help. At least, she hadn't cried out in pain since she took them, which I took as a good sign. I wished I could do more. Wished I could take away the pain entirely.

But this was necessary.

I loved the brand on my own chest. I almost didn't want to treat it. Just let it heal in its painful glory so I could revel in the fact that we shared the same mark.

It was beautiful. Far better than the ring I bought her. Better than declarations. It was a real, tangible wound that would scar and stick with the both of us together.

I stole a glance at the door, half expecting to see her standing in the doorway, watching me with those piercing eyes of hers. But the house remained still, its windows reflecting the setting sun.

I rested my hands on my thighs, feeling the rough fabric of my jeans beneath my fingertips. My mind was filled with a myriad of thoughts, an overwhelming surge of emotions—regret, desire, a twisted kind of affection. All for the woman inside the house, branded by my hand. I'd hurt her, yes, but I'd also cared for her. And I would continue to do so.

The sound of crunching gravel brought me back to reality. Avery's truck pulled up, dust pluming around it as the tires came to a halt. She swung out, the door slamming shut behind her. She was a vision of pure Texan grit; high-waisted denim jeans hugged her figure, a loose flannel shirt was tied around her slender waist, and a pair of scuffed cowboy boots completed the picture.

But what caught my attention was the shotgun.

She held it with surprising steadiness for a woman her size, pointing it square at my chest. I didn't move, not because I was afraid—I'd stared down far scarier things than a nervous cowgirl with a shotgun—but because any movement might be misconstrued as a threat.

"Where's Laura?" My voice broke the tense silence.

Avery swallowed hard, but her grip on the shotgun didn't waver. "She's safe," she stuttered, "and she's gonna stay that way."

I nodded slowly, keeping my eyes steady on hers. It was for the best that Laura wasn't here. Kids complicated things. Besides, the last thing I wanted was her boy to see me put Avery and Laura in their places. I had to take care of them too. Claiming Clover meant claiming them.

"Alright," I said, pushing up from the porch and

raising my hands in a gesture of surrender. I stepped off the porch. "Let's do this, Avery."

Avery's voice had an edge to it, one that hadn't been there before. "Where's Clover? Is she safe?"

I let out a short, humorless chuckle. "Clover's always safe with me."

But even as I said the words, a pang of unease wormed its way into my gut. The branding . . . it had been a spur-of-the-moment decision, one made in the heat of passion and power. I didn't regret what I did, but I couldn't shake the sickening feeling of guilt. The smell of burning flesh, the sight of her wincing in pain —they played on loop in my mind.

Maybe I had gone too far. Maybe . . . No. I shook the thoughts away. I did what I had to do. I marked her as mine, showed her that she belonged to me. If she'd only trusted me, let me take care of her instead of running off . . . maybe things would have been different.

My gaze drifted to the closed door of the house. I just hoped she would come to understand why I did it.

I wouldn't pretend to be sane or even rational.

But I would take care of what was mine.

"You need to let Clover go, Declan," Avery demanded, her determined stare not faltering from me. "We're leaving."

I shook my head, my stance hardening. "No, you're not leaving. You're all under my protection now."

My words hung in the air for a moment, and then Avery did something I hadn't quite expected. She lifted the shotgun higher, pointing it squarely at my chest. Her hands were shaking, but there was a determined set to her jaw. "No."

"Or what, Avery?" I challenged, keeping my voice calm. "You're going to shoot me?"

She didn't answer. Didn't need to. The threat was clear as day.

I let out a scoff, a smirk tugging at the corner of my mouth. "You're not capable of killing, Avery. You're not a killer. But I am."

I hoped my words would unsettle her enough to make her lower the gun. She needed to understand that this wasn't a game—that lives were at stake, including hers.

Avery's fingers quivered around the trigger. Her facade of strength was cracking; I could see the fear swimming in her eyes. Taking advantage of her hesitance, I descended the porch steps, each footfall like a death knell in the pregnant silence.

With a swift move, I grabbed the barrel of the gun, feeling the cool metal under my hand. "You need to understand, Avery," I growled, holding her eyes with mine. "There's no escape. No running away. Clover's mine."

I closed the distance between us, my voice dropping to a menacing whisper. "You can either get with the program or get the hell out of our lives. But Clover isn't going anywhere."

The threat was clear—one last chance for Avery to rethink her actions. One last chance for her to realize the danger she was putting herself in.

I looked down at Avery, her fingers trembling on the shotgun. There was fear in her eyes but also a stubborn determination. Her devotion to her sister was evident, and in a way, I respected it.

"Look, Avery," I began, my voice steady and calm despite the tension between us. "I know you love your sister, and I respect that. But I think you're looking at things from the wrong angle."

She scoffed, her grip on the shotgun tightening. "And what angle should I be approaching this from, Declan?"

"The angle where you're not the center of the world," I said, meeting her penetrating eyes without flinching. "The angle where Clover has her own needs, her own wants, her own life."

Avery's eyes narrowed. "And I suppose you think you're what she needs?"

"I think," I replied carefully, "that Clover needs

someone who sees her as a person. Someone who can give her what she's been giving everyone else for years—support, care, a bit of damn peace."

"Like you?" Avery retorted, her voice dripping with disbelief. "You think you're the peace-bringer? The protector? Clover texted me. You branded her, Declan!"

"Yes, I did," I said evenly, not backing down. "And I'd do it again. It was the only way to make her understand."

"Understand what?" Avery shouted, her chest heaving as her anger flared. "That she's property? That she's yours to mark and control?"

"No, Avery," I said firmly, stepping closer and lowering my voice. "To make her understand that she's not alone. That she doesn't have to carry the world on her shoulders. That she has me."

Avery stayed silent for a moment, seemingly taken aback. "You have a sick way of showing care, Declan," she finally spat.

"Maybe," I conceded. "But at least I'm willing to fight for her. What have you done for her, Avery, aside from leading her into trouble?"

Avery's face fell, but she quickly masked it with renewed anger. "You don't know anything about us, Declan. You don't know what we've been through!"

"Then enlighten me," I countered. "Tell me why

289

you're so hell-bent on leaving. Tell me why you're pointing a gun at me instead of trying to understand what I'm saying. Tell me why you're ready to tear your sister away from me."

The question hung in the air between us, a challenge wrapped in the form of an inquiry. Avery's breath was shaky as she struggled with her reply.

"You're ridiculous," Avery spat, her grip on the shotgun wavering as she glared at me. "You're a killer, a threat. Clover's not safe with you."

"On the contrary," I retorted. "She's safer with me than she ever was on her own. I've got a darkness in me, Avery, that's true. But that darkness can protect her, guard her from the threats you can't see."

"I don't believe you," she said, but her voice lacked conviction.

"I don't care if you believe me, Avery," I said. "I'm not asking for your approval. I'm telling you how it is. Clover is mine. I'll get rid of Hank, I'll keep her safe. She's going to have a life, Avery. A life where she's not constantly looking over her shoulder, not constantly taking care of everyone else."

Avery shook her head, looking smaller somehow. She seemed to deflate, the fight draining out of her as reality set in. "I just . . . I want to see Clover," she murmured, her gaze dropping to the ground.

"I know," I said, softening my tone. "And you will.

But you need to understand, things are different now. Clover is mine. And I'll do whatever it takes to protect what's mine."

"Can I see her now?"

"She's resting. I don't want her to have to worry about what you'll think or about taking care of you. Let her rest, Avery."

Avery nodded slowly, the fight gone from her. "Will you take care of her?" she asked, her voice barely a whisper.

"You have my word."

She chewed on her lip before responding. "And what is your word worth, Declan?"

I considered her for a moment. "Everything," I replied. "My word is my bond. Whatever I say, I'll do it. And Clover will be taken care of."

Avery hesitated for a moment before nodding. "Okay." She lowered the shotgun, no longer pointing it at me.

Relief flooded me. Avery had come to her senses, and for the moment, everything was okay.

"So no more running away?" I asked, my voice gentle.

Avery shook her head. "You've shown we can't escape. I suppose we can stick around to see if you can take care of Hank and his men," she replied.

"What about Laura?" I asked. I needed to know how many people I needed to keep an eye on.

"I insisted she take Carson out of here."

I nodded. "Good. Tell her to stay away until Hank is dealt with. Should be a couple of weeks."

"Alright." Avery took a deep breath before continuing. "You know, I want to believe you, Declan. I want to believe what you said about taking care of Clover. She deserves to be taken care of, and I don't think I can do it."

I smiled, understanding her reasoning. "You don't have to," I said. "But I will. And I'll do it better than anyone."

Avery nodded, her shoulders slumping in resignation. "I suppose we will see," she conceded.

For a long moment, we stood there in silence, the quiet broken only by the chirping of birds in the distance. Finally, Avery broke the silence.

"Can I please see her?" she asked.

"She's resting, but you can see her when she wakes up."

She nodded.

I watched her go, grateful that the situation had been diffused without violence. It seemed that Avery was finally coming around to my point of view.

I had made my point, and now it was time to make sure Avery and Clover both understood what I meant

—and I could think of no better way to do it than to show them.

Hank would die.

I'd find out who killed my mother.

And with a little bloodshed and a little luck, we'd live happily ever fucking after.

CHAPTER 22
The Outlaw's Temptress

CLOVER

The moment I stirred, a dull, throbbing pain from my shoulder yanked me back into consciousness. I winced, the crisp white sheets under me feeling like sandpaper against my stinging skin. Groggy confusion gave way to dread as I remembered what had happened—the branding, the heat, Declan.

Declan.

He was perched on the edge of the bed, concern etched on his face, but his eyes held a certain detachment. He turned, presenting me with a small glass of water and a couple of pills.

"Painkillers," he explained, his deep voice steady.

My eyes darted between the pills and his stoic face. Nerves twisted in my gut. I felt torn, pulled in two different directions. Part of me wanted to reach out and accept his offer of temporary relief. The other part was wary, afraid of trusting him, afraid of what the pills might do.

"It's just ibuprofen," he reassured me, guessing my hesitation. "To ease your pain."

The words were simple, but they resonated with a profound meaning. Yes, I was in physical pain—the burn on my shoulder was a testament to that—but I was also in emotional agony. The fear, the confusion, the sense of betrayal, everything was overwhelming.

He waited patiently, not pressing me but allowing me the space to decide. It was a small thing, but it reminded me of the man I had been drawn to, the man who'd made me feel cherished, cared for. The same fucking man who'd branded me.

"Thank you," I muttered, my voice barely a whisper. I reached out, accepting the water and pills from him. The pills were bitter but I swallowed them down, welcoming the promise of relief.

Declan gave me a small nod before standing up. He was still distant, but I could see the concern in his expression. A part of me wanted to reach out, to unravel the enigma that was Declan, but I was too scared, too confused.

For now, I just needed the pain to subside. I needed

time to think, to figure out what to do next. But the fear was ever present, a constant whisper in my ear. I was in uncharted territory, and I didn't know what would come next.

"Your sister stopped by earlier," Declan said after a long silence. He didn't look at me, his eyes focused on some unseen point on the floor.

I tensed, my heart pounding in my chest. "Avery?" I croaked out, my throat parched.

He nodded, finally turning to look at me. "Yeah, Avery. She's gone now, had to head to work."

I felt a wash of relief, quickly followed by a pang of guilt. I hadn't seen Avery in what felt like ages. We needed to talk, to figure things out, but right now, I wasn't up for it. I was barely keeping it together as it was.

"And Laura?" I asked, my voice just above a whisper. The question hung heavy in the air between us.

He sighed, running a hand through his hair. "Laura and the kid left town for a bit. Probably for the best."

I didn't need him to tell me why it was for the best. She didn't need to be involved in my mess. It was a small comfort, but I was grateful for it. Despite everything, I didn't want my problems to become hers.

I nodded, understanding washing over me. Our lives had become a tangle of peril and uncertainty, and it seemed everyone I cared about was being pulled into it. Despite the agony pulsing from the brand, the guilt weighed heavier on my heart.

"I can see you're nervous, Clover," Declan observed, his tone careful as though he was navigating a minefield. "You don't need to worry. I've got everything under control."

I laughed then, a bitter, humorless sound. "You expect me to trust you, after what you've done?" I said, unable to keep the edge from my voice.

He was silent for a long moment, and I could see the conflict playing out on his face. He seemed to be struggling with something, some inner chaos that he was wrestling with. I saw a flicker of something cross his face—regret, perhaps? Or was it just guilt?

"I didn't want to hurt you," he finally said, his voice so low I had to strain to hear it. "But I need you to understand. This is how it has to be."

"But why?" I shot back, my frustration bubbling up. "Why does it have to be this way? Why can't you just . . . let me go?"

"I don't know why I'm like this, Clover!" Declan's voice reverberated around the room, filled with a raw anger that made me flinch. His fists clenched, and I saw the tension ripple through his muscles.

His chest heaved, his breathing labored as he

seemed to grapple with his anger. I watched him, my heart pounding, unsure of what he would do next.

"I didn't choose this. I didn't choose to be this . . . this monster," he snarled, the word filled with self-loathing. His hands went through his hair, gripping at the roots as if he could somehow pull the darkness out of himself.

I didn't know what to say. I had no words of comfort, no solace to offer. All I could do was sit there, watching as Declan wrestled with his inner demons.

"I didn't want this life," he confessed, his voice filled with a desperation I hadn't heard before. "But that's all I've ever known. Violence, pain, darkness . . ."

"I'm sorry, Declan," I managed to say, my voice weak. I didn't know if my words offered him any comfort, but it was all I had. It felt wrong to be the one apologizing.

Declan swallowed, his Adam's apple bobbing as he gathered his thoughts. His eyes were far away, as if he were watching the memories play out in his mind.

"My foster brother," he said, his voice rough. "He was a member of a gang. Pulled me in before I had a chance to refuse." His fingers traced absent patterns on the worn denim of his jeans, a seemingly uncon-scious gesture. I held my breath, listening to his tale, a striking difference to the tranquility of the room.

"One day," he continued, his tone steady, but I could see the tension in his jaw. "I had to kill someone . . . to prove my loyalty." His confession hung in the air, heavy and foreboding.

I was frozen, torn between wanting to comfort him and the cold realization of who he was, what he had done.

"An ex-military man taught me how to handle a gun. Shoot with precision." Declan's voice had a detached quality to it, as if he were talking about someone else's life. The barest hint of a frown tugged at his lips, the only indication of his discomfort.

"I . . ." He paused, his icy blue eyes boring into mine. "I lost myself in that life." His admission left me breathless, a pang of sorrow seeping into my heart.

"But then," he began, his eyes drifting toward the window, "I found out that Hank knew who killed my mother. That was all I needed. My life became . . . about revenge."

His words stirred up a whirlwind of emotions in me. Shock, sympathy, terror—they all clashed within me, leaving me disoriented.

"But now, Clover," his voice softened, pulling me back from my turmoil. He turned toward me, his eyes radiating a warmth that contradicted his harsh tale. "You . . . you've opened up something in me."

"Me?" I asked.

"Yes."

It didn't fucking make sense. "Why? What's so special about me?"

"Do I need a reason? Do you want me to list what I like about you? Why I'm willing to *kill* for you? Why you're worth the risk?"

I nodded, nervous for his answer.

Declan licked his lips. "I suppose I could say that it's because I want to be the hero, but that would be a lie. Saving you made me feel alive. Like I could actually fucking accomplish something. But I've never been the hero, Clover. I don't think that's it."

I waited with bated breath for him to continue.

"I'm sure some fucking therapist would blame my trauma. Would say I want to save you because I couldn't save my mother."

"Declan—"

"That's the thing about obsessions, Wildflower. They rarely make sense. I don't need a reason to crave you—ache for you. Sometimes, if you're lucky, a spark burns down the whole fucking world. I saw you. I wanted you. I wanted *us*."

"I just don't get it," I admitted.

"I don't pretend to be sane, Clover. I don't pretend to make sense. I don't pretend to fall into logical categories of what feels right. What *seems* right. What's appropriate. Sometimes you just know."

"So, Declan, how do I know that you won't become obsessed with the next girl you see at a rodeo a month from now? How do I know that spark for me won't just sputter out as quickly as it burned to life? How can I build a life with you when we don't have a foundation?"

"I don't want anyone else, and I mean that. There won't be any other girl. This isn't a fleeting spark; it's a flame that won't be kindled for anyone else."

He moved closer, reaching out to lightly touch my arm. "You're right," he admitted. "Words are just words. They don't hold much value without action, do they? You have to just experience it. Try something and see where it leads you. The proof is in the journey."

Looking deep into my eyes, he said, "Give me a chance to build the foundation. I promise it won't be a shaky one. I may not have the best track record, but I've learned from my past, and I'm ready to build a strong, steady future."

A moment of silence passed between us, his last words echoing in my head. I didn't know what to say, how to respond. In this quiet room, amid the remnants of our shared pain, I realized that both of us were lost, adrift in our haunted pasts. And perhaps the only solace we could find was in each other's company.

Declan sat in silence for a moment, as if he was carefully weighing his words. He exhaled deeply before turning to me, his expression sincere. "Clover," he began, his tone gentle, "you . . . you've changed me. You've given me something more than revenge to hold on to."

I stared at him, digesting his words before cautiously asking, "But can we ever move past this, Declan? Can we ever be . . . normal?"

He gave a hollow chuckle, his gaze falling onto the floor. "Normalcy, huh?" he muttered, a bitter smile tugging at his lips. "I'm not sure if that's something I can promise. Not until I get my answers."

The unease swelled within me again, threatening to consume me. I looked at Declan, at the man who was both my captor and protector, and I wondered if we could ever escape the webs of his complicated past. "What do you need to do to get those answers, Declan?" I finally asked, my voice trembling slightly.

He looked back at me, his eyes darkening as he said, "I need to take care of Hank's dirty work. It's the only way he'll give me the information I need."

My heart pounded in my chest at his words. Despite my fears, despite my reservations, I knew I had to stand by Declan. I couldn't abandon him when he was fighting his demons. But the question that remained was, could I survive in his world, the world that was marked by violence and danger?

"Call Judge Mathis," Declan said, his voice breaking through the silence that had settled between us. "Cancel the trail ride."

I blinked at him, taken aback by his request. The trail ride. I had forgotten all about it in the chaos of the past few days. In a way, I was relieved. The thought of being out there again, amongst the towering trees and the wide, open spaces, sent a quake of unease through me. I wasn't ready. Not yet. I couldn't imagine being out there and *not* thinking about what happened to me.

But his command sparked a curiosity, a questioning of his motives. "Why?" I asked, meeting his stare with a hardened resolve.

He looked away, his expression unreadable. "It's better you don't know," he said. "I don't want you involved in this any more than you have to be."

But his response wasn't good enough for me. I needed to know. The fear, the uncertainty—it was eating away at me. "Tell me, Declan," I insisted, my voice quiet but steady. "What does Hank need you to do?"

His words came out in a rush, like they were being dragged from him. "He wants me to kill the judge and his wife," Declan said, his voice raw. He paused, swallowed hard, and then added, "And he wanted you dead, too."

I felt like the floor had dropped out from under me. My heart pounded in my chest as I processed his words. Kill me? Kill the judge? His *wife*? The reality of everything crashed down around me like a wave.

The breath hitched in my throat. I was supposed to be dead. That . . . that was Hank's plan. The terror, raw and unfettered, welled up within me. I didn't know how to respond, how to process this horrifying information. Fear tightened its grip around my heart, squeezing until I could hardly breathe.

I looked at Declan, the man who claimed to care for me yet was admitting to such a horrendous act. He was involved in this dangerous game of life and death, his actions controlled by Hank. But he was also the man who had saved me, who had treated my wounds and offered me comfort in the aftermath of my trauma.

"Do . . . do you still have to . . . ," I started, but the words got stuck in my throat. Could he still do it? Would he still do it? Kill the judge? Kill me? Despite everything, despite the pain and the fear, I needed to know.

Declan leaned forward, his face serious, and there was a strange, terrifying calmness in his penetrating stare. "Clover," he began, his voice as solid as steel, "I swear to you, you're not going to get hurt. Not on my watch."

He ran his hands through his hair, the muscle in his jaw pulsing with tension. "The judge, though . . ." His voice trailed off, and he shook his head. "I have to deal with him. I need the truth about my mother. It's the only way to put an end to all of this."

His penetrating eyes were intense, the honesty in his expression piercing through my terror. "And once I have what I need," he added, "I'm putting an end to Hank, too. I won't let him control our lives anymore."

I didn't know what to say, how to respond to his chilling words. This was the reality we were living, the twisted life that had been thrust upon us.

"Then how do you plan on killing Judge Mathis?" I asked, my voice barely above a whisper. I braced myself, ready for an answer I was not sure I wanted to hear.

Declan's face darkened, a storm cloud rolling in as he wrestled with his thoughts. He sighed, the sound heavy with an uncertainty that seemed out of character for the man who always appeared to know what he was doing.

"I'm not sure yet," he admitted, his words slow as he chose them carefully. "The trail . . . it was perfect. Isolated. An easy target. I tried to give Hank another option, but he was adamant it be done there. That *you* die with them. But now . . ."

His voice trailed off as he stared into the distance, seemingly lost in a world of horrific possibilities. The implications of what he was saying sent a rush of fear through me. This was far beyond anything I had ever dealt with.

"So once the judge is dead," I began, my voice shaking with trepidation, "you'll get the answers you need about your mother? Then we can get rid of Hank?"

I paused, letting the reality of my words sink in. The whole scenario felt like a dark road leading toward an uncertain future. Yet, in some twisted way, it seemed like our only path forward. A way out of the life Declan was trapped in. Maybe, just maybe, once Declan found out who killed his mother, he'd finally be able to let me go.

Declan met my stare, his dark eyes holding a depth of emotion that was hard to decipher. The burden of his past, the mayhem of his present, and the uncertainty of his future—they all reflected back at me, reinforcing my own fears. But beneath it all, I detected something else. Something that resembled hope.

"Yes," Declan responded, his voice barely above a whisper.

Then, mustering the strength I didn't know I still

had, I said, "Then we'll do the trail ride. You're going to kill the judge and . . . his wife. We'll make it look like you killed me too. You'll . . . get the job done." My voice wavered at the end, the weight of what I had just committed to sinking in.

Declan's eyes widened in surprise, and he was quiet for a moment, studying me. I could see a mixture of relief and worry in his gaze. Relief because I was giving him a way to accomplish his mission, and worry about the risks I was willing to take.

"Are you sure, Clover?" he asked gently, the potency of his expression softening. "It's not going to be easy . . . for either of us."

I swallowed hard, bracing myself for the reality of the situation. I was far from ready to confront my trauma, let alone witness a murder. But there was a desperate need within me to move forward, to break free from the hold Hank had over us.

"I trust you," I confessed, locking eyes with him. "For some fucked-up reason, I trust you not to kill me, Declan." I let out a shuddering breath. "You might brand me, own me, *hurt me*, but you won't kill me."

As Declan processed my words, my mind spun off in a whirl of disbelief. Was I really agreeing to this? Agreeing to let Declan commit murder? Agreeing to be his accomplice in this dark and twisted plan?

The rational part of my mind screamed at the

insanity of it all, warning me of the potential consequences. This was beyond reckless. Yet, there was this small, unwavering voice within me that was urging me to trust Declan, to trust this terrifying course we were setting ourselves on.

Trust. It's such a fragile thing, so easily shattered. And yet here I was, placing my trust in Declan, a man I knew was capable of such brutality. In this moment, I felt as if I were staring into an abyss of uncertainty. It was crazy. But maybe it was our only chance to break free.

Declan broke out into a triumphant grin. "I knew I could count on you, Clover," he said, his voice filled with a strange mix of relief and determination.

My heart fluttered uneasily at his words, but I nodded. "The trail ride with the judge . . . it's in three days. I need to be ready," I muttered, mostly to myself.

Then, another thought hit me. I'd tried to give my horses away to our neighbor when I planned on running. "What about the horses?" I asked, turning back to Declan. "I gave them away when I tried . . ." I let my words trail off. I didn't want to anger Declan again.

He snorted. "I took care of that. Told that nosey neighbor of yours to get lost. You're not getting rid of those horses, Clover."

His words sent a spark through my stomach.

Despite everything, I was relieved that my horses were still here, with me. They were the last bit of normalcy in this chaos. As for the trail ride, I knew I had to be prepared. But, for now, all I could do was breathe, try to process all this, and brace myself for what was to come.

CHAPTER 23

Femme Fatales of the West

DECLAN

*N*ext day dawned with the same Texas heat, relentless as the truth I was living. The morning sun was just starting to make its presence known, and I found myself on the porch, watching Clover.

Her skin glowed golden under the soft morning light as she cradled a cup of coffee between her hands. She was wearing a tank top, leaving her shoulders bare. My eyes were drawn to the angry red mark on her shoulder—the brand I'd seared into her skin. It was a harsh reminder of my claim over her.

As she looked out onto the open air, her eyes clouded with unspoken thoughts, I felt a thrill course through me. I owned her. This tough, beautiful woman was mine. It was a savage feeling, a primal possession that left me raw and wanting. I knew I had forever changed our lives, marking her so irrevocably, but the sight of my brand on her sent a wave of satisfaction through me. I owned her. She was mine, in every sense of the word.

"Get your boots on, Clover," I said, my voice slicing through the morning stillness. "We're going for a ride."

Without waiting for her reaction, I strode toward the barn, leaving her to her thoughts. The barn was cool and quiet. It smelled of hay and horses, a familiar scent that calmed my storming mind.

I made my way to Clover's horse. Her coat was a shining chestnut, and she flicked her ears at my approach, recognizing the sound of my footsteps. I ran a hand down her flank, her muscles twitching slightly under my touch. Her saddle was already set out, well-oiled and maintained.

As I started to saddle her up, my mind was busy with plans. Today, I would show Clover where on the trail I intended to make my move on the judge. The thought of it, the planning, the impending violence—it was all familiar territory for me. But involving Clover, having her by my side for this, was new. And somehow, that was the most frightening part of all.

As Clover came into sight, my eyes instinctively swept over her. She had pulled on her boots and a pair of worn jeans, her brown hair tied back with a bright pink scarf to combat the heat. She approached me, her eyes fixed on Ginny.

"Climb on," I instructed, offering my hand. With a moment's hesitation, she took it, and I helped her onto the saddle. I noticed the wince as she adjusted her position, her shoulder likely protesting the movement. But she said nothing, fixing her eyes straight ahead.

I mounted Ginny behind Clover, the heat of her body radiating onto me. I reached around her to take the reins, pulling her back against my chest while being mindful of the painful brand on her shoulder. The contact sent a jolt through me, a sudden and intense awareness of her. Of us.

As we started our ride, I couldn't help but be acutely aware of every breath she took, every shift in her position. We rode in silence, the only sounds the rhythmic clop of Ginny's hooves and the occasional call of a bird overhead.

There was a tension in the air, a silent under-standing of the gravity of what we were doing. It was a strange blend of danger and intimacy. The seductive pull of Clover's body against mine, mixed with the chilling knowledge of the path we were taking, made the ride far more thrilling and daunting than I could have imagined.

I felt her body stiffen against mine as we rode, her muscles coiling tight like a drawn bow. Leaning in, I

dropped my voice to a low murmur. "How you holdin'
up, Clover?"

"I . . . it's . . . strange," she confessed, her voice
barely audible over the sound of Ginny's rhythmic
steps. "The last time I was on a trail ride, I . . . you
know."

Her words hung in the air, a reminder of the
trauma she had experienced. I knew what she had
been through, yet hearing it acknowledged aloud was
a punch to the gut.

"Understandable," I replied gruffly, my grip tightening on the reins. I could only imagine the fear and
unease she must be grappling with, the daunting
memories hovering over her like a storm cloud.

"Take it one step at a time, Clover," I continued.
"We're here to make things right, remember?" Even as
I said the words, I could feel a knot of anxiety in my
own stomach. But I had to remain strong for her, for
us. "You're safe, I promise."

The morning light was just beginning to seep
through the branches of the trees around us, casting a
warm golden hue onto the worn dirt trail. The wind
played with Clover's hair as we rode, stirring strands
into a beautiful chaos. Tension tangled up my insides
as I took in her poised profile. The three-inch brand
on her shoulder stood out raw and vivid against her
skin. It was a symbol of ownership that incited a thrill

deep in me, but it was also a reminder of the path we were treading.

"My dad taught me how to ride." Clover's voice pulled me out of my thoughts. The timber of her voice was soft, wistful, yet there was an undercurrent of tension there that wasn't lost on me. She traced the reins in her hands, lost in a past I could only imagine.

"He found peace in the chaos of bull riding. For me, it was the quiet trail rides with our horses . . . it was almost spiritual. That peace was shattered when . . . when . . ." She didn't complete her sentence, but the pain in her voice filled in the gaps.

I waited, allowing the silence to fill the space between us, only the sound of hooves crunching on the dirt track giving rhythm to our journey.

"He rode for the Nightfall Rodeo for a little while, too. Can't help but feel like we've come full circle. Hank was so mad when he left and got sponsors. Said he'd make us pay all those years ago. Seems he finally got what he wanted," she revealed suddenly, her voice firm.

"That's why you were worried about Avery riding for the Devils, isn't it?"

There was a pause. I felt Clover's back stiffen against me. "Yeah. My father was different when he rode for the Devils. It was very quick, maybe a few months before he was recruited. I was young, but I didn't understand just how risky it was. Looking back, I feel like those years changed him. I'm glad he got sponsored and got out."

I felt Clover tense up as we reached the bend in the trail, her hand gripping the reins tighter. I reached out, placing my hand over hers to offer some semblance of reassurance.

"This is the spot," I said, my voice steady, although I could feel my heart pounding against my rib cage. I pointed out to the bend in the trail. "He won't see it coming."

Her breath hitched at my words, and she looked over at me. "How . . . how are you going to do it, Declan?" she asked, her voice barely above a whisper.

I took a deep breath before pulling the horse to a stop and dismounting. She reluctantly got off with me and with a deep breath, I answered, knowing I needed her to be fully aware of the grim reality. "I'll be hidden in those trees," I motioned to a dense patch nearby. "I'll be armed with a .45 Colt. It's a heavy firearm, reliable. It's done its job for me before."

The mention of the gun had her flinching slightly, and I gave her hand a comforting squeeze. "I'll aim for a clean shot, right in the head. It will be quick, he won't feel a thing. Then I'll shoot his wife."

I could see the fear in her eyes, but she nodded for me to continue. "The gunshot will likely spook his horse. It will bolt, which might buy us some extra time."

"And after . . . after that?" she asked, her voice shaky.

"After that, we will deal with Hank," I replied grimly. "I'll hide you. Tell him the job is done and the bodies are hidden. I'll get our answers from him. Once that's done, we'll take care of him. We'll be free."

The words hung in the air between us. She leaned closer, and I could feel her breath against my neck, quick and shallow. The realization of what we were about to do was sinking in, and the weight of it felt like a storm about to break.

"And then what?" Clover asked again, her voice trembling, her eyes searching mine. "We just . . . move on? We pretend everything is okay?"

"We don't have to pretend, Clover," I said, my voice earnest.

"But how?" she asked, the single word holding a world of uncertainty. "After everything . . . You've pushed me past my limits. You're about to kill a man . . . and you branded me."

The accusations hung heavy in the air between us, the bitter truths hard to swallow. I couldn't deny any of it. I had done those things. I had hurt her in ways I never intended, pushed her into a world she never asked for.

"It's not that simple, Declan," she continued, tears glistening in her eyes. "I'm . . . I'm scared. And yet . . . I . . ."

"Clover," I started, my heart aching at her words. But she held up a hand, silencing me.

"No, let me finish," she said. "You've put me in danger. You're . . . you're a killer. And I don't . . . I don't know if I can live with that. I don't know if I can live with the blood on your hands. But at the same time . . ."

I tried to pull her against me, but she resisted. Her voice trailed off again, and she took a deep, shaky breath, lifting her eyes to meet mine.

"At the same time," she whispered, "I crave you. I want you, despite everything."

My heart pounded in my chest at her admission. I knew she was torn, just as I was. I knew the path I'd chosen was one that might lead us both to ruin. But hearing her admit her fear, her desire . . . it made the stakes feel all the more real.

"I know," I murmured, my voice filled with raw emotion. "I know, Clover."

I reached out, pulling her against me. This time, she didn't resist. Instead, she buried her face in my chest, her hands gripping the fabric of my shirt.

"I know you're scared," I said, my voice steady despite the turmoil raging within me. "I'm scared too.

But we don't have to do this alone. We have each other."

"But how can we be together, Declan?" she asked, her voice muffled against my chest. "After everything that's happened, how can we possibly be together? It's wrong, right? I'm crazy to think we have a future after everything. Crazy to even *want* a future with you."

"It won't be easy," I admitted, my hand moving to gently stroke her hair. "I've made mistakes, I've hurt you. I've made decisions that I can't take back. But I will do everything in my power to make this right."

"Even if it means walking away from me?" she asked, pulling away to look into my eyes.

"If it means keeping you safe, then yes," I said, my voice unwavering. "But I'll fight like hell to make sure it doesn't come to that. We're in this together, Clover. And I'm not giving up on us."

"But what if I can't forget?" she asked, her voice barely above a whisper. "What if I can't forget the hurt, the blood?"

I took a moment to formulate my reply, my heart pounding in my chest.

"Then we'll work through it," I said finally, my voice filled with quiet resolve. "We'll face it together. We'll face it all. We don't have to forget, Clover. We just have to find a way to keep going, to move forward."

"But how, Declan?" she asked again, her eyes brimming with tears. "How can we move forward?"

I paused, my mind racing for the right words. "By learning," I said finally. "By learning to forgive, to trust, and to love. I won't lie, Clover. It's not going to be easy. There will be days when we'll question everything, days when the past will come back to haunt us. But we'll face them, together. We'll learn from our mistakes, from our past. We'll learn to live again. I'll show you that a future with me isn't just pain. It can be beautiful. You'll never want for anything. I'll always take care of you."

I looked at her, my heart pounding with the strength of my feelings. "I can't undo the past, Clover," I said, my voice heavy with regret. "But I can promise you this—I will spend every day of my life making it up to you, making sure you feel safe, loved, and cherished."

She looked at me, her eyes searching mine. "Can you really promise that, Declan?" she asked, her voice shaky. "Can you promise me a future?"

I reached out, cupping her face in my hands. "I can promise you this, Clover," I said, my voice filled with conviction. "I can promise you my loyalty, my protection, and my love. I can promise you that I will fight for us, for our future. It won't be an easy path, but I swear to you, it will be worth it."

For a moment, she just stared at me, her eyes filled with a mixture of fear and hope. Then, slowly, she reached up, her fingers gently tracing the line of my jaw.

"And if I choose to walk this path with you, Declan," she said, her voice soft, "if I choose to face this . . . will you be there, every step of the way?"

"Every step," I confirmed, holding her stare. "Every damn step."

With that, I leaned in, capturing her lips with mine in a kiss filled with promise and resolve. It was a soft kiss, gentle and tender, a stark contrast to the harsh realities we were facing. But it was filled with an underlying passion, a silent vow of our commitment to face whatever may come our way, together.

As we pulled apart, I rested my forehead against hers, taking a moment to relish the intimacy of the moment. "We'll make it, Clover," I murmured, my voice filled with conviction. "We'll make it together."

She nodded, her eyes meeting mine in a silent agreement. We stood there for a moment, lost in each other's eyes, before I helped her back onto the saddle.

We rode in silence for a while, each of us lost in our own thoughts. The tension was still there, an invisible thread that connected us. But beneath that, there was something else. A shared sense of purpose, a common goal. Despite the upheaval that churned within us, we had each other.

As the morning gave way to the afternoon, the sun casting long shadows across the barren landscape, I felt her body relax against mine. I could hear her breath evening out, her heart rate slowing. It was as if some of her fear had abated, replaced by a sense of grim determination.

Turning Ginny around, we started our ride back. As the homestead came into view, I found myself thinking about what lay ahead of us. I had killed before, but it was different this time. The stakes were higher. There was more at risk than just my life. I had Clover to protect, to fight for.

As we approached the barn, I pulled on the reins, bringing Ginny to a stop. I slid off the horse, my boots hitting the ground with a soft thud. Extending my hand to Clover, I helped her down. She winced as her feet touched the ground, her branded shoulder clearly causing her pain.

"Are you okay?" I asked, concern flooding my voice.

She nodded, swallowing hard. "I will be," she said, determination lacing her words.

Suddenly, I found myself pulling her to me, wrapping my arms around her in a fierce embrace. She stiffened in surprise, then relaxed into my hold, her arms encircling me in return.

"Promise me," I whispered against her hair. "Promise me you'll stay safe."

"I promise," she murmured, her voice muffled against my chest. "But only if you promise me the same."

"We're in this together, Clover," I said, pulling back to look into her eyes. "I'm not letting you go through this alone."

And then, without thinking, I leaned in and kissed her. It was a hard, desperate kiss, filled with fear and uncertainty. But it was also filled with passion and a promise of what could be. A promise of a future beyond the violence and the bloodshed.

Pulling back, I looked at Clover, her eyes wide with surprise and something else. Something that looked a lot like hope.

"We'll get through this, Clover," I said, my voice barely above a whisper. "We'll find our way out."

And as we stood there, in the fading afternoon light, I believed it. Because with Clover by my side, I felt invincible. We had a daunting path ahead of us, but whatever lay ahead, we would face it together.

CHAPTER 24

Heartbreakers on the Neon Rodeo

CLOVER

The morning sun had barely broken over the horizon when I found myself in the barn, my hands trembling as I saddled up Ginny, Storm, and Filo. I made sure to select Filo as Judge Mathis's horse. He was the best trained and wouldn't run off after the gun went off. I wasn't sure how Storm would react, though. My stomach churned with a mix of fear and anticipation as I prepared for the day's ride.

The horses sensed my unease, their soft snorts and the shuffle of their hooves were loud in the otherwise somber barn. Ginny, her coat glistening under the soft glow of the sunlight, nuzzled her nose against my palm in a silent show of comfort. I gave her a soft pat, taking a deep breath to steady my nerves.

Beside me, a picnic basket lay open, revealing a perfectly packed lunch that I knew would go untouched. Sandwiches, fruits, a bottle of wine—all intended for a couple who wouldn't live long enough to enjoy it.

The crunch of gravel alerted me to their arrival. I stepped out of the barn, my heart pounding as I saw Judge Mathis's luxury car roll to a stop in front of the ranch house. Even in the early light, the shine of the black paint was obnoxiously bright, reflecting the man's showy nature.

Judge Mathis stepped out, his tall frame impeccably dressed in jeans and a button-up shirt, the fabric straining slightly at his ample belly. His slicked back silver hair and the carefully trimmed beard gave him an air of practiced sophistication, a thin veneer over his corrupt heart. He was a man used to power, used to getting his way.

Beside him, his wife emerged, her coiffed blonde hair shimmering in the sun. She was a picture of polished elegance in her cream-colored shirt, her diamond earrings glittering in the sunlight.

I forced a smile onto my face, stepping forward to meet them. "Judge Mathis, Mrs. Mathis," I greeted, my voice steady despite the turmoil within me. "Good morning. The horses are ready."

Judge Mathis graced me with a curt nod, his eyes

already scanning the vast fields, the showy display of wealth not impressing him as much as it did most. His wife, on the other hand, gave me a smile, her eyes revealing a kindness that seemed out of place beside her husband.

"Thank you, my dear," she said, her voice soft and warm. It was almost a contrast to her husband's gruff demeanor. "We're looking forward to the ride. I told my husband we just *had* to go out for my birthday. It's so fun. A little adventure!"

The words echoed hollowly in my ears, the anticipation of what was to come making them sound like a macabre premonition. I nodded, leading them toward the horses.

The rest of the morning passed in a blur, my mind focused on the grim task that lay ahead. The facade of a pleasant ride, the friendly conversation, the laughter —it all felt like a grotesque charade.

Despite the heaviness in my heart, I continued to play the part, offering polite smiles and responding with rehearsed answers. Underneath it all, the anxiety continued to bubble, the reality of the task ahead leaving me trembling on the inside.

But I knew this was something that had to be done. It was a necessary evil, a path I had chosen, not for revenge but for safety. For Declan's closure. And with that thought in mind, I forced down my fear, focusing instead on the trail ahead, on the mission at hand. The path to redemption was just beginning, and there was no turning back now.

If Declan didn't finish the job, then Hank would come after us. I didn't have much of an option.

The clip-clop of the horses' hooves provided a comforting rhythm against the backdrop of a beautiful Texas sky. Sunlight filtered through the trees, casting dappled shadows on the trail, making the leaves shimmer like tiny emeralds. But beneath this scenic tranquility, a storm of anticipation brewed.

Judge Mathis, riding beside me, broke into a hearty anecdote from his political career. "I still remember, it was 1999, and we were pushing for that bill . . . against all odds, mind you," he said, his eyes gleaming with the joy of past victories.

His wife, Mrs. Mathis, riding slightly behind, laughed, "Oh, Harold, and you haven't let us forget it since."

His chuckle rang out, and I found myself smiling at their banter. It was all a cruelly pleasant distraction from the reality that would soon darken this idyllic moment.

Mrs. Mathis steered the conversation toward their family, her face softening. "Our grandson, Sammy, just turned five last week," she chimed in, pulling a picture from her saddlebag. The photo displayed a wide-eyed boy, grinning from ear to ear as he clutched a new toy truck.

"And Emily, our granddaughter, just turned seven," Mrs. Mathis continued, flipping the photo to reveal a young girl with a toothy smile and pigtails. She looked so much like her grandmother, I thought.

"Emily wants to be a teacher," Judge Mathis added with an affectionate smile. "Just like her granny."

My heart clenched at their words, my mind unwillingly painting a picture of their soon-to-be-grieving grandchildren. I nodded and offered a small smile, the guilt churning like a rough sea inside me.

Our trail ride continued, the pleasant weather and the sound of the bubbling creek running parallel to us failing to ease the tension brewing in me. The benign chatter of Judge Mathis and his wife seemed to fade into the background as my focus shifted to the path unfolding ahead.

As we approached the bend in the trail, I couldn't help but notice the ominous branches of the trees Declan had pointed out to me yesterday. Every stride that took us closer made my heart pound louder against my chest. I could almost feel Declan's presence hidden somewhere within the dense foliage, waiting.

I glanced at Judge Mathis, his face flushed from the sun, laughing at something his wife had said. They were lost in their own world, oblivious to the grim fate that was mere moments away.

I tightened my grip on the reins as we rounded the bend. My pulse roared loudly in my ears, drowning out the tranquil chirping of birds or the rustling leaves. I was part of a picturesque painting with a horrifying twist, and all I could do was hold my breath and pray for the strength to face the aftermath.

The scent of impending doom was heavy in the air, like a thick blanket threatening to smother us all. I looked at Judge Mathis, his mouth opening in mid-laughter, and Mrs. Mathis, her eyes crinkling, and a resolution took root in my heart.

I couldn't do this.

I couldn't kill innocent people.

I couldn't.

I couldn't.

"Stop!" I cut across Judge Mathis, my voice sharp and urgent.

He blinked, confusion clouding his mirth-filled eyes. "I beg your pardon, Clover?" I couldn't afford to let him delay us any further.

"We need to go back. Now," I urged, swinging my horse around to face the way we'd come.

Mrs. Mathis frowned, her gaze darting between me and her husband. "Is something wrong, dear?"

"No time to explain, just trust me," I said, my heart

pounding against my ribcage. I could almost hear the seconds ticking away, each one pushing us closer to the point of no return.

Without waiting for a response, I kicked my horse into a gallop, urging them to follow me. "Come on!" My voice carried the weight of my desperation.

Mrs. Mathis gasped, but Judge Mathis, with a stern nod, quickly followed my lead. Their horses sprang into motion, following the frantic rhythm of my own horse.

Behind us, I could hear the unsteady beat of hoof-beats gaining speed, the shocked exclamations of the judge and his wife blending with the wind. My heart pounded in my chest, each beat a plea to whatever forces were watching us to delay Declan, to let us escape unscathed.

The horses kicked up a cloud of dust as they galloped, the wind whipping past us like a wrathful spirit. The trail seemed to elongate, time and space stretching unbearably as we raced against destiny itself.

I dared not glance back at the spot where Declan lay in wait, praying silently that we had left in time, that our hastily executed escape had thrown off his deadly plan. Fear and hope entwined, the grim dance of life and death etched onto the canvas of a seemingly perfect Texas trail ride.

I didn't want to think about how I'd disappointed him.

There had to be another way.

After a long run that left our horses panting in exhaustion, we stumbled off our horses, our breathing ragged from the frantic ride. The world around us seemed to swirl into a chaotic mess as we stood there, a frantic knot of dread, shock, and disbelief. The horses, equally shaken, pranced and whinnied beside us, their eyes wide and wild.

"There was an . . . an ambush," I gasped out, my lungs burning from the frantic pace. I looked at Judge Mathis, his face a mottled canvas of fear and confusion. "He . . . he was going to . . ."

"Going to what?" Judge Mathis snapped, his eyes darting around the property in panic.

I shook my head, a hollow feeling growing in my stomach. "It doesn't matter now. Just get to your car and leave, don't look back."

"What the fuck is wrong with you?" Judge Mathis shouted, his hands trembling. "You expect us to leave without an explanation? I'll call the police, I'll—"

"No!" I cried, a sick feeling roiling in my stomach. "You don't understand, the police can't help."

Suddenly, the judge pulled out a silver pistol from his waistband, the sun glinting off the ornate engraving. It was an antique, a relic from the old west, yet in his hands, it was as deadly as any modern firearm.

"Now you listen here, young lady," he said, aiming the gun shakily at me. "You better explain what the hell is going on, or I swear—"

"Judge, please!" I pleaded, my hands up in surrender. "This isn't going to help!"

His wife was screaming, her hands clutching her chest as she watched the confrontation unfold. The world seemed to slow down, each second dragging into an eternity. My heart pounded in my chest, the metallic taste of fear coating my tongue.

"Just . . . just get in the car," I said, my voice trembling. "Leave, and don't come back."

Judge Mathis's eyes bore into me, the threat of violence discernable in the air. And as his gaze wavered, a flicker of uncertainty in his eyes, I realized we were all victims in this intricate game of survival. We were all just trying to stay alive, our decisions dictated by the desperate need to keep breathing for another day, another hour, another minute. The line between prey and predator blurred, distorted by fear and desperation.

And in that moment, a profound sadness washed over me. This was the life Declan had sucked us into, a life defined by violence and deceit. As I stood there, under the relentless Texas sun, I knew this was a world I could no longer be a part of.

"He . . . he was going to . . ." My voice trembled, my words tripping over each other in their hurry to escape. "He was going to kill you. Both of you."

A hush fell over us. Judge Mathis staggered back, his face pale. "What . . . ?"

I swallowed, steeling myself. "We planned an ambush on the trail. You weren't supposed to make it back."

His eyes were piercing, the weight of my confession pressing down on all of us. His hand tightened around the gun, the knuckles white.

"You . . . you were in on this?" he stuttered, his face turning a shade of red. "You lured us into a trap?"

"Yes, but I—" The words died in my throat as he took a menacing step toward me.

"No," he spat, his voice a low growl. "No excuses."

His hand trembled as he raised the gun, pointing it at me. His eyes were wild, darting around the property as if expecting enemies to leap out at any moment.

"You think you can just play with people's lives?" he shouted, his words slicing through the silence. "That you can decide who lives and who dies?"

"No, judge, it's not like that. I—" I tried to explain, but he cut me off with a wild shake of his head.

"No!" he roared. "You're a killer!"

His finger twitched on the trigger, and I could see the battle waging in his mind. To pull or not to pull. Life or death. All hanging on a thread.

"I should kill you," he snarled. "For trying to kill us. For leading us into a death trap. It would be self-defense, you know. Easily cleaned up."

"I didn't want this," I pleaded. "I changed my mind. That's why I brought us back."

But it was too late. The judgment was written all over his face. I was the enemy. And enemies were to be taken out.

The judge's wife was a spectator of terror in the background, her anguished cries swallowed by the unforgiving tension between us. And in the silence that swallowed my pleas, the air seemed to crackle with the inevitability of violence. The conclusion was written on the judge's face, the final verdict drawn.

But then, the world exploded.

The gunshot's deafening blow split the silence, ricocheting off the quiet landscape. An anguished cry tore through the air as Judge Mathis's body jerked, the force of the bullet throwing him backwards. Blood blossomed like a grotesque flower on his chest, soaking into his pristine white shirt. His eyes widened in shock, and the gun slipped from his fingers, clattering onto the dirt.

There was another blast, and the judge's wife was

swept off her feet. Her mouth opened in a silent scream as she crumpled to the ground, blood staining her cream-colored top.

A wild, primal fear seized me as I stared at their fallen bodies. Time seemed to have frozen, the silence punctuated by the soft moans of the injured and dying. The taste of death filled the air, sharp and bitter.

It was then that I saw him. Declan emerged from the side of the barn, his silhouette standing out against the setting sun. He was a picture of death, his face hard and unyielding. The Colt .45 still smoked in his hand, its metallic taste hanging heavy in the air. His gaze met mine, and in his eyes, I saw a hardened resolve that shocked me.

The world around me spun. The scent of blood and gunpowder, the moans of the dying, and Declan's piercing eyes converged into a nightmarish assembly of death and betrayal. The grisly scene of violence played out in cruel, high-definition clarity, each minute detail etched into my mind.

The horror of it, the reality of my complicity, crashed down on me. My knees buckled, and I fell to the ground, my world narrowing to the sickening sight of Judge Mathis and his wife, life ebbing away from them.

As their life seeped into the Texas dirt, I could

only watch, the bitter taste of regret and dread etching itself into my soul. I had played with life and death, and death had won. I was a part of this carnage, a player in this brutal game of survival. My mind reeled at the thought, the world blurring as I was swallowed by the tragic reality of what I'd become.

Declan approached me slowly, deliberately, as though he was afraid any sudden movement might scare me away. His boots crunched against the dry earth, a somber drumbeat to our grim silence.

"Clover?" His voice cut through the stillness, sounding unusually soft, almost tender.

I tried to answer, but the words got caught in my throat. Panic bubbled up inside me, threatening to spill over. My breaths came in short, rapid gasps, the world around me tilting dangerously. Would he be mad that I ran?

"Why, Clover?" he asked again, his face a mask of confusion and concern. "Why did you change the plan? Why did you warn them?"

His words, his confusion, it was too much. The world felt too big, too real, and I felt myself shrinking under its weight.

"I . . . I . . . ," I stammered, my voice barely a whisper. "I couldn't . . . couldn't do it."

My words hung in the air, raw and vulnerable. I

saw the flicker of surprise in Declan's eyes, followed quickly by a wave of understanding.

"You're scared," he said softly, his eyes never leaving mine. It wasn't a question. It was a statement, a recognition of the fear that was coursing through my veins. "I knew I shouldn't have dragged you into this. I'm so sorry, Clover."

"No . . ." I shook my head, a desperate attempt to deny what was so evident. "I am . . . I am."

"Hey, hey . . ." Declan knelt down next to me, his voice steady and reassuring. "It's okay, Clover. It's going to be okay."

"I'm sorry," I cried out, not sure if I was saying it to the judge and his wife or Declan.

"You have nothing to be sorry for. I was only worried you'd get hurt. When I saw that gun aimed at you . . . I won't apologize for killing them, Clover. I can't."

His words were meant to soothe, but they only amplified my disgust of what had just happened. I looked at him, really looked at him, and I saw him for what he truly was. He was a killer. He had taken lives, and I had helped him.

Panic surged within me. I couldn't breathe, couldn't think. All I could see was the blood, all I could hear were the dying gasps of the judge and his wife.

And Declan, with his soothing voice and concerned eyes, was the architect of it all.

Suddenly, I couldn't bear to be near him. I couldn't bear the sight of him, the scent of him. I needed to escape, needed to get away from this nightmare.

So, I got to my feet. My legs wobbled underneath me, the world spinning around me. I glanced at Declan one last time, his eyes wide with surprise and concern. Then, without a word, I turned on my heels and ran.

CHAPTER 25

Gilded Guilt, Diamond Dust

DECLAN

*J*saw her bolt. My heart clenched as I watched her brown hair whipping around her shoulders, her strides panicked and wild. I was frozen in place for a moment, her terror slamming into me like a sledgehammer. But then instinct took over. I was after her.

"Damn it, Clover!" I shouted, my voice ripping through the eerie silence left in the wake of the gunshots. My boots dug into the earth, propelling me forward as I pursued her, but she had a good head start.

I could still see her in the distance, a frantic figure tearing through the fields. My heart pounded against my ribcage, each thud mimicking the rhythm of my thoughts. I'd put her in danger, lied to her, pushed her to her limits. I'd placed the burden of blood on her hands, and now she was running, and all I could think of was to chase.

In that moment, all I saw was the back of Judge Mathis, his gnarled hand clutching that gleaming gun, pointing it at her. At *my* Clover. Every muscle in my body had coiled tighter than a bed of rattlesnakes ready to strike.

"Stop, Clover!" I roared again, my voice ragged with desperation. I saw her hesitate, just for a split second, but then she was off again, running like a wild deer escaping a predator.

God, was that what I'd become to her? A predator?

The irony wasn't lost on me. I'd branded her as mine, thought of our relationship as some sort of savage, primal possession. And here we were, the hunter and the hunted. The guilt was stabbing me in the chest, leaving me winded and disoriented, but I couldn't stop now. I couldn't let her run into the wilderness, panicked and alone.

"I won't hurt you!" I tried again, my voice screeching in the vast expanse of Texas land. But it fell on deaf ears. She continued her wild dash, her fear rendering her oblivious to my pleas.

Every breath was a gasp, each stride an exertion. I was a cowboy, a killer, a protector, all rolled into one. And here I was, chasing after the woman I'd unintentionally driven away, my mind a chaotic whirlwind of regret and terror.

Her skin flashed like burnished copper each time she moved, a stark contrast to the clothes that clung to her like a second skin. It was as if the universe were trying to taunt me, to remind me of what I stood to lose.

She was beautiful, even in her fear. I imagined how the frantic beating of her heart matched the pounding in my own chest. I could practically taste the adrenaline that was spiking through her veins, sour and bitter.

Her sobs echoed in my ears, mingling with the rough sound of my own breaths. I was the one who had put that fear in her eyes, made her heart race for all the wrong reasons.

"Stop running, Clover!" I growled, my voice hoarse. But she wouldn't, or couldn't, stop. She was like a wild mustang, desperate for freedom, yearning to break free from the reins that had been thrust upon her.

My strides lengthened, the gap between us slowly closing. Her frantic breaths reached my ears, a sweet yet tragic melody that broke my heart. I reached out, fingers brushing against her shirt, her body warmth seeping through it, igniting a flame deep within me.

With one final leap, I tackled her to the ground.

Her breath whooshed out of her as we hit the ground, her body beneath mine. She was panting heavily, her chest rising and falling beneath me. I flipped her over onto her back and stared deeply into her eyes.

"Clover . . ." My voice was a whisper, a plea. She was trembling beneath me, her fear almost tangible. But underneath it all, there was a spark of something else . . . something instinctive and primal.

With her beneath me, her body writhing and attempting to escape, I felt my own fear. I was afraid of losing her, afraid of what I had become in her eyes.

Her scent filled my nostrils, sweet and intoxicating. It was a moment of raw emotion, a confession of the harsh reality. I had pushed her to the edge, and now, she was running from me.

As I looked into her wide, panicked eyes, the guilt consumed me. It was a bitter pill to swallow. I had caused this, and now, I had to face the consequences. I could feel the tension between us, thick with unspoken words and emotions. Clover's body writhed beneath me, her muscles tensing with every attempt to free herself. But I held her down, my weight a reminder of my control over her.

"Clover," I whispered again, my voice low and pleading. "Please, just listen to me."

Her eyes widened even further, the fear only

growing in ferocity. And yet, there was that spark again, that primal need that burned within us both.

I leaned in closer, my breath hot against her cheek. Our bodies were so close that I could feel the heat emanating from her skin.

"You can run from me all you want," I murmured, my lips grazing her ear. "But I will just catch you, Wildflower. I love the chase."

The words were possessive, almost feral, and I could feel her resistance faltering. She was like prey beneath me, and I was the predator circling her orbit.

"Clover," I whispered, her name on my lips sounding as sacred as a prayer. Her eyes locked with mine, confusion and terror swimming within them. The tremors in her body hadn't ceased, but she had stopped trying to escape from my grasp.

"You killed them," she cried.

"And I'd do it again, Wildflower."

Each violent quake that racked her slender frame made fire rush through my veins. My words hung heavy between us. The sun hung overhead, highlighting the freckles that dusted her nose, the brown strands that escaped her messy bun, the innocence that still clung to her despite the chaos.

"I need you to let go, Clover," I pleaded, my voice barely a whisper. "Let me bear the burden. All of it."

Her eyes never left mine. Her breath hitched, the

silence enveloping us making the moment seem frozen.

"Give me the blame, Clover," I murmured. "I'll take it . . . all of it. You . . . you didn't do anything. This is all on me."

The tension between us was thick, the air around us heavy with unspoken words and unresolved feelings. Our bodies pressed together, the mixture of fear, guilt, and desire creating a blend that sent my senses into overdrive.

Our bodies were locked in a ravishing struggle of power and control. And yet, I was also the one begging, pleading for forgiveness, for understanding, for a chance to rectify my wrongs.

As our bodies lay entangled on the ground, I felt the edges of her fear begin to soften, replaced by a different kind of tension. One that pulsed with need and desire.

My words trailed off as I felt her slowly relax beneath me, the harsh trembles subsiding to softer shivers. Her wide eyes never left mine, and in them, I saw a flicker of something that wasn't fear. It was a spark, small and tentative, but it was there.

She gasped, an almost inaudible sound lost in the wind. It wasn't an agreement, not quite, but it was something. A hint of surrender, a tentative acceptance of my plea—of me.

"I'm the villain here, baby," I murmured, pressing my forehead against hers. Our breaths mingled, our bodies connected in a way that was terrifyingly intimate. "Blame me for everything. I can take it."

The words were honest, exposing every piece of my guilt, every shred of my regret. I felt vulnerable beneath the weight of my confession, more exposed than I'd ever felt before.

I didn't know how she would react, didn't know if she would push me away or pull me closer. But I needed her to know, to understand that I would shoulder this burden, would take on all the guilt and blame, for her.

Her croaked response shocked me.

"Prove it, Declan."

I ground against her, my cock hard as steel. "Prove what, Wildflower?"

She swallowed and looked at me with determination. "Prove you're the villain."

I felt my heart quicken, unstoppable waves of heat radiating throughout my body. My breathing had increased, matching hers as I pulled away and looked into her eyes.

"I'll ruin you. And you'll blame me for all of it," I replied before slipping into the person she wanted me to be. The person she could blame. The person she could hurt.

In a wild moment of need and desire, I tore at her clothes. She fought me, screaming and shaking as I ripped away the last of her defenses. Eventually she lay beneath me, exposed and vulnerable. I wanted to savor the moment, but we both knew there was no time for such luxuries.

As my hands roamed her body, probing for weaknesses and hidden secrets, something changed in both of us. It was as if we had reached an unspoken agreement: I would take the blame, but in return she'd give herself up to me completely and utterly.

She didn't resist as my fingers found their way around her throat, closing tight around the fragile flesh. The pressure felt like a warning, yet it was oddly intimate too, like a brand placed upon her gentle skin that told the world: *this is mine now.*

Her breathing grew shallow as my grip tightened slightly on her neck. I could feel her pulse racing as her body quivered beneath me. She was scared, I was sure of it, but I could also sense that her fear was slowly being replaced by something else.

Determination? Trust?

It didn't matter. All that mattered were those few seconds suspended between us, those precious, lingering moments when I couldn't tell where I ended and she began.

I looked down at her, my eyes blazing with some-

thing I had never felt before. It was a mix of possessiveness, passion and tenderness.

I had found my match in her; I had found something that I never thought I would find.

"Clover," I whispered, sweeping a gentle caress
down her neck. "I'm here. I'm not going anywhere."

Her trembling ceased, and I could see the fear
fading from her eyes. She had given herself to me, and
I knew at that moment that there was no turning back.

My lips lowered to hers and we kissed. It wasn't
gentle, it wasn't sweet, it was raw and passionate and
needy—two souls colliding in the heat of the moment.

She fought me as I unzipped my pants, pulled out
my throbbing cock, and thrust inside of her. But even
in her struggle, I knew this was what she wanted, this
heat, this passion, this connection.

And in that moment, I wasn't a villain anymore. I
was just her lover, her protector. Whatever sins I may
have committed in the past, whatever guilt I may have
held, they vanished like smoke.

We moved together in a harsh rhythm, her tight
walls gripping me as our desire grew and climax
neared. Flesh slapped against flesh as I pounded into
her, pushing her closer and closer to the edge.

"Fuck you!" she screamed, but there was sadness in
her tone. Longing.

As her words lingered in the air, I tentatively let

my fingers roam her body, tracing the length of her arms, each of her fingers, the soft curve of her hips. I felt her inhale sharply as my hands wandered to her breasts, gently kneading the supple flesh. She was warm and soft beneath my roughened touch.

"I love you," I whispered, my voice barely audible over our panting breaths, "Give me the blame, Wildflower. Give me all of it."

I could feel her heart pound against my chest, her lips parting as my words washed over her. I hoped she understood. That in this intimate moment, I was not the monster she had feared.

Our bodies moved together, her beneath me, me above her, in a rhythm as old as time itself. Each thrust was met with a soft gasp, a clinging clutch of her hands on my back, a roll of her hips that made my head spin. She was perfection, a heady mix of desire and fear, of guilt and relief.

All that mattered was her, was us. The world outside ceased to exist as our bodies moved in sync, each breath, each heartbeat shared between us.

The tension built within us, a crescendo of lust and craving that threatened to consume us. Her tight walls clenched around me, a sweet surrender that had me reeling. I buried my face in the crook of her neck, each ragged breath a testament to the impact of our shared passion.

As my rhythm quickened, as my control teetered on the edge, I held onto her. Flesh met flesh, a sinful beat to our shared need. I felt her body tense beneath me, her grip tightening on me, her breaths coming out in short gasps.

"Clover," I murmured against her skin, my voice barely audible over our panting. "Clover . . . fuck, I love you."

And then, everything was silent. The world tilted as ecstasy claimed us, our bodies tightening, releasing in a wave of intense pleasure. The guilt, the fear, the obsession . . . all of it was swept away in the tidal wave of our climax, leaving behind only raw emotion and shared desire.

As our bodies slowly came down from the high, as our breaths steadied and our heartbeats slowed, I held her close. I held onto her as if she were my lifeline, as if letting go would mean plunging into a world of guilt and remorse.

The zeal of the moment faded slowly until all that was left was tenderness and peace. I lay there beside her, listening to each other's heartbeats in sync—two souls forever bound by this sinful act.

As I lay spent, our bodies melting together in a pool of sweat and tears, I knew this burdensome guilt was no longer mine to bear. Together we had proven there could be redemption even amidst the blame and guilt.

And finally—finally—she whispered those four words neither one of us expected to hear: "I love you, too."

CHAPTER 26
Stardust Secrets, Desert Flames

CLOVER

The living room was shrouded in silence as I sat on the worn-out couch, my knees tucked up to my chest. The fabric felt rough under my hands, grounding me in the harsh reality. Beside me, my sister Avery was a comforting presence, her eyes heavy with concern as they bore into me.

"I just . . . ," I began, my voice trembling as I tried to form the words. "I don't know, Avery."

My eyes dropped to the coffee table in front of us, littered with empty tea cups and tissues. My thoughts were a whirlpool of guilt, fear, and confusion. Declan had saved me. He had taken the bodies away, had swept in like some dark avenger, carrying the weight of my sins.

And then he left to confront Hank.

And I was scared out of my fucking mind.

"Avery," I whispered, the name a plea for understanding. I turned to face her, my eyes brimming with unshed tears. "He . . . he took the blame. All of it. Said it was his fault . . . that I should blame him."

Avery's brow furrowed, her lips parting as if to speak. But then she seemed to change her mind, her lips pressing together as she searched my face for answers. "And do you?" she finally asked, her voice barely above a whisper. "Do you blame him, Clover?"

I shook my head, the movement slow and lethargic. "I don't know," I admitted, my voice barely audible. The confusion was overwhelming, clouding my judgment, suffocating my rational thoughts. "I just . . . I don't know."

Silence fell between us once again, the ticking clock on the wall a cruel reminder of the passing time. The shadows in the room seemed to grow longer, the soft glow from the lone lamp casting eerie shapes onto the faded wallpaper.

"But he saved me, Avery," I said, my voice a desperate whisper. "He keeps saving me."

Avery sighed, reaching over to grip my hand, her fingers warm and steady against mine. "I know, Clover," she murmured. "I know."

The conflicting emotions inside me were a raging storm, one that threatened to tear me apart. I wanted to blame Declan for what had happened. I wanted to let him carry all the guilt, the shame. But I also knew that he had saved me *again* and had put himself at risk for my sake. And that knowledge was like a beacon in the dark, a glimmer of hope amidst the chaos.

"So what do I do?" I asked, my voice choked with emotion. "What am I supposed to feel, Avery?"

Avery didn't respond immediately. She seemed to be weighing her words, her gaze distant as she mulled over my question. When she finally spoke, her voice was soft but steady.

"Clover," she said, her voice barely a whisper. "Feel what you need to feel. There's no right or wrong here. It's your emotions, your conflict. And no one but you can figure out how to navigate it."

I knew she was right, but that didn't make it any easier. The guilt, the fear, the relief . . . they were all tangled together, creating a web that I didn't know how to sort through. But I had to try. For myself, for Declan, for us.

I sat back, releasing a shaky breath as I nodded. "Okay, Avery," I murmured, a tear escaping my eye. "Okay."

For a moment, we sat in silence, the soft hum of the air conditioner and the ticking clock the only sound in the room. It was a lot to process, a lot to accept. But I knew that I had to do it.

"Where's Declan now?" Avery's question pulled me from my thoughts.

I swallowed hard, feeling the sting of unshed tears at the back of my eyes. "He went to Hank," I said quietly, "to end all this. To get answers."

Avery nodded slowly, taking in my words. She didn't say anything for a moment, just studied me, her eyes a deep well of concern. "Are you worried about him?" she asked eventually, her voice soft.

It was a simple question, but it brought forth a tidal wave of emotions. I took a deep, shaky breath, my fingers tightening around the hem of my shirt. "Yes," I admitted, my voice barely more than a whisper. "I am . . . I love him, Avery."

Tears filled my eyes as I finally let the words out, letting the truth spill from my lips. It was both terrifying and liberating at the same time. I felt Avery's hand squeeze my own, a comforting, grounding pressure.

"Are you sure?" she asked, her voice gentle, careful. "Could it be . . . trauma bonding or something?"

I bit my lower lip, contemplating her words. It was possible, wasn't it? Everything that had happened . . . it was enough to mess with anyone's head. But when Declan had left, when he'd stepped out into the night to face Hank, the worry that had filled me was undeniable.

"I don't know," I confessed, tears spilling onto my cheeks. "But when he left, Avery . . . I was sick with worry. I still am."

She watched me for a long moment before speaking. "You know, Clover," she started, her voice thoughtful, "you've never let anyone in before. It's . . . it's scary, I know. But it could also be . . . good."

I looked at her, my heart pounding in my chest. I knew what she was saying. It wasn't approval, not exactly. But it was understanding, empathy. She knew that I couldn't control how I felt, no matter how complicated or potentially misguided it might be.

"I just . . . I don't know what to do," I admitted, my voice a broken whisper.

Avery squeezed my hand again, offering a small, comforting smile. "You don't have to do anything right now, Clover," she said softly. "Just . . . just be. Feel what you need to feel. And when you're ready . . . we'll figure it out together, okay?"

And in that moment, amidst the chaos and confusion, I felt a glimmer of hope. Maybe, just maybe, I wasn't alone in this.

Sitting on the couch, I found my attention returning time and again to the small, lifeless screen of my phone. I couldn't stop the scenarios that played out in my mind, each more frightening than the last. Was

Declan confronting Hank right now? Was he fighting for his life? Or worse . . .

He'd told me to stay at home. Lock the doors. Wait for word from him. I wanted to run, but he promised it would be handled before Hank even knew I was alive.

Declan was cocky, but I trusted him.

The knot in my stomach tightened, the anxiety gnawing at me, an incessant reminder of the precarious position we were in.

Suddenly, a loud knock jolted me out of my dark thoughts. My heart skipped a beat. Declan?

I scrambled to my feet, stumbling in my haste to reach the door. I yanked it open, a breathless greeting already forming on my lips. But the sight that met my eyes was far from the relief I was hoping for.

There, standing on the porch, was a man I didn't recognize. His expression was harsh, eyes cold and unfeeling. And in his hand, pointed directly at my chest, was the gleaming barrel of a gun.

Fear gripped me, an icy chill spreading through my veins. I stood there, frozen, my breath caught in my throat as I stared into the dark abyss of the gun barrel.

Avery's gasp filled the small hallway, a chilling harmony to the pounding of my heart. Her voice was a trembling whisper, loaded with bravado she did not feel. "Who the hell are you?"

The man didn't so much as flinch. His stare was a deadly weapon in itself, shifting toward Avery before settling back on me. "That's none of your concern, girlie," he grumbled, his voice was like a rock slide down a mountain. "You," he commanded, jabbing the gun toward me, "you're coming with me."

Avery launched herself forward, a protective wall between the man and me. "No way in hell!" she spat, venomous. But her body shook, and her eyes flared with terror beneath her defiance.

With a growl that was more beast than man, he swiveled the gun toward Avery, the barrel gleaming menacingly under the dull hallway lights. "Stay put or I'll put you down right here, right now," he hissed.

Terror coiled around my heart like a vise, squeezing till I couldn't breathe. The taste of salt hit my tongue as a tear slid down my cheek, unchecked, unnoticed. In that moment, the world narrowed down to the icy metal of the gun, the sneering man, and the precious life of my sister hanging in the balance.

"I'm . . . I'm coming," I stammered, forcing my numb legs to move. As if she were released from a spell, Avery's fingers slackened, falling from my arm. Her eyes were wide, pleading. I met her gaze and nodded—a silent promise. I was walking into the lion's den, but I was doing it on my own terms. For her. I

359

was the one knee-deep in this mess of bloodshed. I'd save her. I'd *always* save her.

With a grunt that sounded oddly pleased, the man stepped aside, gesturing with the gun for me to move past him. His lips pulled back in a snarl of a smile; the eyes, however, were empty and deadly.

I took a deep breath, turning one last time to look at Avery. I memorized the fear in her eyes, the determination on her face, the way her lips moved as she mouthed "be careful." It would be my lifeline in whatever was about to come. Then, with a shudder of terror, I stepped out into the swallowing darkness.

The cab of the truck reeked of oil and smoke, a potent mix that made me choke. He grunted and gestured with the gun again, this time for me to buckle up. His demeanor was all cold detachment and efficiency, as if kidnapping were second nature to him.

He was older, maybe in his late fifties. His face was a roadmap of lines and scars, each etching a story that I was sure was darker than the last. Despite the gruff exterior, there was a familiarity about him that I couldn't shake. The shape of his nose, the squareness of his jaw—it stirred something in me, a deep-rooted memory I couldn't quite grasp.

"Who are you?" I blurted, my voice sounding small in the cold, metallic confines of the truck.

He grunted, a noise that vibrated deep in his chest.

"Didn't anyone ever teach you manners, girl?" His tone was gruff, but there was a hint of amusement there, too.

"I . . . I think I know you," I ventured. "You look . . . familiar."

He glanced at me, his eyes sharp beneath the bushy brows. For a moment, there was a flicker of something akin to surprise before it was quickly masked. He nodded. "Yeah, you probably do. Knew your father. Knew him well."

Father? He knew my father? "What's your name?" I demanded, trying to keep my voice firm.

He gave a chuckle, more of a bark really, and finally turned to look at me. His eyes bore into mine, a cold blue that mirrored the chill running through me. "Name's Jim," he said, his voice low and rough, "Jim Harlow."

My heart froze. Harlow. That name, it was like a ghost from the past. My father's past.

"You used to ride bulls for Nightfall," I said.

He smirked. "I was a better rider than your father. But he had no loyalty. The moment he got sponsors, he was out of there. Guess he was smarter than me."

I swallowed. "Did Hank send you?"

He shook his head. "Hank *warned* me. Said trouble was brewing. Said I made too many enemies in my younger years."

361

"I don't understand. What does this have to do with me?" I asked, my heart racing.

Jim took a deep breath, keeping his eyes on the road. "I was jealous of your father," he confessed, the words slipping from his lips with a bitterness that surprised me. "I thought he was the golden boy, got everything handed to him on a silver platter. And that drove me mad."

His confession was a naked truth that I was struggling to process. I had known my father had left Nightfall, but to hear Jim's side of the story . . . It felt as if I were peeling back layers, revealing a side of my father I never knew.

"I thought that if I couldn't have the fame, the glory, I could at least have his happiness," Jim continued, his voice tinged with regret. "So, one night, when I saw him on a date, I . . . I saw him so happy. I decided he didn't deserve a pretty woman *and* a rodeo career."

The words died in his throat, his grip on the steering wheel tightening. I watched him, my mind reeling. He had killed the woman my father was with . . . I didn't even know Dad had been dating someone.

The puzzle pieces started to click together. This strange man. This story . . .

"Hank wanted to punish your father," he continued, a bitter chuckle escaping his lips. "For leaving

Nightfall. I was killing two birds with one stone, so to speak."

A cold dread sunk into my bones. "And now, her son is out for blood," I murmured, my heart pounding in my chest. "You killed Declan's mother. All because she was on a date with my father."

There was so much to process I could barely think.

"Didn't realize her son would grow up to be a cold-blooded killer."

I swallowed. "Are . . . are you going to kill me?"

"You're nothing more than a worm on a hook. Bait," he grumbled, snapping me out of my reverie. "Although it would make me *very* happy to punish your father even more, I need you alive to get what I want. As long as you do as I say, no one has to get hurt."

My mind was a whirlwind of confusion. Why would Jim Harlow want me as insurance? My stomach churned with a mixture of fear and confusion. It felt like I was on a collision course with my past, and I had no idea how to steer clear.

"I'm leverage. You're going to use me to draw out Declan," I croaked.

He was silent for a moment, his grip tightening on the steering wheel. "That's right," he said finally. The calmness in his voice contrasted starkly with the trembling fear I felt.

"I'll kill him, just like I killed his mother. And if you obey, I'll let you live."

The realization knocked the wind out of me. "Where are you taking me?" My voice was a shaky whisper, the lump in my throat making it hard to speak.

"Get comfortable, Clover." Jim's voice was malicious, unsettling in its calmness. He didn't look at me this time, his gaze fixed firmly on the darkened road stretching out before us. "We've got a long ride ahead."

A shudder coursed through me at his words. The uncertainty of what lay ahead, the dread that clung to each passing moment, it threatened to consume me. But I knew I had to stay strong, had to hold on, for Declan . . . for myself.

CHAPTER 27
Torn Lace and Broken Promises

DECLAN

The air in the dimly lit room hung heavy with the scent of stale cigarettes and tension. I took a seat at the worn-out wooden desk, my heart pounding in my chest like a caged beast. Anxiety coursed through my veins, fueled by the knowledge of what I had done, the gas line I had cut. Time was running out, and Hank's den could go up in flames at any moment.

I'd get my answers.

Hank would get a meeting with the devil.

As I settled into the chair, my eyes involuntarily drifted to the objects on the table beside me: a pack of cigarettes and a silver lighter. It was a simple, innocent setup, but it held the potential to ignite disaster. If Hank reached for those cigarettes and flicked open that lighter, the entire place would go up in a fiery inferno.

The horror of the suspense weighed heavily on me, the knowledge that my life teetered on a fragile balance. I had to be careful, keep Hank occupied, and prevent any careless movements that could trigger the catastrophe waiting to happen.

Hank's arrival shattered the uneasy silence, his heavy footsteps echoing through the room. His eyes were cold, devoid of any mercy or compassion. He took a seat across from me, a sinister grin curling his lips as he surveyed the table.

We couldn't smell the gas leak.

Yet.

But it would quickly fill this entire room.

A risk I had to take.

"The judge, his wife, and the trail guide," Hank said, his voice low and gravelly. "Are they all dead like I asked?"

I met his stare, my expression impassive. "They won't be troubling you anymore," I replied. With a swift motion, I reached into the waistband of my jeans and dropped Judge Mathis's bloodstained gun on the table.

Hank's eyes narrowed, his attention fixated on the evidence before him. A twisted satisfaction skipped across his face.

"I buried the bodies somewhere no one will find them," I continued. Each word carried the weight of the secrets I held, the grave acts I had committed. It was a necessary evil, a means to an end, and I had to see it through.

A glimmer of amusement danced in Hank's eyes, a sadistic pleasure at the control he held over me. "Good," he chuckled darkly. "You've done well, Declan. But this is just the beginning."

I fought to keep the chaos within me hidden, the rising anger and desperation threatening to consume me. This man, Hank, he reveled in the pain he inflicted, in the power he wielded. But I couldn't let my emotions betray me. I had to play his game, navigate the treacherous path laid before me.

"What's next, Hank?" I asked, my voice tinged with a calmness. "You've got your proof. Now it's time for you to hold up your end of the deal."

Hank leaned back in his chair, a wicked grin spreading across his face. "Oh, don't you worry, Declan," he sneered, relishing in the torment he inflicted. "I always keep my promises. But remember, the devil always collects his due. And you, my friend, are dancing with the devil himself."

The weight of his words settled upon me, a chilling reminder of the game I had willingly stepped into. I had to tread carefully, maneuver through the darkness, and ensure that I emerged victorious. The lives of Clover and everyone else who had suffered were at stake.

As we continued our twisted conversation, I couldn't shake the gnawing feeling of the impending disaster. The gas leak was a ticking time bomb, its presence a constant reminder of the risks.

The cruelty in Hank's expression softened for just a moment, replaced by an emotion I couldn't decipher. "Your vengeance is closer than you think, Declan," he began. "The man you're looking for is Jim Harlow."

The name scratched my mind, sending a surge of shock through me. "Harlow . . . ," I whispered, as if trying to summon a memory from a forgotten past. "He killed my mother?"

Hank nodded, a sinister seriousness casting a shadow over his usually gleeful countenance. "Indeed, he did. And I can tell you where to find him."

The room seemed to spin as I grappled with the information. My mission, my vengeance, was right within my reach. "Where is he?"

His lips curled up into a smirk again, the temporary lapse of joviality replaced by his usual malicious grin. "Well, that's the best part," he sneered. "You know, Declan, the death of the trail guide wasn't just business. It was my present to you."

My brow furrowed in confusion. What was he

playing at? My eyes narrowed as I leaned in, waiting for him to elaborate.

"Your mother," Hank said, slowly, carefully, "was on a date with Clover's father the night she was killed."

The world stopped. The sounds of the room dulled as I focused on Hank's words, the implications ripping through me like a bullet. "What?" I managed to choke out, the words barely a whisper. "Clover's father?"

Hank nodded, his eyes gleaming with malicious satisfaction. "A tragic tale, isn't it? Jim had a vendetta against Bill—that's the trail guide's father. Your mother was caught in the crossfire. As for Bill, he died in a rodeo accident years later. I figured killing his daughter was the next best thing for you. I'm a good leader. I like helping my hard workers."

I sat in stunned silence, the information crashing over me like a tidal wave. I loved Clover and had been drawn to her resilience, her spirit, from the moment we'd met. Now, to learn our lives were so tragically intertwined . . . it was a revelation that threatened to drown me.

My heart pounded in my chest as I wrestled with my thoughts, my emotions. Anger. Betrayal. Love. Grief. They swirled within me, a whirlpool threatening to consume me. Yet, I had to remain composed, not let Hank see the distress ripping through me.

The knowledge of the gas leak became an

afterthought, overshadowed by the revelations of the past. Hank was weaving a tale, revealing secrets that painted the world in shades of gray, obliterating the lines between friend and foe. It was a dangerous game, and the stakes were higher than ever before.

For Clover. For my mother. For myself. I had to stay in control. I had to win.

My thoughts spiraled, and just when I thought they couldn't twist any further, Hank leaned forward, his mud brown eyes boring into mine. "But you didn't finish the job, did you, Declan?" His voice was a razor-sharp whisper, cutting through the fog of my shock. "Clover is alive."

The room spun. The frail thread holding my emotions together snapped. "She's . . . dead." Even saying it made my chest clench.

Hank leaned back, a deep, chilling laughter erupting from his throat. The sound echoed through the room, bouncing against the walls, and seemed to seep into my bones. His gaze never left mine as he fished his phone out of his pocket and tossed it onto the table, its screen glowing with an unread message.

"Then why did Jim just text me, saying he had her?" Hank drawled, his laughter subsiding into a cruel grin.

A gasp ripped through my throat, and my eyes locked onto the screen. A heavy silence filled the room, the gravity of his words hanging in the air. The taste of betrayal was bitter on my tongue, a deafening drum of despair in my chest. But within that turmoil, there was a glimmer of hope—Clover was alive. I just needed to hold onto that as I braced for the storm that was sure to come. The ticking time bomb of the gas leak had taken a back seat again; my focus was now saving Clover and defeating Jim Harlow. And Hank, too, if I could manage it.

Hank's smirk widened, his eyes glinting with a malevolent delight. "I suppose you could save her, if she really means that much to you," he taunted. "She's where it all began. A few towns over. Poetic, really. She'll die in the same spot your mother did."

His words fell like a hammer onto my already shattered world. Hank had played us all like pieces on a chessboard, setting a deadly endgame into motion. But there was a fire burning in my veins now, a potent mix of anger, desperation, and determination.

"But I don't like being disobeyed. And I don't like loose ends. She knows too much. Jim is loyal. With any luck, he'll kill you all. But you better hurry."

Every fiber in my being screamed to lunge at him, to wipe that smug smile off his face, but I knew better. I had a greater mission, a higher purpose. Clover needed me.

Pushing back from the table, I picked up the worn silver lighter. My heart pounded a frenzied rhythm against my ribs, each beat an echoing affirmation of what I was about to do. Hank's laughter still followed me, a haunting melody that filled the air, as I walked across the room. The worn wooden floorboards creaked under my weight, singing their own swan song.

Reaching the door, I paused for a moment, the lighter's cool metal casing pressing into my palm. Turning back, I locked eyes with Hank. He sat there, his bloated form lounging in the chair, a smug smile playing on his lips. For a moment, it felt like the world had come to a standstill. Hank, the room, the city outside—it was all bathed in an uncanny stillness, as if waiting with bated breath for what was to come.

"See you in hell, Hank," I muttered, my voice barely a whisper. A final goodbye to the monster before me. Hank's smile faltered, replaced by a look of confusion. But I didn't stick around to see it evolve into realization.

In one swift movement, I flung the lit lighter over my shoulder. It spun in the air, a spinning orb of metal and flame, drawing an arc toward its destined end. I didn't wait to see it land.

The explosion hit just as I stepped out into the cool night air. A monstrous roar filled the night, accompanied by a shockwave that ripped through the compound, shaking the earth beneath me. I fell to the ground and felt the heat of the inferno on my back, a hot breath from the hellfire that was consuming Hank's den.

Glancing back over my shoulder, I saw the compound engulfed in a violent blaze. Flames clawed at the night sky, hungrily devouring everything in their path. Hank's laughter was replaced by the scream of the inferno, a deafening sound that drowned out everything else. The compound, once a testament to Hank's cruelty, was now a beacon of justice.

But there was no time to savor the sight, to relish in the retribution. Hank's death was but the first step on a longer path, a single note in the symphony of vengeance that awaited. My heart pounded in my chest, a steady drum in the urgency of my mission.

I stood up and turned away from the blazing ruin, the heat of the flames becoming a distant warmth against my back. As I moved into the night, a single thought consumed me, driving me forward.

I had to find Jim Harlow. For Clover. For my mother. And for myself.

CHAPTER 28

Seductive Showdown in the Desert Sands

CLOVER

J im Harlow drove in silence. The landscape outside the window was ablur, blanketed in darkness. I lost all sense of direction as the time passed, my anxiety reaching a fever pitch.

Eventually, the truck came to a halt in front of a decrepit old barn. The wood was weathered, the red paint chipped and faded. I trembled as I looked at it. It felt isolated, forgotten, a mirror to the chaos inside me.

"Out," he ordered, his voice brooking no argument. I hesitated for a moment, my eyes flicking to the barn, then back to him. But his cold determination left no room for negotiation.

I stumbled out of the truck, the gravel biting into

my bare feet. The chill in the air made me shake, the distant hoot of an owl echoing eerily in the silence. He came around to my side, his eyes scanning the area with a predatory edge.

"Now listen," he said, his voice low and threatening. "You will do as I say, understand? Your life, your sister's life, depends on it. Screw up and I won't hesitate to pull the trigger. I killed Declan's mother in this barn, and I won't hesitate to kill you, too." He smiled to himself, as if relishing in the memory. "Your father was so fucking romantic. Brought her to dinner, then they came out here. Probably fucked her on a bale of hay. Guess he didn't want to bring that whore back home."

I shivered in disgust.

"And maybe I'll have some fun with you, too," he rasped. "Maybe I'll give your father one last *fuck you*."

The threat hung in the air between us, a terrifying promise. I trembled, the lump in my throat making it impossible for me to speak. I didn't know what was going to happen next. All I knew was that I was far from home, far from Avery, far from Declan.

I was led into the barn, my eyes taking in the details in the dim light. Haystacks were piled up in the corners, their musty smell filling the air. A few old tools lay scattered around, their metallic gleam dull and forgotten. It was as if the barn hadn't seen use in years.

The shovel in the corner of the barn caught my eye, its rusted edges bearing stories of hard labor and time. An involuntary spike of adrenaline surged through me as I contemplated its new sinister potential.

Jim huffed in annoyance, thrusting his phone back into his pocket. "Hank's not picking up. But no worries," he sneered, locking his cold gaze onto me. "Declan, that loyal mutt, he won't be able to resist coming here. He always shows up."

He leaned against a worn wooden pillar, crossing his arms over his chest. A cruel smirk twisted his lips as he began to share his gruesome plan. His words slithered through the chilly air, landing heavily in the silence of the barn.

"See, once that boy gets here," he started, the light in his eyes dancing with sadistic delight, "I'll be waiting for him. Maybe I'll surprise him from behind, take this rusty old shovel"—he gestured toward the tool that had caught my attention earlier—"and swing it right at his head."

His laughter bounced off the barn walls, a chilling sound that twisted my stomach into knots. "Or maybe, just maybe, I'll go for a slower approach. I'll tie him up, just like his dear old mom. Watch the fear build in his eyes. Just the way I like it."

He paused, savoring the terror that must have shown on my face. "Oh, and don't you worry. I'll make sure you have the best seat in the house. You can watch as I tear him apart, bit by bit."

His laughter filled the barn once more, echoing my rising fear. I clenched my fists, my nails digging into the palms of my hands. The terrifying image he painted was too much, too real. I couldn't let it happen. I couldn't let Declan walk into this nightmare. I had to act, had to find a way to prevent his dark plans from becoming a reality. With each laugh from Jim, my resolve hardened. I had to save Declan. And I had to do it soon.

Jim stalked closer, his breath a sickening cocktail of whiskey and stale smoke. He let out a low, cruel laugh, his eyes glinting with a sickening joy in the dim barn light. "Clover," he drawled, letting my name hang in the air like a predator toying with its prey. "You know, I've been contemplating a fitting punishment for your little boyfriend, Declan."

The echo of his words held a promise of sadistic intentions. "I bet you can't even begin to imagine what I have in store for him. But first . . ." He paused, licking his lips. "You."

I felt my blood run cold as he continued, his words painting a grotesque image. "Can you imagine, Clover? Declan watching while I . . ."

His sentence hung in the air, unfinished yet filled with the horrifying details left unsaid. A spark of rebellion ignited within me, a protective fury that blazed against the chilling terror. I remembered the feeling of violation, of being helpless, of being a plaything for a monster. I refused to live that nightmare again.

"No," I muttered under my breath, my voice barely a whisper but firm with conviction.

Jim's laughter ricocheted around the barn, bouncing off the musty hay bales and rusty tools. My eyes were drawn to the shovel. The once mundane tool now seemed like a beacon, its edges illuminated ominously in the dim light.

"Nobody will hear you scream," Jim sneered, a sickening pleasure lining his words. "Just like his mother."

"No," I repeated, louder this time. His words were fuel to the fire within me, the heat of my rage growing with every syllable he uttered. The shovel no longer looked like an ordinary farm tool; it was now a symbol of defiance, a way to regain my power.

Jim's words added weight to my resolve, each vile comment, each repugnant detail, solidifying my determination. His laughter boomed in my ears, a chilling soundtrack to the scene unfolding in my mind's eye. I envisioned myself, not as a victim, but as a woman reclaiming her power.

"No!" I shouted, the word filling the barn. It was a declaration, a promise to myself and to him. I wouldn't be a victim again. I wouldn't allow him to take anything more from me.

With a battle cry in my mind, my pledge of defiance, I lunged.

I sprang forward with a speed and strength I didn't know I possessed, my hand wrapping around the cool wooden handle of the shovel. My heart pounded in my chest, the beat a thunderous drumline in time with my thoughts: No more. Not again.

That was it. The dam holding my rage back exploded, a storm of fury that had been brewing ever since this nightmare started. All thoughts of fear were erased by a white-hot determination.

"No!" I bellowed, my voice a clarion call piercing the oppressive tension in the barn.

The texture of the handle was rough, splintered from years of use and neglect. Each ridge and groove dug into my palm, grounding me, anchoring me to this singular moment. The weight of it felt both comforting and terrifying, a responsibility and a weapon rolled into one.

I wheeled around, fueled by a raw surge of adrenaline. The shovel sliced through the air, its path a deadly arc. It found its mark on Jim's body with a sickening thud. Jim gasped, a strangled sound of shock and pain, his body staggering back under the force of the blow.

"You won't hurt me!" I roared, my words whipping through the cold air. The declaration was as much for me as it was for him. A promise and a war cry that echoed off the barn walls. "Never again!" My voice pitched higher, charged with adrenaline and rage, each syllable syncing with the brutal rhythm of the shovel slamming into Jim's body.

The impact jolted up my arms, the tremors shaking me to my core. But there was a grim satisfaction in it too. Each strike was a blow against my past, against the terror that had held me captive.

I hit him.

I hit him again.

I hit him again.

Jim's form crumbled, his knees buckling beneath him. His body folded onto the barn floor, creating a cloud of dust that hung in the air, a grim tableau of our final confrontation. His fall was a cruel mockery of his earlier bravado, the sight of him so diminished fueling my fury.

I stood over him, my breaths coming in ragged gasps, the sharp sting of exertion shooting through my arms. The weight of the shovel felt different now, a symbol of my strength, my survival. I lifted it high, the edge catching a glint of the weak light filtering through the barn slats.

With a yell that scraped raw against my throat, I brought the shovel down. The rusty edge bit into his neck, the resistance giving way to the relentless force of my strike. The sound of tearing flesh and splintering bone was grotesque, the silence that followed even more so.

Jim's life seeped out of him, pooling on the dust-covered floor, his eyes losing their cruel light. The moment was brutal, harsh in its finality. But in the aftermath of that violence, I felt a sense of relief wash over me. A certainty settling in my bones. It was over. Jim Harlow would never harm anyone again. I had ensured that.

At that moment, with the weight of the shovel still heavy in my hand and the metallic scent of blood lingering in the air, I realized I had done more than just defend myself. I had reclaimed my power, my dignity. This was more than survival. This was a victory. I had stood up against my nightmare, faced it head-on.

I killed.

I endured.

I saved my fucking self.

CHAPTER 29
Riding on the Edge of Shadows

DECLAN

*T*he barn haunted the horizon like a tombstone, its decrepit figure a chilling echo of a past I wanted to bury. My grip on the steering wheel tightened, the leather groaning a soft protest under the pressure of my white-knuckled hands. This was a battleground, a place of violent loss and harrowing truths. I had to face it. For myself, for my past, and for her. For Clover.

I still remember when the police told my foster mother that they'd found blood at a barn one mile from the river where her body was found.

I still remember running away to see for myself.

The yellow tape. The blood-stained hay.

I stepped out of the car, the scent of aged hay and rusted metal hung heavily in the air. Each stride toward the barn felt weighted, as though every footfall was weighed heavily with the harsh reminder of my mother's end. But it wasn't her blood that had me pressing forward, it was Clover's. Her life was intertwined with my demons, and I would rip those beasts apart to keep her safe.

The barn door protested under my push, creaking open to reveal a sight that shattered the world around me. There, amidst the scattered tools and dust-laden floor, stood Clover. The faint light that managed to breach the old wooden boards of the barn danced on her figure, painting her in a spectral glow. She held a shovel, its edge shining with a vicious promise under the ambient moonlight.

But it was the sight beneath her that struck me the hardest, Jim Harlow lay at her feet, his life's essence pooling around his lifeless form. His once threatening presence was now nothing but a silenced menace, vanquished by the woman who dared to stand against him.

She killed him.

The object of my obsession. My affection. My world.

She killed the man I'd been searching for. My life's purpose. My revenge.

Her skin was adorned with crimson, the blood painting her in a morbid masterpiece of survival. Her eyes met mine, glowing with a fierce determination that eclipsed the tragedy of the situation. At that moment, she was no damsel. She was a warrior. A survivor. An avenger.

My breath hitched in my throat, every fear, every doubt, drowned under the wave of gratitude that surged within me. The sight of her, standing tall and victorious, was more beautiful than any sunrise, any rainbow, any star-lit sky. She was beauty personified, not in the traditional sense, but in a way that resonated deep within my soul. She was beautiful not because of her symmetry, but because of her strength, her courage, her defiance.

The gun slipped from my numb fingers, its impact against the barn floor distant against the thunderous drumming in my ears. I was drawn to her, my steps unsteady as I closed the gap between us. When I reached her, it was as if a seismic shift occurred within me. My arms wrapped around her, holding her to me as if our survival depended on that singular act.

Her arms reciprocated my hold, her touch a grounding force amidst the chaos that surrounded us. I buried my face in her hair, the faint scent of her shampoo clashing with the metallic tang of blood that permeated the air. We clung to each other, two survivors in a sea of past and present horrors.

Clover clung to me as if I were her only tether to

reality. Her voice, usually so soft and soothing, was raw and fractured as she whispered my name.

"Declan."

"Wildflower, I was so fucking worried about you."

Her arms tightened around me, her fingers digging into my back through the fabric of my shirt.

The warmth of her lips crashed against mine, a storm of emotions conveyed in a single act. The taste of her was mingled with the iron tang of blood, a haunting reminder of the violence that had just taken place. She was fervent, almost frantic, her hands roaming across my skin, leaving smears of red in their wake.

Her nails scraped down my back, each mark a fiery line of possession. It was as though she was trying to burrow into me, seeking solace within the contours of my body. Her need was noticeable, wrapping us in a shroud of vulnerability.

The sharp sting of her teeth against my lip jolted me, a sharp contrast to the sweet taste of her mouth. I could taste her tears now, the saltiness intermingling with our shared breaths. They were echoes of her fears, her traumas, her fight for survival.

This wasn't a simple act of intimacy. It was a communion, a mingling of our shared turmoil and relief. It was Clover marking me as her refuge and, in turn, my silent vow to always be there for her. It was us, reclaiming our story, our bodies, from the night-mare of past and present monsters. We were survivors, painting our defiance in shades of crimson and tears.

The power of the moment faded, though our hold on each other remained. I pulled away, my eyes tracing her face, looking for any wounds or signs of distress. Her eyes were bright with a fierce determination, and I could feel her skin radiating with heat against my own.

She touched my face, her fingertips light against my stubbled jawline. Then, she smiled, the expression tinged with sadness but bursting with strength.

"I'm alright," she murmured, almost as if she had to convince herself of the fact.

I nodded, pressing a kiss to her forehead before I stepped away from her and guided her toward the barn wall on the other side, away from Jim's body.

I held her clothes in my hands, the fabric heavy with Jim's blood. I could no longer stand the sight of them on Clover, so I started stripping them off without a word.

Her breathing had become shallow and rapid, a moan accompanying each movement of my hands. She kept reaching for me, desperately clasping onto me as if I could remain her anchor throughout this storm.

I ripped off her shirt, pulling it away from her body before tossing it aside. Her jeans were next. The zipper stuck at first before being forced down with one tug. My fingers fumbled around the clasp of her bra before finally successfully tugging it apart.

Once all of her bloody clothing was gone, she stood in front of me, clad only in pale skin and determination. Though she was shaking slightly from adrenaline and fear, there was an undeniable strength radiating from her body that filled me with awe.

I took a step back, admiring her beauty and power. The moonlight cast a soft glow on her skin, making her appear ethereal.

I reached out for her, and she hesitated at first before finally taking my hand. I felt a jolt of electricity when our skin touched, a promise of something bigger yet to come.

"Show me your brand," I said softly, gesturing toward her shoulder, where I knew the evidence of our bond still bloomed.

I needed to see it.

Feel it.

Trace it with my tongue.

Clover nodded slowly and then stepped forward, bracing against the wall with her palms as I moved her hair to the side so I could see it. My heart stopped when I saw the angry, healing scar that seemed like a badge of courage and defiance on Clover's delicate skin. Tears stung my eyes at the thought of how close she had come to ending up like Jim. I couldn't imagine never seeing this again. This mark of possession. This testament to us.

I moved closer, pressing a gentle kiss to the top of her shoulder blade before tracing my fingers along the perimeter of the brand. A shiver ran through Clover's body as my fingers traced their way down her spine before coming to rest on her lower back.

She looked over her shoulder, and our eyes met. We were lost in each other's gaze and understanding what this meant for us both—that though we had been through so much darkness, this was the light that would guide us out into safety.

"What happened to Hank?" she asked.

"Bastard's dead."

She chewed on her lip. "Is my sister okay?"

"Safe."

"What about you? Are you—"

I was done letting her worry about everyone else. "Shut the fuck up, Wildflower. The only person I'm concerned about is *you*. And I'm going to spend the rest of my life keeping you safe."

She leaned into me then, as my arms wrapped around her waist tightly. We stayed like that for what seemed like an eternity before finally separating again.

She held onto my hands as if they were life lines; I could feel how desperately she was clinging onto me even though she never said a single word out loud.

"Wildflower," I breathed out, feeling my heart swell with pride and love. Clover was more than a survivor; she was a fighter who refused to let her past define her.

I unbuckled my jeans.

I pulled out my cock.

Her gasp caressed my ears as I pressed myself against her. I felt the warmth of her flesh against mine, and my mind spun with the sensation of it all.

"Don't take the blame this time, Declan," she whispered, so softly I could barely hear. "I did this all on my own. I survived . . ."

Fuck, I was hard as a rock at her words. She survived. She was here. She healed wounds I couldn't even process yet.

I sunk down to my knees as she spun around, worshiping at the altar of her sweet pussy. The smell of blood still lingered on her skin, and I wanted nothing more than to lick it all away. I placed my hands on either side of her hips, as if they were guiding me down so that I could kiss the red marks that marred her skin.

The taste of her was pure pleasure, a remedy for the raging storm inside me. I licked and sucked her clit until her breathing grew ragged and her hips couldn't keep still. She tasted like woman, all woman, honey and sugar. She was the taste of a decadent treat, the kind I could taste on my tongue for hours.

I kept going, pushing her past her limits until she screamed out my name and started grinding against my tongue. Her orgasm flooded over me in waves—a flood of love and pleasure that I wanted to ride out forever.

I held her tight as she came, her pussy milking me with pleasure. I slowly rose to my feet, sopping wet and smiling with satisfaction as I held Clover close.

"You're so fucking strong, Wildflower," I praised. "So brave."

"I killed him," she whispered.

I couldn't even be angry that I didn't get the satisfaction of murdering my mother's killer. It was pure serendipity that the woman I loved would find her power by ending his life. Karma coming full circle.

I held her up against the barn wall and entered her, her heat wrapping around me like a cocoon of pure bliss. "You squeeze my cock like such a good girl."

Her back slammed against the barn wall, but she hunched her shoulders forward to keep the wood from dragging against her brand. She cried out. "Fuck, Declan. Yes. Yes . . . fuck."

I pumped into her as she screamed my name, my

hips slapping against her. We moved to the ground. I wanted deeper. I wanted her to be fuller. Of me. Of us.

I thrust deeper, feeling my desire for her swell inside me with each movement. My heart pounded in my chest as I felt my body responding to hers. She was everything I could ever want: passionate, strong and full of life.

Clover moaned softly, her hands gripping onto my shoulders tightly as she moved against me. We were both lost in our own world of pleasure and sensation, completely oblivious to anything else happening around us. I looked into her eyes and saw true passion blazing there; it made me even more driven to make this moment last forever.

We moved together, passionately lost in the moment until all I felt was her. I thrust in and out of her with a combination of urgency and gentle love.

"You're so fucking strong, Clover," I grunted.

She cried out.

We moved together, sweaty and raw, until I could feel the orgasm building in both of us.

I grabbed her by the hips and pounded into her, faster and harder as I felt her tighten around me. I roared out in pleasure, my body shaking with exhilarating waves of ecstasy, and Clover soon followed, screaming out my name and gripping me tight. Her hair was wild and untamed. Her body reeked of sex, death, and sweat.

We both collapsed into a pile of boneless euphoria, panting and grinning.

I kissed Clover softly, relieved that she was safe. "My Wildflower," I whispered. "My survivor . . ."

EPILOGUE

CLOVER

TWO YEARS LATER

The pulsating energy of the Fort Worth Stock Show & Rodeo enveloped us, the clamor of enthusiastic spectators, the rhythmic cadence of horses, and the distant drone of the announcer filling the air. Amidst it all, Declan and I were perched on the bleachers, his arm securely draped around me. I watched as my younger sister, Avery, made her preparations in the ring. I was a mix of nerves and pride for the daredevil sister of mine.

"Your grip could crush steel, Clover," Declan's deep voice playfully teased in my ear, causing a tremor of amusement to course through me. His presence was as calming as it was grounding.

"Sorry," I replied, loosening my vise-like grip on his hand. But as I turned my attention back to the ring, I couldn't help but tighten it again.

With a hearty chuckle, Declan assured, "She's going to do great."

Anxiously, I traced my thumb over the back of his hand as I watched Avery. She had always been braver than most, a female bull rider in a male-dominated sport. I was nervous for her, yet I had never been prouder.

"I know," I said, turning to him with a smile. "Did you know she got another sponsor?"

Declan feigned surprise. "Another? Your sister is going to be a rodeo star before we know it."

"She already is," I corrected him with a grin.

My gaze found Avery across the ring, her figure vibrant and full of life despite the distance. She had been my rock in the storm, her protective nature a constant source of strength in the face of adversity. When Declan and I first came home, covered in Jim Harlow's blood, she wept at my feet, terrified that something bad would happen to us again.

It had taken time for her to see that Declan was safe, that he didn't carry with him the pain of our past, but the promise of a peaceful future. He understood our pain, our fear, but he was determined to offer something else. Hope. Stability. A love that wasn't marred by darkness.

Watching Declan from the corner of my eye, I could see the quiet determination etched on his face. He'd borne Avery's initial distrust with patience and grace, unwavering in his commitment to prove himself to her. To prove that he could bring me peace and normalcy outside of his past.

And he had.

Looking at our life now, it was clear that Declan had made good on his promises. He'd gifted me a life where I could pursue my passions without fear, where I could watch my sister thrive, and where I was loved unconditionally. The journey had been far from easy, and it had taken a lot of time and effort from all of us. But it had been worth it.

"Big weekend coming up at the Wilder Barn," he said, his thumb drawing circles on my hand. "All prepped for the Smith wedding?"

I let out a laugh, shaking my head in wonder. "Yes. She loves the flowers I picked out for the centerpieces. Still can't believe you built that for me, Dec. It's perfect. And yes, we're ready. The barn's never looked more beautiful." When I told Declan about my dream to host events and weekend rides on my property, he made it his life's mission to make it a reality. He bought the property behind ours, expanding our land to forty acres. We had a new barn, an event center, and were in the process of building cute cabins at the edge of our property for people to rent. At first, it made him uncomfortable to invite people into our space, but he overcame that.

His responding smile was filled with pride and adoration. He leaned down, pressing a soft kiss to my temple. "And the new horses?"

"Settling in well. They're a handful, but a wonderful one. Ginny likes having younger horses to mother."

The small talk continued as we watched the event unfold, Declan's voice a comforting background hum against the thrilling excitement around us. We chatted about life—the new horses that we were trying to acclimate to our herd, the upcoming wedding we were hosting at the event center he'd built for me, and our plans for the weekend trail rides.

We were just two ordinary people living an extraordinary life, a life we had fought tooth and nail for. Our past was a chapter that we had decided to close. We had survived and emerged stronger, refusing to be defined by our scars. Today, we were thriving.

Just as I was lost in my thoughts, a pair of familiar figures approached us. Laura, her smile as bright as the Texas sun, led her eight-year-old son Carson toward us. With his shock of bright blond hair and freckled face, Carson was a bundle of endless energy, one that reminded me of the simpler times of childhood.

"Hey there, troublemaker!" Declan greeted Carson, ruffling his hair playfully as the boy waved around a bright, flashy toy in his hand.

"Declan, Declan! Look!" Carson was practically bouncing in his excitement. His light-up toy danced in the evening glow, painting swirling patterns in the air. "It's a space sword!"

Declan laughed, bending down to Carson's level to take a closer look at the toy. The way they interacted was heartwarming. It was clear Declan had a soft spot for the little guy, and the feeling was mutual.

As the two of them were engaged in a detailed discussion about the mechanics of a space sword, Laura sidled up next to me, her eyes twinkling.

"I swear, Carson is more excited to see Declan than anyone else," she said, shaking her head. "Says he's the coolest cowboy he knows."

"I bet. Declan has that effect on people," I responded, watching them with a smile. Declan was teaching Carson how to swing his space sword like a true space cowboy now, the sight making me smile.

"He sure does," Laura agreed. "Thanks to him, Carson's riding is getting better and better."

As we watched Declan and Carson, I felt a swell of

gratitude. Our lives had changed so much. Laura had quit her job at the supermarket and joined me in planning events. We were a team, and we were happy. The past was behind us, and the future was bright.

The announcement of Avery's name echoed around the arena, jolting me back from my thoughts. I clung tighter to Declan, my breath hitching in anticipation. This time, Declan didn't tease me about my grip. Instead, he held me closer, whispering comforting words in my ear as Avery took her place in the spotlight.

The roar of the crowd made me look at Avery. She was perched on the bucking beast, her focus entirely on the bull beneath her. Even from this distance, I could see the determination etched into her features, the fire of excitement in her eyes. I gripped Declan's hand tighter, my heart pounding in sync with the pulsing rhythm of the rodeo music.

"Here she goes," Declan murmured, his warm breath tickling my ear. His arm was secure around my waist, a steady anchor in the sea of excited spectators.

Avery's ride was intense, the powerful bull giving its all to throw her. Yet my sister held on with the tenacity that was a trademark of our family. She rode with the ease of a seasoned professional, every jerk, every attempt to dislodge her, met with a matching countermove. Her stubbornness was a sight to behold.

Time seemed to stretch, the eight-second ride feeling like an eternity. But finally, the buzzer sounded, signaling the end. Avery dismounted, landing with cat-like grace on the dirt, the crowd erupting into deafening applause. A broad grin spread across her face, the thrill of her successful ride clear.

"Your sister is something else," Declan commented, his voice filled with awe.

"She always has been," I agreed, my voice brimming with pride. Avery had found her calling in the rodeo ring, just as I had found mine in the event center Declan built for me, in the trail rides I led, in the simple, peaceful life we'd created together.

It hadn't been easy getting to this point. There had been many sleepless nights, filled with worries about Avery's safety. But I'd come to realize that I couldn't shield her from the world. She had to live her own life, chase her own dreams. And she was doing it fearlessly.

She was even living on her own now, having moved out into a place of her own a few months ago. It was tough, the old fear still gnawing at me some-times. But seeing her tonight, how radiant and alive she was, it was clear that she was on the right path.

Looking at Avery, then at Declan, Carson, and Laura, I realized just how far we'd all come. We'd survived, we'd thrived, and we'd done it together. It was a beautiful journey, and I couldn't wait to see where it would lead us next.

As the dust settled and the crowd began to disperse, we made our way through the chaos to meet Avery. The triumphant grin was still plastered across her face, her eyes sparkling with joy and adrenaline. Before words could be exchanged, we all pulled her into a tight group hug, her victory the glue bonding us all together in the moment.

Pulling back, I looked at the faces of the people who made up my world—Avery, Laura, Carson, and Declan. My heart fluttered with a mix of anxiety and excitement, the news I was about to share causing a whirlwind of emotions.

Taking a deep breath, I squeezed Declan's hand. His eyes met mine, curious and reassuring. The noise of the rodeo seemed to fade away as I opened my mouth, my voice small yet steady against the quiet hum of the departing crowd.

"I'm pregnant," I announced, my eyes scanning the faces of our family. Avery gasped, a hand flying to her mouth, while Laura squealed with joy, pulling me into a tight embrace. Carson looked confused for a moment, then his face lit up as he processed the news.

"Does this mean I'll be an uncle?" he asked, bouncing on his toes.

It was Declan's reaction that I was most focused

on. His eyes filled with tears, his strong cowboy exterior crumbling as the news sank in. He pulled me into his arms, his voice a choked whisper in my ear. "Clover, baby, this is the best news."

Our cheers of celebration filled the night, the rodeo lights illuminating our shared joy. As our family reveled in the news, Declan gave me a look filled with so much love that it made my heart skip a beat. With a grin, he scooped me up into his arms, ignoring my startled yelp.

"C'mon, Wildflower," he said, his eyes twinkling with mischief and happiness. "We've got a baby to celebrate."

And with that, he carried me off into the night, our laughter filling the cool Texas air. It was a perfect beginning to a new chapter in our story—a testament to our journey, a beacon of hope for the future. As the lights of the rodeo faded behind us, I knew that whatever the future held, we would face it together, as a family.

DEAR READER

Before you close this book, I'd like to ask you a favor. If you enjoyed the wild ride and the beating heart of this story, please consider leaving a review. Your words are a guiding light for both me and future readers.

Now, I am so thrilled to share that I'm currently working on Avery's book. I can hardly wait for you to dive into her thrilling journey and watch her story unfold. I am sure you will embrace her adventure just as warmly as you have this one.

And finally, I want to thank you for being an adventurer, for trusting me, for coming along on whatever journey I choose to write about. Your faith and openness to explore new narratives and characters is what truly makes storytelling an exhilarating endeavor.

In the end, this isn't just my story—it's ours. Thank you for being a part of it.

With much love and gratitude,

Coralee June

ACKNOWLEDGMENTS

This journey, the culmination of every word on these pages, is a testament to the unwavering support and countless hours of dedication from so many incredible individuals.

Helayna Trask, your eagle-eyed attention to detail and your insightful guidance were invaluable to the crafting of this story. Your editorial prowess was nothing short of magic, and I am forever grateful. Brittany Franks, you gave life to my words with your dazzling designs. The world I imagined was made tangible, vibrant, and beautiful through your creative expertise.

My June Bug team, you are the backbone of this endeavor. A special shout-out to Quincy Mayes, who was always there with innovative ideas, unending encouragement, and the steadfast belief in my vision.

To my beta readers, your invaluable feedback and relentless cheerleading provided the final polish this story needed to truly shine.

I would be remiss not to mention my loyal readers, who have stuck with me on this rollercoaster of a ride.

Your endless support and engagement are the fuel that keeps my creative engine running.

Finally, my deepest gratitude goes to my late Paw Paw. His love for the western genre inspired me to venture into uncharted territories and write a western romance of my own. He always believed that I could capture the heart of the Wild West, though he probably never imagined I'd write a story like this. Love you, big guy. Hope you're riding horses and tinkering on cars up there in heaven.

Dear Reader,

Coralee June here! If you enjoyed the pulse-pounding excitement and deep emotional resonance of this book, you might want to explore more of the worlds I've created. Each story is its own thrilling adventure, filled with unique tropes that I've come to love writing about. Let me guide you through some of them.

For those of you who can't resist the seductive allure of a dangerous underworld coupled with undeniable love, my Sunshine and Bullets series might be the next thrilling experience for you. It features a mafia romance trope with raw power dynamics that's sure to keep you on the edge of your seat.

If you're drawn to a blend of passion, power, and intrigue set in a grand stage, my Bloody Royals series is the perfect pick. This is a royal reverse harem romance that throws a luxurious, passionate love story into the fascinating world of nobility and power.

My book Burnout is an emotionally charged romance between a student and a teacher. It's a rollercoaster of emotions, self-discovery, and a love story that defies societal norms, wrapped up in the popular student-teacher romance trope.

For those who love a touch of the forbidden, my Twisted Legacy Duet offers an engrossing narrative involving a stepfather's uncle. This one spins around the forbidden romance trope and delivers a story that will make your heart race.

Lastly, if you're intrigued by the idea of a dangerously obsessive love, A Lovely Obsession will be a captivating read. This dark stalker romance features a significant age gap, treading the thrilling line between desire and obsession.

Each book I write is a journey into the intricate world of human emotions, tangled with love, danger, and thrilling desire. I'm so grateful to share these worlds with you, and I hope you find the same joy in exploring them as I do in creating them.

Happy reading,

Coralee June

ABOUT THE AUTHOR

Coralee June is an *USA Today* bestselling romance writer who enjoys engaging projects and developing real, raw, and relatable characters. She is an English major from Texas State University and has had an intense interest in literature since her youth. She currently resides with her husband and three children in Dallas, Texas, where she enjoys long walks through the ice-cream aisle at her local grocery store.

www.authorcoraleejune.com

Made in the USA
Monee, IL
01 July 2023